The Thirteenth Child

By Mark deMeza

The Thirteenth Child

First published in 2024

Copyright © Bebetter Publishing 2024

ISBN: 978-1-7384541-0-5

TAUK Publishing

DEDICATION

To Sophia and all the children needlessly lost.

AUTHOR'S NOTE

This novel is a fictional recreation of the Nazi invasion of the Netherlands during World War II and the resultant impact on the Jewish population. It represents the events, dates, and locations as accurately as possible, while occasionally taking liberties to condense a tragedy which affected an entire nation into a more manageable fictional narrative. Most of its characters are based upon real people, the major exceptions being the five members of the Kisch family, who have been invented. However, the story of the Kisch family has been drawn from historical events, and as such, I believe they are fair representations of the lives and fates of Dutch Jews living there during this period. I discuss the history of the period further at the end of the novel.

Mark deMeza
Summer 2023

SOPHIA – ONE OF THE ONE HUNDRED AND TWO THOUSAND

I was apprehensive, my fingers poised motionless above my computer keyboard. I took a deep breath and slowly and deliberately typed the letters *"d e m e z a"* in the search box. I pressed the enter key and waited.

A small clock icon appeared, pulsing silently, but almost immediately disappeared, to be replaced by the message *"results below."*

My gaze ran up and down the screen as I read the names:

Esther deMeza
Birthdate: 9-9-1923 in Amsterdam
Murdered: 4-6-1943 in Sobibor

Jechiel deMeza
Birthdate: 15-2-1890 in Amsterdam
Murdered: 3-9-1942 in Auschwitz

Sophia deMeza

Birthdate: 25-4-1931 in Amsterdam

Murdered: 26-1-1943 in Auschwitz

Raphael Siegfried deMeza

Birthdate: 16-12-1912 in Amsterda

Murdered: 2-7-1943 in Sobibor

Mietje deMeza-Glazer

Birthdate: 5-6-1892 in Amsterdam

Murdered: 26-1-1943 in Auschwitz

Frederika deMeza

Birthdate: 30-6-1907 in Amsterdam

Murdered: 25-1-1943 in Auschwitz

Arie deMeza

Birthdate: 13-2-1929 in Amsterdam

Murdered: 26-1-1943 in Auschwitz

Betsy Estella deMeza-Maarzen

Birthdate: 4-5-1913 in Amsterdam

Murdered: 2-7-1943 in Sobibor

Marianne deMeza

Birthdate: 9-8-1923 in Amsterdam

Murdered: 21-5-1943 in Sobibor

Clara deMeza
Birthdate: 7-4-1894 in Amsterdam
Murdered: 25-1-1943 in Auschwitz

Johanna deMeza-Hamburger
Birthdate: 20-1-1887 in Nijkerk
Murdered: 4-6-1943 in Sobibor

David deMeza
Birthdate: 11-12-1885 in Amsterdam
Murdered: 4-6-1943 in Sobibor

I was stunned. Prior to the advent of the personal computer and the internet, stories of my ancestors had been passed down by word of mouth or cocooned in the long-forgotten archives of religious or civic buildings. Occasionally, a faded black-and-white photograph might be discovered in a dusty storage box in a relative's loft.

I had always known that my Jewish forebears had originated in Portugal and, because of the Spanish Inquisition of the late-fifteenth century, had made their way across Europe to the Netherlands and then onward to England at the end of the nineteenth century.

I had remained in this state of relative ignorance until 2021, when I was researching a planned holiday in the Netherlands and chanced upon a news report about the Holocaust Names

Memorial in Amsterdam. Out of curiosity, I searched for the memorial's website and started investigating.

When visitors enter the memorial, they find themselves in a series of passageways formed by two-yard-high brick walls that, when viewed from above, spell out the message *"In memory of"* in Hebrew. Inscribed on each of the bricks is the name, date of birth, and age at death of a Dutch Jew killed by the Nazis during World War II in their network of concentration and extermination camps.

There are in excess of 102,000 bricks in these walls, and the name of every victim is searchable on the memorial's website.

Scanning the list on my computer, my gaze settled upon the name Sophia, who perished in Auschwitz aged eleven. She was one of five family members killed on January 25 and 26, 1943. It was the thought of this little girl, about whom I knew absolutely nothing, that inspired me to gain an understanding of the plight of the Jews during those terrible times.

The following pages are dedicated to Sophia deMeza, one of the 102,000 and one of the approximately six million Jews murdered by the Nazis.

ONE

Amsterdam – May 16, 1940

It was Hannes's seventh birthday when the German army rolled into Amsterdam.

Hannes rode up Weesperstraat as fast as his legs and brand-new bicycle would allow, closely followed by his best friend, Isaac. They pedaled furiously alongside the River Amstel before abandoning their bikes against a lamppost on Dam Square.

On that spring afternoon, the sun shone brightly, and the square and surrounding areas were thronging with people. The crowds that lined the streets were four or five deep, and the boys could see nothing of what lay beyond, so they squeezed their way through the masses until they found themselves at the front with a view across the square with Raadhuisstraat stretching out to their left. It was a wide street with plenty of space for cars, trucks, trams, and pedestrians. However, today, there were no trams and no cars. All that could be seen was the advancing army.

The boys watched in wonder as the Germans passed, armored jeeps that looked like they carried senior officers in black uniforms, troop carriers holding eighteen or twenty soldiers with their rounded helmets and field-gray uniforms, and the foot soldiers marching to the rear, whose metal-heeled boots rapped out a metronomic beat that echoed around the square and streets.

A black limousine passed by with its top open. Hannes noticed that unlike the other vehicles, which were dull and matt, it was painted a polished black with chrome trim that sparkled in the rays of the sun. Sitting in the rear, two soldiers wearing peaked caps and with multicolored medals on their chests were making the Nazi salute, familiar to him from pictures in his father's newspapers. As he watched the crowds, he saw a number of the spectators saluting in return, and amidst the general hubbub, he thought he could hear both cheers and jeers.

To his right, a woman darted forward. For a moment, Hannes thought she looked so alone, stranded in the empty space between the crowds and the passing army. Dressed in a red skirt and white blouse, with a red headscarf to cover her hair, she rushed across the carriageway toward the limousine. Immediately, the soldier driving the vehicle stopped, disembarked, drew his pistol, and leveled it at the woman. He lowered the weapon when she timidly raised her arm to reveal a red flower. She then proceeded to offer it to one of the seated officers, who nodded solemnly, took the flower, and repeated his salute. The driver replaced the pistol in its holster, resumed his position behind the steering wheel, and the convoy moved on.

"Look, look, look!" Isaac's voice was full of excitement as he pointed into the distance. Several hundred yards to the left, there was a bend in the street, and the boys could see an armored tank rolling slowly into view. They waited with nervous anticipation for it to draw level. They watched and marveled as its continuous track smoothly propelled the vehicle forward and admired the goggle-wearing soldier whose head protruded above the gun turret like a mole peeping out of its hole. The boys waited for more tanks to arrive, but there were none. In fact, they were disappointed to discover that the parade of the German army did not finish with modern, state-of-the-art equipment, but small artillery guns and carriages pulled by pairs of horses.

When the convoy had passed, the crowd started dispersing. Some continued to gather in small huddles, deep in discussion. The two boys remained, fascinated by the army, and on this beautiful, sunny day and without a shot being fired, it seemed to them that many of the Dutch people were of the same mind.

They loitered for a while, drifting between groups of people, trying to catch snippets of conversations. Hannes led the way, slightly taller than his friend and broader in the chest, his blond hair partly covered by an old black cap he had received from his father. His brown eyes darted around with a natural and wondering curiosity. He wore a white shirt and oversized gray short pants that reached below his knees, a hand-down from the wardrobe of his older brother, Hendrik. Clothes that had been clean that morning were now dirty after their earlier games in Plantage Park.

The park was situated at the far end of Weesperstraat. An expanse of wide walkways and lush, exotic plants, it housed the city's botanical gardens and provided the boys with a myriad of opportunities to play games and ride their bikes.

"Come on, Zac, let's get back. I want to tell Papa what we've seen," Hannes said.

"Han, I need to go for my dinner," Isaac replied. "I'll see you tomorrow."

With that, the boys retraced their steps to where they had abandoned their bikes. They then headed back at a leisurely pace until they parted when Isaac took a right turn down Lapelstraat.

The Kisch family lived at Weesperstraat 47, a pleasant middle-class house no bigger or smaller than those in its immediate vicinity. It was on four levels, and its narrow, redbrick facade was decorated with a mixture of square and rectangular windows, those on the second floor being elongated to allow more natural light to pass into the rooms beyond.

When Hannes entered the living room, his father was sitting by the open window, reading his newspaper by the afternoon light. This was where Franck could be found every day, without fail. The gold fountain pen, which had been an eighteenth birthday gift from his own father, would always be resting in his fingertips, even after he had completed that day's crossword puzzle.

As soon as he saw his son, he put down his paper.

"Hannes!" he exclaimed. "Happy birthday!" He dropped to his knees so he could look his son straight in the eyes before the two hugged warmly. That morning, he had left for the university before his son had risen.

"And did you like your gift?" he added.

"It's exactly what I wanted!" the boy exclaimed. "Thank you, Papa. Thank you!"

"You're growing so fast; I'll need to buy you a new bike every six months at this rate."

"Papa!" Hannes said breathlessly. "Guess what?! Zac and I have seen the German army! We saw a tank!"

"Slow down!" his father replied. "There's no reason for celebration when it comes to the Germans."

"But there was a tank! And Zac's papa said this is a neutral country, so the Germans will leave the Dutch people alone."

"It may be a neutral country, but I'm not so sure the Germans will leave us alone."

As he spoke, Hannes noticed that his father's brow was furrowed like a crumpled piece of paper.

"Why not?" the boy asked.

At that moment, his mother entered the room.

He ran over and threw his arms around her. She bent over and kissed the top of his head.

Elizabeth Kisch was thin but strong and wiry, as befitting someone who had been brought up on a farm. Her hair was light brown, although at that moment it was not visible, tucked beneath a white headscarf. In her arms, she was carrying five empty dinner plates, which she swiftly distributed across the dining room table. She swiveled on her heels, and before returning to the kitchen, spoke to her husband.

"Come on, Franck! It's Hannes's birthday, and he's only seven! Please don't expose him to such serious issues."

"He's bright. I'm sure he can understand how evil the Nazis are. Who knows how long they'll be with us and what they may do? He really should learn about these matters sooner rather than later." He took hold of his son's hand, let him sit on the windowsill next to his chair, and looked earnestly into his son's expectant face.

"Adolf Hitler is the leader of the Nazis and the Germans and isn't a man to be trusted. He said he wouldn't invade Poland, yet he invaded Poland. He promised he would be a democratic ruler, and now he's a dictator. An evil dictator!"

"But we don't have any Nazis here, do we, Papa?" Hannes asked.

"Well," he replied with a grimace, "we have a few Nazis. They call themselves the NSB, but they're still Nazis. No doubt they'll encourage more Dutch Nazis to come forward here. I've worked with many Germans over the years, and they all seemed to be respectful and decent people, but they've done dreadful things to the Jews over there. They have destroyed their shops, their businesses, their livelihoods, their religion. To do all this, many Germans have been involved, and many have stood by and watched." He sighed.

"So, why did we let them into our country?" the youngster asked.

"We're a small nation. We can't match the strength of a country of that size. And we're neutral and have been proudly so for years. A neutral country only needs a small army. When the German army arrived at our borders a few days ago, there were very few Dutch soldiers to fight them. The German Air Force destroyed Rotterdam, and our government had no option but to surrender."

Hannes thought his father's voice was not as strong and confident as usual.

"What's happened to Rotterdam?" he asked, remembering his Uncle Solomon, who lived there.

"The Germans threatened to bomb the city unless we surrendered. Our government knew their air force was strong enough and ruthless enough to do it. We had no option. We were going to surrender, but they didn't wait for the paperwork to be signed and bombed Rotterdam anyway. That's how much we can trust Hitler and the Nazis. Today, there's hardly a building still standing there. Tens of thousands of people are homeless."

At that moment, two more people entered the room, Hannes's sister, Rachael, and his older brother, Hendrik.

"Hello there, little man! Happy birthday!" Hendrik smiled, ruffling his brother's hair playfully.

"Happy birthday!" Rachael said, stooping to embrace him. She had also left for work early that morning, and it was the first time she had seen him that day. Then she bent over to kiss her father's cheek. Hendrik nodded toward their father, who reciprocated. Both then went into the kitchen to greet their mother.

The family took dishes and crockery out of a sideboard and set five places around the table. They washed their hands, took their seats, and listened to the customary prayer offered by their father.

"Ah, roast lamb, my favorite!" Franck said, closing his eyes and inhaling the seductive aroma of the meat lying on a large oval plate, surrounded by potatoes, carrots, cabbage, and shiny, deep-brown gravy. "Let's hope the Nazis don't interrupt our lamb supplies!"

Hendrik spoke before anyone could consume their first mouthful of food. "We're going to have to do something about those bloody Nazis! We can't just stand by and watch."

"Well, whoa, Hendrik!" Elizabeth interrupted. "No talk of that at the dinner table. And mind your language, please!"

She turned to her daughter. "How was your day, darling?"

"Fine, thank you, Mama," Rachael answered, smiling.

Hannes loved his sister's smile, which seemed to spread across the whole of her face, flowing beyond her lips to emphasize her round cheeks, crinkled nose, and wide, animated eyes.

"I've got enough problems keeping all the school children in order without having to think about the Nazis as well," she added.

Hannes noticed the older brother did not speak for the rest of the meal, repeatedly biting his bottom lip, which turned its pink skin white.

TWO

The Hague – June 1940

Arthur Seyss-Inquart looked in the mirror and smiled. He had been appointed by Adolf Hitler himself and was standing in an office within the Dutch government building in The Hague. The government ministers, together with the royal family, had fled and dispersed to Britain and Canada, leaving the way open for him to preside over the entire country as Reichskommissar, the most senior representative of the Reich. He had progressed a long way from his birth town in Bohemia to a Czech father and German mother.

There had always been a fierce rivalry between the German and Czech populations, so he was forever indebted to his father for changing the family name from Zajtich and moving to Vienna, where he had gone on to study law at the university. By the end of World War I, the twenty-six-year-old was a qualified lawyer who had served in the Austrian army, as evidenced by a variety of wounds and medals he had received. He was rapidly rising to the top.

Thanks to his successful law practice, he had cultivated a position of prominence within Viennese political circles and, in 1933, joined the Dollfuss government. He had become obsessed with the Aryan theories of racial purity expounded by the leader of the SS, Reichsführer Heinrich Himmler and, by 1938, was the respectable public persona of the Austrian National Socialists.

Pressure placed on the Austrian leadership by Hitler left the way for Seyss-Inquart to be appointed Chancellor. He promptly invited the German army to annex the country, which was then renamed Ostmark, a province of the German Reich. He found himself in the unusual position of drawing up the legal documents for the creation of Ostmark and also signing them.

Hitler's appreciation was further demonstrated when he was appointed Governor of Ostmark, reporting directly to the Führer. The Austrian government immediately adopted Nazi policies. An honorary SS rank and place in Hitler's cabinet soon followed.

When the Dutch had capitulated in May 1940, Seyss-Inquart was an obvious candidate for a senior role in the new regime.

It was his task to embed those concepts of racial purity that were already prevalent in Germany and Austria. Hitler himself believed that the Dutch nation had Aryan origins and would readily embrace the Nazi philosophy. Seyss-Inquart had not been so sure; the NSB, the Dutch Nazi party, had existed for several years and had made little or no impression during recent general elections. Indeed, the documents he had read indicated that support for the NSB was actually declining. Although the Netherlands was only small in terms of land mass, its population of almost nine million people would require a great deal of persuasion, he suspected.

He would relish this challenge. His new position was a senior civilian role and also held one of the highest SS ranks, that of Obergruppenführer. Together, they lent him the power and authority to enforce Nazi ideology. He believed in Germany, and time was on his side.

It had been no problem persuading his wife, Gertrud, and their three children to come to The Hague with him. He had been furnished with a large, detached house outside of the city and a team of servants.

In his new role, he had sequestered the office of the recently departed prime minister. It was a sizable corner office with an imposing mahogany desk and four large windows that looked out across the city in two directions. He had already removed the pictures from the wall, as he did not recognize any of the faces on display. He presumed they were former politicians who had served in past Dutch governments. They would soon be forgotten now the Netherlands had become part of the German Reich. He would find more appropriate pictures to decorate his office. In the interim, he had left a mirror hanging on the wall, and he was now gazing into it. It was framed in wood with an ornate, gilded design, which he considered decadent.

All things considered, he believed he had weathered tolerably well. His brown hair was neatly parted and flecked with a small amount of gray. His face was lean, and he thought that the small, circular, metal-rimmed glasses and impeccably knotted tie gave him an air of gravitas without being obtrusive.

Suitably satisfied with his appearance, he turned, strode over to his desk, and made as if to sit in the soft-leather chair standing behind it.

Without warning, he screamed as a searing pain ran the length of his left leg. He lowered himself into the chair and started rubbing his thigh vigorously. Years earlier, a skiing accident had shattered his knee, and the best surgeons in Vienna could not reconstruct it satisfactorily, leaving him with a permanent limp and these sporadic, excruciating bouts of pain.

"Bloody leg!" he shouted.

In the intervening years, he had successfully passed the injury off as a war wound, and while this had garnered him some expressions of admiration, he could not help but feel that people were smirking behind his back. The man who so strongly allied himself to the purity of the Aryan race was a cripple.

There was a pile of papers positioned neatly on the varnished oak surface of the desk. To the side lay a notebook, a fountain pen, and a bottle of ink.

Once the pain had subsided, he pushed the papers to one side, opened the notebook, picked up the pen, and started writing swiftly but neatly. He wrote without pausing for an hour before calling his secretary Ingrid.

When he had arrived, he had found Ingrid sitting at her desk outside his office door. Alone. Since the government was in exile, the entire floor was otherwise deserted. She was immaculately presented with a smart blue dress, carefully styled fair hair, and an acceptable amount of makeup. She had a pleasant demeanor and a ready smile, which was adequate for the time being.

He asked her to fetch him a cup of coffee and request that Mussert attend his office immediately.

*

Seyss-Inquart knew Anton Mussert was not an Aryan. This inconsequential man had set up the NSB in 1931 and, in almost ten years, had taken it absolutely nowhere. He scoffed inwardly when he thought of the progress Hitler had made with the German Nazis in the same period. Mussert had no proper authority and would continue to have no authority, Seyss-Inquart thought, but he would have his uses.

Mussert edged into his office with obvious nervousness and slowly approached the desk. Seyss-Inquart looked at him without comment. He would make the man wait and suffer.

Mussert was wearing his full NSB uniform: shirt, tie, jacket, and trousers, all in black. The only items that disturbed this curtain of darkness were the polished silver buttons on his jacket and a triangular badge on his left sleeve with the letters NSB stitched into it with white thread. His dark hair was short, thinning on top, and shiny with oil. He looked remarkably similar to the picture Seyss-Inquart had seen in one of his files, always with an austere expression on his face. His immediate impression was that the NSB leader did not possess the gravitas to match his uniform.

"Excuse me, sir," Mussert mumbled.

"What do you want?" he barked.

"You wanted to see me, sir?" Mussert spoke so weakly that there hardly seemed to be a question there.

"Sit down, man!" He was enjoying his new role.

Mussert made as if to speak, but the Austrian interrupted. "You need to call an NSB meeting for this weekend. It has to be an open meeting for all members, those contemplating becoming members, and anybody else who wants to know more about what's going on in their country."

"It's not usual—" Mussert started plaintively, seeming to shrink into his chair.

"I don't care what's usual," Seyss-Inquart interrupted loudly. "It's not usual for a country to be in the privileged position of being assimilated into the German Reich. So let me tell you what's going to happen. You'll stand with me and other officials and inform those in attendance that the queen and the royal family have deserted the nation. They've been exploiting the people of the Netherlands for centuries. Everybody should celebrate their cowardly departure, never countenance their return, and support the new Nazi government, which will create a much more equitable society for all citizens."

Mussert looked excited, like an eager child.

"Not only that, but the Dutch government and its politicians have also behaved reprehensibly, acting only in their own self-interest. They too have deserted the people after decades of neglect. We should rejoice in their flight as well."

He gestured toward the door and ducked his head as if to start writing again. Mussert rose silently and shuffled toward the exit. As he placed his hand on the handle, Seyss-Inquart said, "I'll need to see your speech in its entirety the day before the meeting."

Mussert left the room.

Seyss-Inquart clicked the top of his pen firmly into place. It was proving to be a very productive day for the Reichskommissar.

There was a large bookcase running along the internal wall of the office. He took the opportunity to inspect the shelves. From the briefest of perusals, it was obvious most of the books and documents were written in Dutch. He could barely understand the language, and the little he did grasp was because of its passing similarity to German.

"Ingrid!" he shouted.

Within moments, his secretary appeared in the doorway. "Is there something you need, sir?"

"Come in and look at these books. Do you know what they are?"

"I'm sorry, but no, sir." After a second, she added, "Would you like me to catalog them for you?"

"Catalog them? There're shelves upon shelves to go through."

"I'd be happy to do that for you, sir."

He smiled at his secretary. "Thank you for the offer, Ingrid. However, I have a better idea. Throw them out."

"All of them?" she said with surprise. "There may be legal documents and important books here."

"Dutch law's the past. German law's the future. Throw them all out. With one exception."

"Yes, sir?"

"If you come across any items written in German, please keep them."

"Of course. I'll start first thing in the morning," she said before leaving the office.

THREE

Westerbork – June 1940

Kristallnacht had taken place in Germany in 1938 on the night of November 9. The pretext for the event was the assassination of a German diplomat by a seventeen-year-old Polish Jew in Paris. Spurred on by the Nazi party's SA paramilitary division, a pogrom by German civilians was carried out against the Jewish population.

During that night, approximately seven thousand Jewish businesses were damaged or destroyed, together with over two hundred and fifty synagogues. Thirty thousand Jewish men were arrested and incarcerated in concentration camps.

It was called Kristallnacht after the glistening shards of broken glass, which lay scattered across the streets of German towns and cities from Jewish shops, buildings, and synagogues that had been smashed and vandalized.

Once Hitler came to power, some Jews had foreseen their fate and had already emigrated. However, Kristallnacht was a tipping point, and there followed a flood of emigrations from the country to all points of the compass.

The Netherlands was a popular destination. Regarded as a multicultural, politically neutral, and liberal nation that enjoyed relative stability, and with a significant and settled Jewish population, the country was also regarded as a stepping stone to Britain or the United States.

At first, the Dutch people received these refugees. However, theirs was a relatively small country without the infrastructure required to manage and accommodate large numbers of refugees. For that reason, in the summer of 1939, the government resolved to build a refugee camp to address the problem.

As a location, the government chose a small piece of land in the Drenthe region, approximately twenty miles west of the German border, close to a small village. The camp took the name of the village: Westerbork.

D. A. Syswarda, an administrator in a psychiatric hospital, was appointed as the first director of Camp Westerbork and received the first twenty-two refugees on October 9, 1939.

Leo Blumensohn was the first refugee to register at the camp, having fled Germany in the wake of Kristallnacht.

He had met Jakob Schulz on the train from Hanover. With brown, curly hair that was neatly oiled and combed into place, he had worn a smart, dark suit. Leo had seen the nervous-looking eighteen-year-old and sat with him to provide moral support, although he himself had only recently passed his twenty-second birthday.

While he looked strong and fit, Jakob was leaner and shorter, and his jacket seemed to weigh heavily around his shoulders. They had struck up a rapport immediately and had stayed close ever since.

The two men, together with around forty of the younger and fitter refugees, had been selected to help build the permanent camp. Leo had immediately been chosen, but he had needed to exaggerate the younger man's physical abilities to persuade Syswarda to add him to the group.

It was tough work, as the barracks were being built to a high standard with sturdy redbrick walls supported by solid foundations, but additional rations were granted to those involved.

The Dutch Jewish community did not initially welcome the camp, especially as the government insisted that they contribute more than one million guilders toward its construction.

In the early months, the camp was being built while the first refugees were arriving. By the time the Germans invaded in May 1940, there had already been a significant increase in numbers from 22 to 749. This would lead to people being accommodated in half-finished barracks, or with local villagers.

This part of Drenthe was an unprepossessing area of monotonous, treeless scrubland. Refugees arriving with dreams of onward travel had their expectations dashed when they first set eyes upon the expanse of mottled green that lay in every direction. Those building the camp complained that the tangled mass of grass and weeds that covered the ground constantly thwarted their spades and pickaxes.

The fears of the refugees were partially assuaged when they witnessed the solid construction of the barracks and heard the promises of a hospital, a school, a synagogue, and proper sanitation. Families were housed in two hundred interconnected cottages, each comprising two rooms, a lavatory, and a small yard. The single inmates were accommodated in the barracks.

*

Having just finished the forty-ninth of the planned fifty barracks, Leo and Jakob sought shelter from the burning sun in the empty canteen building.

"Syswarda has gone," Leo said.

"What do you mean, *gone?*" Jakob asked.

"Gone. Replaced." He tugged at the collar of his shirt to ventilate his sweating body and passed his fingers through his hair, only to find them coated in dust and dirt from the worksite. He usually made a point of maintaining the standards of his appearance no matter the circumstances in the camp, but not today.

"Do we know who the replacement is?" Jakob asked nervously.

"A Dutch guy called Schol, so I hear. Syswarda's a good guy. It can't be a coincidence that the Germans have just invaded, and already we're seeing a new commandant in the camp. He'd only been here a few months. Why the change? Somebody new can't be good for us." He picked up his metal cup and took a sip of the coffee he had made in the nearby kitchen.

"Don't worry, Leo," Jakob said. "The camp's so small it can barely accommodate two thousand people squeezed close together. It's of no consequence to the Nazis, a tiny dot on the map. If, as you say, this Schol guy's Dutch, then any Dutchman's got to be better than a Nazi."

"Yes, much better," Leo agreed thoughtfully.

At that moment, a man in a dark suit entered through the canteen door. He walked with a sense of authority, and the two refugees automatically rose to their feet as he approached. Leo noticed the man's light-brown, cropped hair, which was visibly thinning and carefully combed. His spectacles were barely visible, so thin were their pale frames.

"My name is Schol, Captain Jacques Schol. I'm the new camp commandant. Please confirm to me which one of you is Leo Blumensohn."

"I am," Leo replied.

Schol continued without reference to Jakob.

"I've been told you're one of the founding refugees here, and you've earned a reputation as a fair-minded and hard-working man. When you talk, the others listen. You also speak both German and Dutch fluently." He paused. "And you have construction skills."

Leo nodded but did not reply.

Schol took a seat opposite the two men and opened a cardboard folder, in which there was a solitary sheet of paper. Leo could see it was neatly typed but could not read it from his angle.

"There are certain aspects of the camp that we're going to have to change. To make improvements." The commandant spoke firmly but without aggression. "We must ensure that the administration of the refugees is efficient and speedy. From now on, we'll have a roll call twice a day, and if any refugees wish to leave the camp, they'll be obliged to get a travel permit first, signed by myself.

"The management of the postal service will also be changed. All letters and parcels, both incoming and outgoing, will be censored from now on. By me in the short term, but I'll pass this task on to others at some time in the future.

"And lastly, we'll be employing several policemen from the Royal Constabulary to guard the perimeter of the camp and escort refugees who have a valid travel permit."

Leo was relieved, as he had feared regulations significantly more draconian than those now being proposed.

"I'm no supporter of the Nazis," Schol added. "The best way to keep them away from this camp is to manage it as efficiently as possible, giving them no cause to meddle. Most of the refugees here are German. I'm a Dutchman who speaks and writes very little German. I'd like your help to write up these new improvements and rules, then get them circulated and understood. This would be of benefit to you, as well as myself."

"That's fine." Leo nodded. "I don't want too many Nazis around either. I came here specifically to avoid them, so I'm happy to assist you in making the refugees traveling from the east as welcome as possible."

On this pleasant early summer's day, none of these three men could have envisaged what lay ahead for Camp Westerbork and its inmates. Nor could they have known that the horrors to come would not be traveling from the east to the west, but in the opposite direction.

FOUR

The Hague – August 1940

Sitting behind his desk with his chin resting upon his hands, Seyss-Inquart asked himself which of the two men in front of him he disliked the most. Mussert was Dutch, weak, and spineless. Rauter was an Austrian like himself and seemed to believe in Germany, but he was arrogant in a way that annoyed Seyss-Inquart intensely. Had he been honest with himself, he would have admitted that he hated Rauter the most.

Rauter was a threat. Although he reported to Seyss-Inquart, he was also a member of the SS and a commissioner for police and security. In that role, he reported to Heinrich Himmler, head of the SS and the most powerful man in the Reich after the Führer himself. Rauter was forever referring to telephone conversations or written communications he had exchanged with Himmler. Almost without exception, whenever Seyss-Inquart inquired about the work he was undertaking, Rauter would include a reference to Himmler in his explanations.

Having two bosses, his position lacked clarity and his arrogance was annoying. Nonetheless, they had to work together. The needs of Germany came first.

Seyss-Inquart started with Mussert, the NSB leader, who was an easy target and would allow him to warm up before tackling Rauter. "We've received new regulations to implement. You'll need to get your rabble to assist with the necessary communication. They're all effective from tomorrow, no exceptions."

He watched Mussert drop his notepad, pick it back up in a flustered manner, and start making notes with a pencil retrieved from his top pocket.

"There are to be no Jews in the Dutch Civil Service," he continued.

"No Jews," Mussert murmured.

"What about the Jews already working in the civil service?" Rauter interrupted. "There are lots of them. We'd be screwed without them."

"I was coming to that," Seyss-Inquart replied in a consciously condescending tone. "There'll be no more Jews recruited to the civil service. If a Jew leaves, then a non-Jew must replace him. Jews already employed can stay employed." He added, "For the time being."

In contrast to Mussert, who was writing feverishly, he noticed Rauter remained motionless, his hands resting on his crossed legs.

"I have a copy of the new regulations." Rauter smiled. "From Himmler."

"Then why did you ask about the recruitment of Jews?" Seyss-Inquart demanded.

Rauter continued to smile and shrugged his shoulders.

Seyss-Inquart had little option but to turn back to Mussert, who had by now ceased his note-taking and was watching him like a timid schoolchild.

"The ritual slaughter of animals is also forbidden," he continued.

"Good idea! The Jews won't be able to observe kosher rules," Mussert said enthusiastically.

"We'll stipulate that certain ways of slaughtering animals aren't hygienic," Rauter explained, "so it won't appear that we're directly forbidding kosher meat. It's just that kosher practices won't be possible under the new hygiene regulations."

"And we're going to ask for all civil service employees to complete an Aryan attestation to confirm they have pure blood," Seyss-Inquart added without acknowledging Rauter. "Every employee will need to confirm their religious and racial backgrounds."

"Good God!" Rauter exclaimed. "There are over two hundred thousand employees in the civil service. How on earth will you get hold of the manpower to complete all those attestations?"

"It's an enormous task, but the Dutch administrators are very efficient. And it's the best way to record the Jews' details."

"Why not get the Jews to do it themselves? Appoint a Jewish board, committee, or council. The best way of getting information from the Jews is to have them asked by other Jews."

"Such a Jewish board won't be necessary. We can do this with our existing Dutch resources." Seyss-Inquart could not help adding, "But thank you for the suggestion."

Rauter shrugged once more, and Seyss-Inquart thought he saw a disrespectful smirk on his colleague's face.

"That's it! Go, go! Get this done now," he urged.

With that, Rauter and Mussert left the office.

Seyss-Inquart looked around and considered that the appearance of his office was much improved. Against the far wall, he had unfurled two Nazi flags. On the left-hand wall, he had hung a portrait of the Führer. On the right-hand wall, there was a gap that he still had to fill. Upon his desk lay a copy of *Mein Kampf*, with its spine visible to visitors, and on his filing cabinet there were two smaller picture frames, one containing a photograph of himself with the Führer, and behind that, one of Gertrud and the children.

He walked over to the mirror and sighed at his reflection. His tie was crooked. It must have been like that throughout the meeting, he realized.

FIVE

Amsterdam – October 14, 1940

Although it was still light outside, the curtains at Weesperstraat 47 were shut. Franck was sitting in his armchair. Above him, a wall lamp gave off a warm but weak glow. He was straining to read his newspaper, moving it back and forth to obtain a clear and focused image. Decades spent immersed in books had taken their toll on his eyesight.

The room was quiet. The only sound was of Hendrik scribbling on sheets of paper strewn across the dining room table. Hannes was sitting on the windowsill absorbed in a book, an adventure story for youngsters, which he was following with keen interest.

Elizabeth walked into the room carrying a dish of steaming hot potatoes smothered in a mixture of butter and margarine, which left a sweet, sticky aroma in the air as she placed them on the table.

"What about Rachael?" Franck asked, laying down his newspaper. "We never start a meal without Rachael."

"She's working late tonight," Elizabeth replied. "Hendrik, move your papers off the table, please."

"She's a teacher. Teachers never work overtime!" their older son joked. "What's she doing?"

"She said something about marking test papers."

"Tests at that age?" Hendrik exclaimed. "Kids at primary school are too young for exams! What do you think, Father?"

Franck rose to his feet and approached the dining room table. "For once, I think you and I are in agreement. I'd prefer to let young children develop their curiosity and enjoy learning for a few years before experiencing the intensity and pressure of examinations. Can't we wait until she comes home? We always eat dinner as a family."

"She was insistent that we start before her," Elizabeth said, bringing a casserole dish to the table. "She wasn't sure when she'd be back. Hendrik! Wash your hands before dinner and set a good example for your little brother! We're having stew today. Willem de Leeuw, the butcher, could only sell me braising beef. He says the Nazis are severely restricting his meat supplies, and it's certain to be rationed shortly."

"Mama, please don't call me little anymore. I'm seven years old and I'll soon be a man!" Hannes protested.

Hendrik ruffled his brother's hair, smiling. "Well done, little man! I'm sure you'll be a great man one day soon! But even great men must wash their hands before dinner. So, get going!"

Franck recited a prayer, then each member of the family took a helping from the dishes laid out before them. Without Rachael's presence, it was quieter than normal. Her convivial nature would often be the catalyst for their conversations.

It was ten minutes later, while Franck was cutting a piece of beef, that his eldest son addressed him.

"Are you going to sign it, Father?"

Franck paused, a forkful of meat hovering between the plate and his mouth.

"Well?"

"Come on, Hendrik!" his mother beseeched. "Not at the dinner table. And not in front of Hannes! We've already discussed this! It's happening too often."

"This is too important to hide away from, Mama. This is an escalation by the Nazis who're running the country. It's a test for us all, Jews and Gentiles. Who'll comply, who'll disobey? Sign the Aryan attestation and the Nazis will learn the details of every single Jew and non-Jew working in the civil service. That's every teacher, tram driver, civil administrator...and university professor."

"Is that right, Franck?" Elizabeth asked.

"As ever, Hendrik, you make things sound simpler than they are. But it's never that black and white."

Hannes peered up at his father's impassive face.

"As ever, Father, you make things more complicated than they are. You look for every conceivable shade of gray. This *is* a black-and-white question, a matter of choosing between right and wrong." There was a growing anger in Hendrik's tone, and his face had reddened noticeably.

"Lower your voice and show your father a bit of respect," Elizabeth interceded.

"We've had many censuses from the civil service over the years, all requesting similar information. Race and religion included. What if this is just another census, Hendrik?" Franck asked. "The Germans have always been regarded as a very well-organized people, often asking for all sorts of forms to be filled out. Just like this attestation. The Germans have treated us reasonably well so far. We're not overrun by the SS, like the other countries they've invaded. We know the stories coming out of Germany and Poland. If we antagonize them by not signing, what's stopping them from resorting to those tactics here? Nobody wants that."

"Father, it's no census! The form for non-Aryans must be filled out in duplicate, but only once for the Aryans. Who and what is that extra copy for? This is a Nazi trick to identify us Jews, discover where we live, and find out as much information as they can about us! They need that extra copy for something, and knowing the Nazis, it won't be pleasant."

"From what I've heard," Franck said, "most of the civil service employees are going to sign the attestation anyway, Jews and non-Jews. The outcome of non-compliance will be reprisals and violence. If we sign the attestation and the Nazis misuse the information, we can always frustrate them at a later stage.

"Members of the business community say that the Nazis have had a positive effect so far. They're selling many more goods and services to Germany itself. Apparently, Seyss-Inquart has an enormous pile of purchase requisitions ready to be given to Dutch companies."

"Businessmen are only ever interested in money, never values or morals," his son complained. "The Germans would make everything themselves if they could. Has it ever occurred to you that the products our companies are selling to them are being used to make military equipment and weapons? They may be contributing to the deaths of French, British, or Dutch people. They're only using us while it suits them and could change their minds tomorrow.

"Once an attestation is submitted, it can't be changed or withdrawn. It's permanent," he concluded.

Elizabeth coughed timidly, then asked her husband, "And will you sign it, darling?"

He found his wife was gazing directly at him, and, despite his strongest hopes to the contrary, she showed not a flicker of backing down.

In the circumstances, he felt he had no option but to reply to her. "Yes, I probably will."

SIX

Amsterdam – October 1940

"This is the first time I've taken an attendance register at five o'clock in the afternoon!" Rachael said, speaking with a clear and simple German accent.

She was standing in her classroom in the day-care center on Middenlaan, a few hundred yards to the northwest of Plantage Park, directly opposite the Dutch Theater. Two trams, 9 and 14, regularly trundled past on their way to Dam Square.

The building itself was three stories high with a steep, gabled roof. Its plain brick facade was much improved by unusually tall windows on the first floor.

The center had started out as a crèche for babies and young children whose mothers were out working. It could accommodate up to a hundred children a day. Most of the children who attended were Jewish, as were the teachers and carers. Over the years, the age limit of the children attending had steadily risen. At the time of the Nazi invasion of the Netherlands, the oldest child in attendance had been seven.

Henriette Pimentel had managed the center since 1926. By October 1940, she was sixty-four years old. Her hair was gray, but the laughter of young children had sustained her spirit and left a youthful gleam in her brown eyes. She would still be the first to arrive at the center each day and the last to leave. At that time, she employed nineteen members of staff.

Her organizational and management skills were exceptional. A stranger visiting her office for the first time would have seen a jungle of exotic plants and piles of books sitting on every surface and maybe interpreted this as a sign of disorganization, but they would have been incorrect. She knew every aspect of the center in minute detail, and the curling palm fronds and oversized cacti were because of her addiction to books about foreign travel. Having dedicated herself to childcare since the age of seventeen, she had never visited the places where these plants came from.

Some weeks earlier, she had asked Rachael if she would be prepared to teach Dutch to young German refugees.

"The refugees have had a frightful experience," she said. "Losing their businesses, their jobs, their homes. And now, they're cooped up in camps or have fought their way to cities like Amsterdam and just aren't prepared for life here. There's a large group of children who would benefit from your knowledge of German and Dutch. I know that you've got a kind soul, which is why I've asked you.

"Unfortunately, we can't pay you. There are no funds available, and the refugees are too poor to pay anything," she added.

"It would be a pleasure," Rachael replied. "I'm more than happy to spend a little of my time to help these children. The poor things must be frightened to death by all these changes."

She had studied German at the University of Amsterdam, and although she had only completed her degree during the previous year, she felt more than competent and confident enough to teach it.

And now, she found herself in front of a room of German children on a chilly October evening. She had attempted to create a more formal classroom environment, but the tables and chairs were intended for younger children and made the older refugees look like giants. However, the pupils were arranged in neat rows and were watching her expectantly.

"I'm going to read the register out. Please tell me if you don't hear your own name being called," she announced, speaking in slow and well-articulated German. "Is that understood?"

She held up the sheets of paper that comprised the register and began reading aloud.

"Bachmann Helmut, Bloch Walther, Drechsler Beate…"

When she had finished, she asked, "Is there any boy or girl whose name I didn't call?"

She scanned the faces of the children in front of her, their expressions covering the full spectrum from relaxed to anxious, enthusiastic to uninterested. This was not surprising under the circumstances.

She was about to put down the papers when an arm was raised hesitantly near the back of the classroom.

"Yes?" she asked softly. "What's your name, young man?" She watched the boy's lips moving but heard nothing.

She asked him again, but his voice was still inaudible, so to avoid him further discomfort, she walked up to his desk and kneeled beside him.

The boy was about eight years old, but the usual verve and energy associated with a child seemed to have drained from him. He was worryingly thin, and his cheekbones looked as if they were about to burst through his pallid, paper-like skin. His eyes had receded into their dark sockets as if they no longer wished to confront the outside world. They were so deep set that she could not readily determine their color. His black hair was short and disheveled but recently washed. He wore a white shirt, which was clean but frayed.

She glanced around the room, noticing that the boy's condition was not significantly different from that of the other children. She knew from the registration documents that the children varied in age from five to fourteen and shuddered to think that some of these children were the same age as Hannes. How they had suffered in comparison!

"So, what's your name?" she asked.

"Karl Zimmermann," the boy replied, appearing to strain every sinew and muscle in his body to squeeze the words out.

"Thank you, Karl," she answered, smiling. She returned to her desk at the front of the classroom, picked up the sheets of paper once more, and silently reread the list. She turned the last sheet over. There, on the back, was a single name—Karl Zimmermann. She marked his name on the register and then addressed the class.

"You and your families are going to be living in the Netherlands for a while, and in this country, we speak Dutch, which is quite like German. I hope I can teach you how to read, write, and talk a little. Perhaps I can also help you learn more about our way of life and customs. If you're lucky, you'll be able to go to a shop and buy sweets or chocolate using the Dutch you have learned!"

The mention of candy had an immediate and noticeable impact on the children; their attention sparked, their eyes wide with excitement. She made a mental note to buy some boiled sweets from Jansen's Candy Emporium and bring them along to their next lesson.

"Okay. Now I've gained your attention, shall I teach you how to say your name in Dutch?" she asked.

SEVEN

The Hague – November 1940

Seyss-Inquart turned over the last sheet of paper on his desk and leaned back in his chair. Circular 47176 had proved to be a resounding success. Remarkably, the vast majority of the employees of the civil service had completed the Aryan attestation, including the Jews.

He wished he had been stationed in Amsterdam. Most of the Jews were concentrated there and therefore most of his work too. There was nothing much happening in The Hague, but there would be plenty happening there over the coming months. Hours earlier, he had received his latest orders from Hitler and was keen to see them carried out as soon as possible.

There was a timid knock on his office door. "Come in!" he bellowed.

The oak door creaked on its hinges as it opened, revealing Mussert standing in the corridor, not daring to venture beyond the threshold.

"Come in!!"

Mussert entered cautiously and approached Seyss-Inquart's desk, glancing briefly at the two empty chairs.

"No need for Rauter's presence today. It's just a few minor circulars and regulations for us to deal with. No doubt he's already received them," the Reichskommissar explained, anticipating the question on the other man's lips. "I suppose you'll be wanting to take notes."

He felt particularly satisfied with himself. Rauter was sure to feel affronted by not being invited to the meeting, whether he had been informed by Himmler or not. The fact he had invited Mussert, and not Rauter, would add insult to injury.

"Having obtained the attestations, we have identified the Aryans and non-Aryans in the civil service. I believe we can now effectively use this information. All Jews are to be removed from civil service positions."

"Excluding those who are already in employment?"

"Don't be an idiot, man! That rule's already in place. This regulation is specifically intended for the Jews employed in the civil service. They're all to be removed. With immediate effect."

"All of them? Even those in senior or essential roles?" Mussert asked.

"We'll have no people of non-Aryan blood operating anywhere within our administration, no matter what position they occupy."

"For instance, there's Lodewijk Visser, the President of the High Court, the most senior person in the whole legislature," the NSB leader countered. "He's very well regarded and has a broad base of support among Aryans and non-Aryans alike. I appreciate he's Jewish, but shouldn't we retain him?" Having summoned the courage to utter these words, he cowered like a school pupil awaiting a reprimand from the principal.

"One day, you'll learn not to query orders. All Jewish civil servants are to be dismissed with immediate effect. The remaining Aryans will cope admirably, I'm sure."

Mussert wrote this down in his notebook and rose to his feet as if to leave.

"Sit down, man!" Seyss-Inquart ordered. "We still have more regulations to go through. The attestations have given us a clear picture of the number of poisonous Jews infecting our civil service, so we can now move our attention to the Jewish businesses that are exploiting and choking our commercial activities. We now require all Jewish businesses to be registered before Christmas to give us a good start to 1941. The NSB must communicate this forthwith and make sure the Jews are quite aware of the ramifications if they don't comply. I'll deal with the administration of this regulation. Is that clear?"

"Yes, very clear, sir," the NSB leader replied, keeping his mouth open as if to speak further.

"If you've anything interesting to say, say it. If not, then say nothing and go away!" the commissioner interrupted.

"I thought you'd like to know that membership of the NSB has reached one hundred thousand. A few months ago, it was only ten thousand. And from now on, all new mayors appointed across the country must be members," Mussert said sheepishly.

"Good grief! I don't believe it! A piece of good news. You've actually done something worthwhile. Congratulations! Let's hope we have another one from you before the end of the war!" his superior exclaimed before adding, "Obviously, the NSB's now the only political party legally permitted, so it's not as if you've much in the way of competition."

"There's more," Mussert continued with a marginal increase in confidence. "Our members have been instigating unrest and rioting in the main Jewish living areas in Amsterdam."

"And why on earth would they do that?"

"Well, it builds up nervousness and friction among the local communities, both Jewish and non-Jewish. We arrest anybody who retaliates. To be honest, the new members want to be involved in the action, and we need to show that we're an organization of actions, not just words. Beating up and arresting Jews can never be a bad thing!"

"Who gave the order for this to happen?"

"Well…we…we just did it," Mussert replied, his confidence draining away, as the Austrian had hoped.

"In the future, behave like a soldier and only respond to orders from your superiors. Is that understood?"

"Fully understood, sir."

"Out of curiosity, how many Jews did you arrest because of these fabricated riots?"

"Over fifty, sir."

"Well, since you've arrested them, you might as well do something with them rather than have them lying around in the police cells. They can be classified as political prisoners and sent off to Mauthausen forthwith."

"Yes, sir!"

"And Mussert. You're right, of course. Arresting Jews is never such a terrible thing. You have my permission to conduct raids and cause riots regularly from now on. Provided you continue to make arrests, the biggest troublemakers will be taken off the streets."

"Will there be a circular or regulation for this, sir?"

"None is required. This is a straightforward order from me to you. It's normal day-to-day business. You may go," the Reichskommissar concluded.

Mussert rose and briskly made his way out of the office.

It was a shame about Visser, Seyss-Inquart thought. The man was, from what he had heard, a deeply knowledgeable and respected public servant. His loss would undoubtedly have a negative impact on the judicial system in the short term and be likely to reduce morale. However, once the Jews and the civil service had seen the Nazi plans for 1941, any lingering concerns about Lodewijk Visser would quickly evaporate.

EIGHT

Mauthausen – December 1940

Mauthausen was a small town close to the city of Linz in Upper Austria. Its surrounding hills contained immense seams of fine-grained granite, which had been widely used in the construction of the splendid edifices of the Austro-Hungarian Empire.

By the start of 1939, it had a population of approximately three thousand. The quarry was owned and run by the German Earth and Stonework Company Limited, whose managing director was Oswald Pohl, the head of business and administration for the SS, an appointment made by Himmler himself.

In August 1938, the Nazis sent several hundred political prisoners from the Dachau concentration camp to Mauthausen with the specific task of building a forced labor camp to increase the output of the quarry.

The labor camp was the responsibility of Franz Ziereis, who had recently been promoted to SS-Sturmbannführer, a senior rank that granted its owner four silver pips on the black collar of his uniform. He was a lifelong soldier, having joined the German Army in 1924 at the age of only eighteen. The military life had nurtured within him a fanatical obsession with discipline and Nazism. His uniform and dark-brown hair were immaculate, matching his severe expression and small, dark, emotionless eyes.

The camp had been financed to a large extent by goods and property taken from its own inmates, together with loans from German banks. By the end of 1940, the main camp was complete and operating profitably.

One evening, Pohl and Ziereis were in Pohl's house. It was, from the outside, an unprepossessing building situated on a low hill overlooking the camp, painted green to match its natural surroundings. The quarry lay to the west, at the far end of which they could see the 186 steps, nicknamed the Stairs of Death, which rose from the quarry floor up to a large, flattened, level area about fifty yards above, from where the granite blocks were dispatched on trucks.

Notwithstanding the plain exterior of the house, Pohl had acquired extravagant furnishings for the interior, many sourced from his contacts in Vienna. He was extremely pleased with the mahogany desk and the two deep-red velvet armchairs in his study. There was a scratch on the desk's surface, probably caused by its previous owner, but overall, it was an excellent piece. It was in this room overlooking the camp where he felt most comfortable.

After serving in the German navy during the World War, he had studied business and law at college. Having rejoined the navy, his skills in finance, accounting, and administration were soon noticed, so much so that Himmler himself recognized his work and put him in charge of the SS Administration. This role included managing the growing number of labor camps that were being created to satisfy the demands of the Reich. Pohl established a reputation for getting things done and recruiting people who did the same.

He was a decade older than Ziereis, born in the latter years of the nineteenth century, bald from the middle of his forehead to his nape, with slicked-down patches of black hair on either side. Where Ziereis was austere, Pohl was jovial, his jowls and mouth resting naturally in a half smile. His quick-witted business mind had been of considerable benefit to the Reich but had also given him access to certain extravagances in his personal life that may well have contributed to his contented demeanor. In his SS uniform, Ziereis looked like a pencil, upright and uptight. Pohl's paunch caused the shiny silver buttons of his jacket to stretch their buttonholes, and he looked louche and decadent in comparison.

Snow was falling outside, leaving a white blanket across the landscape. From the house, it seemed to Ziereis as if the camp below them had disappeared. The roll-call yard was barely distinguishable from inmates' barracks. Thin wisps of gray smoke plumed out of the chimneys of the SS accommodation blocks. Beyond the camp perimeter fence, the open quarry loomed, its sheer, vertical sides untouched by snow and looking like a dark, gaping mouth.

Ziereis turned toward the fire burning warmly in the hearth. Pohl was sitting in one of the velvet chairs, swirling brandy around his glass.

"Franz, there are too many inmates in the camp," Pohl said. "We really only have space for a thousand and we've now got three."

"But we have plenty of work for them to do," Ziereis replied. "We're operating two quarries and can always send surplus men out to work in the farmers' fields. There are also ongoing discussions about the introduction of specialist manufacturing in the camp. A lot of these political prisoners aren't so stupid and can carry out more complicated tasks than lugging slabs of granite around. We have doctors, architects, lawyers, the lot. They can build and work in factories of almost any kind, whatever products we require. We keep them here, use them as best we can, safe in the knowledge they'll never ever set foot outside the camp to spread their pernicious views or dilute the Aryan bloodstock. If we get too many prisoners, we can use them to build another camp."

"Keep this to yourself, Franz, but profit per ton of quarried granite is higher than it's ever been!" Pohl's tone bordered on excitement. "We're making a serious amount of money.

"I've been informed that we'll soon be receiving Poland's political prisoners as well, to add to the Spanish partisans from earlier this year. Poor sods escaped from Franco by entering France, then the French handed them over to us!" He laughed. "As the war proceeds, it's logical that we'll receive more and more prisoners. Whether they'll be good for complex manufacturing work or for lifting stone up the Stairs of Death, the labor's free! It's a big win either way!"

"So, let's send surplus inmates to Gusen to build another camp. They can walk there from here. Work them hard. We've got plenty of spare men who can die," Ziereis said thoughtfully. "However, hard labor and your *little games* might not reduce the numbers quickly enough, I fear."

"What do you mean by *little games*?" Pohl snorted, taking a swig of brandy to empty his glass.

"I saw one only yesterday evening. Your SS guys put an inmate in the yard, soaked him in cold water, and left him standing there in the snow. He didn't even have a pair of clogs on his feet."

"Of course. It was carried out for the benefit of the doctors! A scientific experiment to establish how long the human body can withstand exceptionally low temperatures. It'll be useful knowledge when we take Nazification to colder countries like Finland and Russia." Pohl grinned. He stood up and walked over to the drinks cabinet to replenish his glass.

"And what were the results of this experiment?" Ziereis asked doubtfully.

"Ah, well, that's unfortunate. We had to abort." The businessman could barely suppress his laughter. "It was extremely cold last night, well below freezing. Anyway, it was too cold for our men, so they went back inside before the prisoner died. He was definitely dead by the morning, though. We'll have to perform the experiment again, I suppose."

Ziereis paced up and down the room, taking measured sips from his glass. It was so cold outside that, despite the strong heat from the fire, he could feel the temperature dropping each time he neared the window. He watched his colleague, who had resumed his position by the hearth.

"Our objective isn't to play games or to make a pile of money out of forced labor. It's to carry out the orders of Himmler, whose instructions come directly from the Führer."

"It's not so bad to make money at the same time, though. This brandy isn't cheap," Pohl replied, holding his glass up.

"I like you, Oswald, but sometimes I think you put money ahead of the Party rather than the other way around. For me, the Party always comes first." Ziereis stood upright and puffed out his chest as he spoke.

"I like you too, Franz, although sometimes you're a little too serious. I like you so much that tomorrow, I'm going to requisition materials to build a new camp at Gusen *and* a new factory. We'll let the surplus main camp prisoners walk over and work there each day until it's built. And I'll make sure there's enough in the budget to purchase a mobile gas chamber. In fact, our profits are so good at the moment, I'll order two mobile gas chambers to make us twice as effective in managing the number of inmates. Let's aim to reduce the overall number of inmates by a thousand over the next couple of months." He gestured for Ziereis to take a seat. "Come on! No more serious talk! Grab hold of that bottle and let me tell you what happened on the Stairs of Death today."

"Another experiment, I presume?" Ziereis asking, taking his place by the fire.

"This one's more to do with the laws of physics!" Pohl took another sip of brandy. "The prisoners are all carrying one block of granite on their backs. Each block weighs about a hundred pounds, give or take. The stairs are wide enough to accommodate five prisoners at a time, and there are one hundred and eight-six steps.

"So, the experiment is a bit like a game of human skittles. How many prisoners can a soldier knock over by pushing one of them off the top stair? There's a good deal of thought necessary, I'm telling you. You need to consider the weather, which currently makes the conditions slippery underfoot. Then there's the strength of the prisoner. If he's too weak, he simply collapses on the spot. If he's strong, he may not fall over at all. It's best to select someone between the two extremes. If he's of average strength, he'll try to stay upright, totter, flail his arms and, in doing so, collide with prisoners next to and behind him."

"I hope this experiment isn't impacting the amount of granite being processed each day," Ziereis interjected.

"Of course not! Assuming the steps are fully loaded, that's nine hundred and thirty people carrying about ninety-three thousand pounds of granite at any point in time. That's an acceptable weight of granite. Our experiment is a tiny pebble in comparison." He smiled, watching Ziereis. "There are five soldiers guarding the top of the stairs, and each one's allowed one push per day. The rest of their time's spent making sure the carriers keep up the pace. Remember, it's their job to shoot the prisoners who can go no farther. That's strenuous work. Our men *do* need some light relief."

"Okay, come on, Oswald! Tell me the results of this so-called physics experiment," Ziereis blurted, unable to wait any longer.

"Very well. The most effective push should be around the fifth ascent of the day. Before then, the prisoners still have some energy and might withstand a push. Too long after, they can be too weak and just collapse. And we need to select a man in the middle of the row—"

"So he can fall into the prisoners on either side," Ziereis interjected.

"Exactly. Then you want somebody reasonably big and strong who, if he falls, will collide with the most people. Lastly, the soldiers need to watch the first few lifts carefully to look for the most likely candidates. By lift five or six, even the strongest inmates begin to tire."

"And the result?"

"The best result has been seven," Pohl said proudly. "The winning prisoner didn't fall straight away but staggered sideways first, then backward, and then plowed into two columns of men instead of one. We knocked over seven inmates carrying seven granite stones from one firm push. We'll try again tomorrow and see if we can improve on that."

"And what about the granite that the inmates have dropped? How do we get it carried to the trucks?"

"Always the pragmatist, Franz! We let the fallen man pick it up himself. If he can't do it, he'll be shot. Then we get somebody else to carry it. You can imagine it can become quite messy if seven skittles fall at one time."

Pohl could not resist a smile and was pleased to see Ziereis reciprocate.

"Oswald, do you have any of those nice Cuban cigars? I appreciate they're tricky to get hold of, but I think one might help take the chill out of my bones."

"Funny you should ask!" Pohl replied. "Only today, I was able to do a nice little exchange with an acquaintance who needed some US dollars. I happened to have some dollars, he happened to have cigars! All the way from Cuba!"

He rose from his chair, walked over to the desk, removed a wooden box from a drawer, and carried it back to the fireplace with a satisfied look on his face.

NINE

Amsterdam – New Year's Eve, 1940

Although she was lying in bed with her back to him, Franck knew Elizabeth was still awake. He was not sure how he knew. Perhaps it was the cadence of her breathing. Or that after thirty years of marriage, he had developed a sixth sense.

"Are you having difficulty sleeping, my love?" he asked, placing his book on the bedside table.

"Are we safe here, Franck?" Her voice wavered as she fought to deliver the words. There was a directness in her question he had rarely heard before.

He paused and drew in a long, slow breath. He realized that, over the years, he had paid scant attention to their bedroom, but now he found his eyes lingering and appraising the objects that furnished it. In the soft glow of his reading lamp, the brass bed knobs shone like gold spheres, and the crystal baubles of the ceiling light glimmered like stars. It was warm and comfortable, a pleasant and homey room, he thought.

He recalled the birth of each of their three children in this very room. How Hannes had arrived so quickly that Franck had rushed back from the university and heard a baby crying as he dashed up the stairs, just in time to see his son being passed into the arms of his mother. That day was one of unbridled joy. Without looking, he could clearly envision the antique silver-framed picture standing on the dressing table and portraying the new family sitting on the bed, proud: father and mother, daughter, son, and baby. The children were smiling, young and carefree. Whatever worries the parents might have harbored had been washed away by a tide of elation.

In May 1926, this young university lecturer was aiming to become a professor of German and English. One of the sitting professors was due to retire in another two years, and Franck had been given a strong hint he would be the one to take over the faculty. And so it had proved in 1928, when he received his promotion.

He mused that when his youngest son was born, he could have predicted the path of the family for the next five to ten years with a good deal of confidence and accuracy. But now they had arrived at the end of 1940, and he didn't have the slightest inkling of what might happen in the next five to ten months.

For the first time in his life, he was unemployed, together with the other 2,500 Jews who had been employed by the civil service. They had all been sacked on the same day, based on the Aryan attestations. They had even fired Visser.

Damn that attestation, he reproached himself. As suspected, Seyss-Inquart had abused it, allowing the Nazis to act much more efficiently and quickly. So much for delay.

He wondered what would have happened if he had not signed it. Or if all the Jews had refused. Or the whole of the civil service had refused. He concluded that ruminating about the past would not be helpful. His actions in the here and now were all that mattered.

During this extended silence, he knew full well the answer to his wife's question. No, they weren't safe. The myth about the Jews being treated reasonably by the Nazis had been well and truly exploded. He had hoped his son's views were those of a defiant teenager holding idealistic and radical opinions, but Hendrik had been correct all along, and he, the experienced and logical university professor, had been wrong.

He suddenly felt nauseous, as if bile were forcing its way up from his guts and into his mouth, burning his throat and making him heave. His eyes were watering, he felt dizzy, and the room swirled. He felt as if he were floating in nothingness. The Nazis had uprooted his whole life and existence, stealing his job, threatening his family, and seeking to wreck his future.

He took another deep breath and coughed into his hand to clear his throat.

"There's no reason to worry, my love. We're all safe," he replied. "We'll all stick together and find a way. We always do."

"Are you saying that to placate me?"

"Not at all. We still live in a country experiencing minimal interference from the SS."

She turned over so she could face her husband.

"So, what will the Nazis do next?" she asked.

"Who knows? My guess is that they'll soon realize that people like Visser and university professors are a vital part of society, and they'll reemploy us during the coming months," he responded without enthusiasm. "They're a practical race. When they need people, they tend to keep them around."

"And is Hendrik safe?"

"The Nazis will probably have him expelled from the university in the next few months. With the other Jewish students."

"And his views? They're quite strong."

"The Nazis don't tolerate dissenters," he reflected with furrowed brow. "Hendrik, like many young people, does have radical views. This happens in every generation and is part of a normal, developing society. But there's no way we live in a normal society anymore. Hendrik can have his views but must express them carefully. Saying the wrong thing within earshot of the wrong person will cause him gigantic problems." He slowly shook his head.

"My family's being torn to pieces," she sobbed.

He moved closer to her, wrapping his arms around her shoulders and drawing her to him.

"The five of us will stick together until this situation ends," he said. "It will be soon, I'm sure."

"Can we escape the country?" she asked in a voice that carried a mix of desperation and hope. "Away from the Nazis?"

"We're surrounded by Germans to the east and south of our borders. There's only the coastline to the northwest where it's possible to escape by sea to England. Then maybe on to the United States of America."

"America!" she said, energized, and propping herself up on her elbow. "We have relatives there! Cousin Belle and Auntie Irma live near New York."

"But the Germans understand that the coastline's a way out for Jews. And a potential way in for the Allied Forces. They've been deploying masses of soldiers and equipment right along the coast. For us to escape, we'd have to be like ghosts, traveling the roads unseen, breaching the Nazi coastal defenses undetected, then finding somebody to take us to England, probably in a small boat in the rough seas of winter! It's possible but exceptionally risky."

"But it's possible? I'd risk everything to keep the family together and safe," she said.

He waited to gather his thoughts. He opened his mouth, then paused again before speaking. "I'm not sure it would be five of us, my love."

"What? It has to be all of us! We can't split the family up! Why not five?" she demanded.

"Hannes would come with us, of course. However, Rachael and Hendrik are adults and would need to make up their own minds."

"Hendrik's twenty and barely a man! And would you leave Rachael here on her own?" she countered vehemently.

"We'd try our best to persuade them, but it'd still be their decision. But you're right. I'm not sure I could leave Rachael."

There was silence as she contemplated his words.

"Are you saying that if Rachael chooses to stay, then so do we? We'd stay here with Hannes?"

"I'm really not sure," he answered. "All options are risky."

She sank back down on the mattress and turned away from her husband.

He understood the bleakness of the picture he had painted—and the impact of these words on his wife.

"Look, nothing's impossible," he placated. "I'll tell you what I'll do. Tomorrow, I'll go to the bank and draw out our savings. Then we'll have ready access to cash, should we need it." He forced a more positive tone of voice. "I'll also make discreet inquiries about how we might escape to England or even France. Nothing ventured, nothing gained, as they say."

He looked at his wristwatch, lay down beside his wife, and drew her close to him before speaking.

"I've just looked at the time. Happy New Year, my love."

He felt his wife's slow, shallow breaths and knew she was crying.

After a while, her chest swelled as she prepared to speak. "Happy New Year, Franck," she said. Although her voice faltered, he noticed a determination in her words.

"We *must* keep the family together!" she stressed. "At all costs, we must keep the family together."

TEN

Amsterdam – January 1941

To deter the winter chill, Hannes and Isaac walked briskly along Keizersgracht. They talked incessantly, never interrupting one another, seeming to possess an innate and mutual understanding of the moment when the roles of speaker and listener needed reversing. Each of them held a bag of candy, and with the same apparent telepathy, they would swap or consume items of confectionery without disrupting the flow of conversation. This continued all the way from Jensen's Candy Emporium to the Pathé Movie Theater on Schapensteeg.

The boys came to a halt on the opposite side of the street to the theater. Their conversation petered out as they marveled at the ornate, art deco facade of the building and the brightly lit sign that outlined the words *Walt Disney's Snow White and the Seven Dwarves*. They had eagerly anticipated watching the Walt Disney movie. Almost all features were shown in black and white, and the prospect of the sheer brilliance of Technicolor enthralled them. The theater auditorium was always warm, which provided another benefit on a cold winter's day. They would gulp in its heady atmosphere, laden with the smells of cigarette smoke, alcohol, and sweet perfume.

Seeing that the line was longer than normal, they quickly crossed the road. Ten minutes later, the friends reached the front of the line and approached the ticket office window.

"Two children's tickets, please," Isaac asked politely, his head pushed close to the glass separating him from the ticket attendant, a man in his twenties with straggly, long black hair that looked incompatible with his pressed white shirt and black bow tie.

"Are either of you two Jewish?" the man whispered.

"Why do you want to know that?" Isaac asked in return.

Hannes squeezed up close to the glass next to his friend.

"They are new rules," the man explained unconvincingly, looking from one boy to the other. "Are you a Christian?"

"I am a Christian," Isaac said, "although my mum says I won't be if I don't pay more attention in church."

"And you—are you a Christian?" the attendant asked Hannes, raising his eyebrows expectantly.

"No, I'm Jewish," he replied.

The attendant took a breath and lowered his gaze.

"Well, *you* can buy a ticket," the attendant said, waving his hand at Isaac, "but *you* can't," he added, gesturing toward Hannes.

"But we always go to the movies together," Isaac complained, "and there's no point watching a picture on your own. It's crazy!"

"I'm sorry, but the government has only issued the rule today. Jews aren't allowed in the picture house anymore," the ticket seller replied, his hand still pointing.

"He's not Jewish. He's my best friend," Isaac insisted. "Look, nobody knows he's Jewish apart from us three. Just sell us two tickets and nobody will find out. He looks the same as I do. He's more or less my brother. We're the same age, go to the same school, like the same candy." He held out his bag of candy in front of the glass screen. "Want one?"

The attendant looked up sheepishly and appeared to be considering the situation, tugging at his shirt collar as if it had suddenly become tight around his neck.

"Come on, get a move on or we'll miss the start of the movie!" a voice shouted from somewhere in the line behind them. This seemed to reset the ticket vendor's resolve.

"Sorry, no Jews allowed. Do you want one ticket or none?"

"None, obviously!" Isaac said firmly.

"You can watch it if you want," Hannes said, turning to his friend.

"None!" he repeated without taking his gaze off the attendant. "Why can't you give a ticket to my friend?"

"Sorry, it's more than my job's worth," the attendant replied.

"Then your job's not worth much!" Hannes mocked.

The attendant lifted his head and looked beyond the two boys. "Next, please! Next for tickets!"

The boys slowly walked away from the theater. Neither spoke.

"I'm sorry," Hannes muttered after a while.

"Sorry for what? It's not your fault. It's the theater's!" Isaac said with a smile of empathy for his friend.

"My brother says the Germans don't like the Jews."

"That can't be right!" Isaac scoffed. "Everybody likes you, and you're Jewish!"

"I suppose so."

"There are lots of other things to do rather than watch a dumb movie, anyway. The ponds in the park are frozen over. Let's play there."

With that, the boys started to walk more swiftly, and as they did, took their bags of candy from their pockets.

ELEVEN

Amsterdam – February 11, 1941

In 1882, the Houtgracht canal had been filled in, creating a large and pleasant area of open space in the center of the city. Stretching in front of the Moses and Aaron Catholic Church, the new square was called Waterlooplein and, situated on the western edge of the Jewish Quarter, many of the nearby buildings were homes to Jewish businesses and families.

The Jewish market had been relocated from its former location in Jodenbreestraat, and its traders pitched their stalls among the elm trees that had once lined the canal. Some stalls were set up under the shelter of tarpaulin sheets while others were open to the elements.

The Jewish Quarter was not the wealthiest part of the community, and the square was not the wealthiest part of the Quarter. The Great Depression and the collapse of a large proportion of industry had left many Jews without work. Over time, the once-proud houses standing around the perimeter of the square had fallen into disrepair and were often shared by several families or a mixture of families and businesses.

The businesses that traded there sold basic household goods, many of which were secondhand. The market stalls themselves were rudimentary with worn-out tarpaulins draped over rickety steel frames. They were dark and shabby, like ink stains against the background of the white, two-towered facade of the neo-classical church.

During the latter months of 1940, the Jewish population had become the target of acts of harassment by the NSB. Until then, these had been restricted to barrages of abusive and obscene comments with the occasional incidence of physical violence. The younger and more adversarial Jews might have returned comments to their compatriots or raised their fists in defiance, but the victims had, in the main, simply ignored them.

However, since the start of 1941, the defense section of the NSB, known as the WA, had become more active. The WA's primary aim was to attack and intimidate its enemies by physical force, and the Jews were their enemies. Their attitude was one of contempt, irrespective of age, sex, or appearance. The Jews believed that the members of the WA simply liked to fight and brawl in the streets, their bravado fueled by an excess of alcohol. The equivalent young and antagonistic men within the Jewish community engaged with the WA, fighting for five or ten minutes before breaking away and disappearing into the nearby streets. With their thirst for violence assuaged, the WA gangs would then retreat, either to visit a bar or to return to their barracks.

*

That morning, snow still lay on the ground in Waterlooplein. Men with shovels had cleared pathways around the immediate vicinity of the market stalls, but there were patches of ice in the outer reaches of the square. The leafless elms were like skeletons silhouetted against the slate-gray sky.

Hendrik was buying vegetables for his mother from the de Jongs' stall. His cold and dark mood matched the weather, his anger toward the Nazis and their Dutch sympathizers growing within him.

He heard the WA before he saw them. The thudding of their boots as they marched could have been mistaken for the thunder of a breaking storm. Then they appeared, wearing their customary black uniforms, from behind the church and entered the square.

Hendrik was immediately on his guard; this group consisted of forty to fifty men, considerably bigger than the usual gangs, and was arriving in an organized, marching formation as opposed to the usual inebriated and disorderly mob. A brawl between two small groups would have quickly subsided. Not this one. This WA group was fanning out to present an extended attacking line. They all carried sticks or clubs clasped in their hands.

Although the sound of marching had announced their

arrival, the WA reached the first market stall before the Jews could react. Five men promptly destroyed the nearest stall, kicking its metal supports away and tipping boxes over, scattering carrots and cabbages across the ground. The woman who managed the stall recoiled in fear. A WA man stepped forward and struck her on the side of the head with his stick, making her stumble. As Hendrik watched her fall over backward, he instinctively strode forward.

The WA soon lost their formation, screaming and shouting and waving their wooden clubs indiscriminately. "Jews out!" were the only words Hendrik heard. In the din, he could decipher nothing else.

Then, he heard a clear, resounding cry from behind, "Don't stand by and let them get away with it!"

As he hurried past a market stall containing boxes of fruit, he noticed a wooden pole about three feet long. He grabbed hold of it and brandished it like a club.

The WA men were continuing to demolish market stalls and threaten their owners. When they felt the presence of the approaching Jews, they squared up to them.

Hendrik did not know how many Jews had fought back, but by the time he reached his nearest adversary and brought the pole down hard on the man's forearm, he was aware of similar confrontations breaking out to his left and right.

He heard the roaring and shouting of the opposing groups and found himself screaming at the top of his voice. He thought of his jobless father sitting at home and his brother standing outside the theater, and a rage surged in him as he watched these sinister black figures silhouetted against the snow-covered ground.

The man he had struck was holding his arm and retreating. Hendrik looked around and saw two others kicking a Jew who was on the ground, curled up to protect himself.

"Hey, get off him!" Hendrik bellowed, whirling the wooden pole above his head.

The men looked at each other and abandoned their victim to fight Hendrik. To him, they were not people. They were featureless shadows. He ran straight at them, waving his club and screaming, "Bastards! Bastards!"

Afterward, he supposed they had both struck him at the same time, so strong was the impact. The blows lifted him right off his feet, throwing him to the ground, and he immediately felt a searing pain in his head. The cold concrete against the back of his skull sent a jolt through him, and he felt warm blood seeping through his hair, forming a red stain in the snow like ink on blotting paper.

When he recovered consciousness, he found he was lying on his back. Attempting to look around, he discovered he could not open his right eye. Using only his left eye and by gently turning his head, he determined he was still in Waterlooplein, and though the WA had disappeared completely, there were some Jews remaining. A small number were lying on the ground being treated for their injuries. The others were gathered in groups or attempting to make good the damage caused to their stalls.

"How are you feeling?" Hendrik recognized mevrouw de Jong's voice but could not see her until she leaned over him. She was holding a piece of wet cloth, red with blood.

"Looks worse than it is," she added, seeing him anxiously looking at the cloth. "Blood makes such a mess. I've patched up the cut on the back of your head. You should wait until tomorrow and then see if you need a trip to the hospital. Probably not. The eye's badly bruised. There's nothing we can do about that. It'll just take time for the bruising to go down." She spoke in the soothing manner of a nurse.

"Thank you," he murmured. "What happened?"

"Well, we gave as good as we got, so my husband tells me. Plenty of cuts and bruises, much like your own. On both sides. Only one problem really," she said, her voice deepening and a shadow falling across her face.

"What's wrong?" he asked. "Has somebody been killed?"

"No, but one of them has been seriously injured," she said solemnly. "He was struck on the head, slipped on a patch of ice, and smashed his skull on the edge of a paving slab. By all accounts, he's in a bad way."

"Better a Nazi than a Jew!" Hendrik sneered. "That'll teach them! He's a Dutch Nazi, and the Germans don't consider them to be proper Nazis."

"I'm not so sure," mevrouw de Jong replied with a shrug. "Whether Dutch or German, a seriously injured Nazi spells trouble. Who knows what they'll contemplate in retaliation?"

She dabbed his head wound one more time with the cloth.

"If you're feeling strong enough, it makes sense for you to make your way home, clean up, and get some rest. Your mother will be worried about you. Let's see what tomorrow brings."

TWELVE

Amsterdam – February 12, 1941

Although the office was dark, untidy, and dirty, Seyss-Inquart had a smile on his face. By calling the meeting at short notice and changing its location from The Hague to Amsterdam, he had excluded Rauter.

It had been a logical decision to change the venue. After all, the riots had taken place there, and most of the Jews in the country and their council leaders were also located there.

The downside was that he could not exclude Mussert, who was responsible for procuring a suitable office for the meeting and inviting the relevant contacts in the Jewish community.

Mussert's office and the headquarters of the NSB were in Utrecht, housed in a grandiose building on a wide and imposing boulevard flanked by mature lime trees. Their district office in Amsterdam, close to Museum Square, was a similarly prestigious address. Yet the room Seyss-Inquart now occupied appeared to be little more than an old, dusty storeroom without windows and hastily equipped with a table and a few flimsy wooden chairs.

Based upon the commissioner's initial impressions, the NSB man had failed in the first of his two tasks. The two men sat opposite him were about to show the degree of success of the second.

The riot that had taken place on the previous day certainly provided an opportunity, Seyss-Inquart thought. On its own merits, the serious injury to the Dutch Nazi was of no consequence, but it could certainly be turned to his advantage as the pretext to launching the next round of anti-Jewish measures.

The meeting had been scheduled for four-thirty in the afternoon, allowing time for Mussert to provide him with background notes on the two men. These notes lay on the table before him. He sighed as he looked at the hastily typed sheets, which contained several corrections and spelling mistakes. Amateur, he thought.

According to his notes, the two men were both around sixty years old, but their physical appearances were considerably different. Abraham Asscher sat bolt upright, his arms crossed tightly to his chest. He possessed a wavy mop of blond hair and a full mustache, neither of which showed any signs of graying. He wore a dark-blue three-piece suit, white shirt, and blue bow tie. His face was calm but stern, and he stared directly at the Reichskommissar. This was the businessman whose family owned and ran the world renowned

Asscher Diamond Company. Seyss-Inquart seemed to recall that it was Asscher's who had been commissioned to cleave the Cullinan diamond. He admitted to himself a certain admiration for the bearing and gravitas of this man, even as a Jew.

Professor David Cohen was sitting next to Asscher. He was shorter and stooped slightly, which made it appear as if the top of his bald head barely reached his neighbor's chin. He fidgeted with a pen on the table, keeping his head down and not raising his gaze. This was the academic, the professor of ancient history. The thinker, not a man of action, whose demeanor seemed weak and conciliatory compared to the strong features of his neighbor. Seyss-Inquart was not impressed.

"Shall I set out the agenda?" Mussert asked.

"No! That's for me to do," Seyss-Inquart barked. "You can take the minutes."

The Austrian had been preparing his words since the previous evening when he had first been told about the riots. *Velvet glove and iron fist*, he reminded himself.

"Firstly, gentlemen," the Reichskommissar said. "Thank you for attending this meeting. You've been asked to attend because of your long-standing and undoubted status within the Jewish community.

"You've possibly guessed that we're here to discuss the ramifications of yesterday's riots. The situation has been deteriorating for weeks, and I think it's in everybody's best interests to take decisive action to prevent further damage to

our respective communities. Do you agree?" His tone was
emotionless.

The Jews nodded, but neither spoke.

"Do you agree?" he repeated.

"Agreed," the two men replied.

"Good." The Austrian continued, "After yesterday's
terrible events, we don't want the SS let loose in the Jewish
areas. Obergruppenführer Rauter wants to do that, but I'm
resisting in order to protect you. But I'm wondering how we
can make sure that these few, violent elements in your
community act in the best interests of the majority rather than
pursue their narrow, radical, and selfish objectives. It strikes
me that the Jews themselves would be the best people to do
this rather than the SS. Gentlemen?"

"Are you suggesting that we set up some sort of
organization to lead and represent the Jews?" Cohen asked.

"Good idea! Who better?" Seyss-Inquart replied. "You
keep the Jews in order. I keep the NSB and SS at bay. Of
course, if you don't wish to take part, I can ask others. I'm sure
that leadership of such an organization would be a role which
attracts widespread interest."

"David and I will take on the roles of joint chairmen,"
Asscher replied immediately and confidently. "Nobody else
needs to be considered. We're best placed. We'll appoint
members to represent all parts of our community."

"Yes, by all means," the commissioner said, "appoint as
many members as you wish, but as the chairs of the council, I

expect my communications to be solely with yourselves.

"There's a lot of bad feeling on the streets at the moment," he continued. "One of our WA men was seriously injured yesterday, and they're screaming for revenge. You must convene your first council meeting tomorrow. Agreed?"

"Agreed," Asscher replied, addressing the Reichskommissar directly and without turning to his colleague.

"We'll need to react quickly to keep public order," he continued. "Tonight, I'll arrange for some sort of cordon or barrier to be erected around the Jewish Quarter. I'll keep the factions apart by forbidding the NSB and WA from entering that area unless they've received my written permission. In return, the new Jewish Council must ensure *everybody* has the necessary ID card."

"Excuse me, sir," Cohen asked. "What do you mean by a necessary ID card?"

"Oh, something on the existing ID card to make it clear the owner's allowed into the Jewish Quarter," he replied. "A stamp with the letter J perhaps? Those without a J on their ID card can't enter. So the Jews will be safe. Sounds like a logical solution to me. Are you making notes of all these agreed items, Mussert?"

"Yes, sir," the NSB leader replied, scribbling intensely.

"How would you suggest that your new council can communicate its activities and messages to the wider community?" Seyss-Inquart asked, turning back to the men sitting opposite.

"A sort of newsletter or pamphlet?" Cohen replied.

"A splendid idea! Why not a weekly newspaper to keep your people abreast of everything that's happening? The *Jewish Weekly*, to go with the Jewish Council?" he said enthusiastically, placing a tick mark on one sheet of paper in front of him. "This will keep a printing business running as well. I can sell paper to you if you need any."

"If that's all, we need to call our first meeting for tomorrow and think about the membership of the council," Asscher said, rising from his chair.

"Not finished yet!" Seyss-Inquart interrupted. "After the unprompted and violent behavior of the Jews yesterday, it's only reasonable that we must insist on the confiscation of all objects that may cause harm. The SS wishes to search every house in the Jewish Quarter, turn them upside down and inside out to find weapons. You can save your community a great deal of aggravation if the first *Jewish Weekly* advises everyone to hand in their clubs, knives, guns, et cetera. That would be so much better for all parties. Do you agree?"

"Agreed," Asscher replied before Cohen could open his mouth. "Are we finished now?"

"One more area where I'll be able to help you. I've got access to buildings 117 and 119 on Waterlooplein. That would be a suitable location for your Jewish Council offices. You're welcome to use them. And the rent's more than reasonable."

With that, the commissioner stood up, brushed a speck of dust off his lapel, and left Mussert scurrying after him.

Cohen looked up at Asscher, who had barely moved, his arms still crossed.

"What do you think of that?" he asked.

"We started the meeting with nothing and ended up as co-chairmen of the Jewish Council," Asscher replied. "I firmly believe we're the best people to act as chairmen. We must try our utmost to protect the rights of our fellow citizens, make their difficulties as bearable as possible, and never do anything to harm them. Let's hope our stewardship achieves this."

"Seyss-Inquart's implying he's helping us. I'm not so sure," Cohen mused. "I do wonder if we'll just be a mouthpiece, a puppet of the Nazis, a means of smoothing the introduction of their rules and regulations."

Asscher shrugged.

The two men stood up and walked toward the door. Cohen reached it first and held it open to allow his companion, arms still folded, to pass.

THIRTEEN

Amsterdam – February 19, 1941

Hannes had witnessed family arguments before. In fact, he had seen and heard his papa and brother argue many times. But tonight was different, and Hannes was so nervous that he could not face his dinner.

Hendrik looked ready to explode. His face ordinarily turned livid red whenever he became irate, but after his recent fight, it was covered in bumps and bruises, which were a deep, smarting crimson color.

Hannes usually remained in the living room as the two of them quarreled, taking up a semi-secluded position in the corner. They would argue, then stop, and everything would return to normal. Today, his mother sent him out. That was fortunate because the shouting was very loud and gave him a strange, gripping pain in the pit of his stomach he had not experienced before. He lay on his bed, barely able to move.

The thick walls of the house prevented him from clearly hearing the argument that was taking place, and he could only decipher the odd word. *Immature, coward, Nazis, reckless, danger, Nazis, action, Jewish Council, Nazis.* He understood little of it, but it was only when the shouting stopped that the tension in his stomach subsided. Five minutes later, his mother returned to bring him back. There was no greeting smile from his father, no ruffling of the hair by his brother. The silence was so overwhelming he could hear the mantelpiece clock ticking, throbbing like his heart, though nowhere near as fast.

"When do you think I'll be able to go to the movies again?" he asked casually, trying to break the tension.

It was as if all the air had been sucked from the room. The family held its breath. Hendrik paused with a forkful of food touching his lips; Rachael's knife and fork hovered above her plate. Only Hannes was moving, his head turning from side to side.

Papa and Hendrik looked at each other intently, too preoccupied to answer the boy. So, he turned to his sister. Rachael would know, he was sure.

"Will it be soon?" he asked.

She considered her younger brother, then smiled. "That's not a straightforward question to answer," she began.

"I like to go to the pictures with Zac, and we've done it loads of times before. So what's changed, and what's the harm?" he asked quietly determined.

"Okay," she replied, breathing deeply. "We've told you about Hitler before. He's a very bad man who doesn't like Jews and tries to make life as hard as possible for us."

"But what have I done to Hitler for him to ban me from watching *Snow White*?"

She carefully placed her cutlery on her plate and stared at him with what he recognized as her *teacher's face*.

"Hitler's not banning you. He's banning all Jews." Her tone was mildly chastising. "He hates us."

"How can he hate Jews when he hasn't met them all? I don't like Aron Deldin because he keeps pushing me at school. Even so, I wouldn't stop him going to watch *Snow White*…as long as he stopped pushing me."

"That's why Hitler's an evil man. He tells lies about Jews."

"But most Jews I know are good. So why does the ticket man at the movie theater hate Jews as well?"

"He may not hate Jews. Perhaps he's frightened of the Nazis."

"He did look more frightened than hateful," Hannes mused. "I think he would've let us in if there hadn't been a long line. And he's Dutch. Surely, they don't all hate Jews?"

"I'm certain that most of the Dutch don't hate us," Rachael agreed.

"So, do you think I'll be able to watch *Snow White* next week?" he persisted.

"For fuck's sake, stop going on about *Snow White*." Hendrik blurted out, immediately realizing his error under the angry stares of the others. "There are more important things in life than Walt Disney!"

Hendrik had never sworn at Hannes before. Never. Ever. Part of him was pleased that his brother was addressing him as he might an adult. Yet another part was wounded, and the nausea surged inside him once more. He desperately wanted to hold back his tears, but they were welling up behind his eyelids.

Hannes stuffed a forkful of food into his mouth, but the liver tasted bitter. He faked a cough, which allowed him to use his napkin to wipe his mouth, nose, and watering eyes. But it was too late. There were tears already rolling down his cheeks. He could taste their salty wetness as they dribbled into his dry mouth, and he realized that he too would end up with a red face.

*

Hannes had gone to bed early, and Rachael had returned to her room to prepare for her lessons the following day. Elizabeth was ironing shirts in the dining room. This was a chore she usually performed in the kitchen, but her presence provided a calming influence on her husband and son.

After a sustained period of silence, Franck spoke.

"There's a tidal wave coming."

"What do you mean?" Hendrik asked.

"I was at the Jewish Council meeting today. There's a flood of decrees and regulations on the way. The Nazis are trying to isolate us completely." There was quiet resignation in his voice.

"How?" his son asked.

"Where do I begin? You know the *Jews Only* signs that were put up after the riots? They're being made permanent. We can now call the Jewish Quarter a ghetto. Radios are also being banned," he said, pointing at the brown Bakelite radio set on a nearby bookcase. "Soon we'll have no access to the outside world. We'll not be able to find out who's winning the war or listen to the government in exile."

"It couldn't be worse," Hendrik complained.

"That's only part of it," the professor continued. "They're also going to round up all the Jews across the country and transfer them to Amsterdam."

The student sensed his father's voice trembling.

"Jews and non-Jews will no longer be allowed to live in the same parts of the city, and contact will be further reduced by forbidding Jews and non-Jews from working with each other. Jewish doctors, dentists, lawyers, and such like can only have Jewish clients. Our schoolchildren and students will go to different schools. Poor Hannes, it will be impossible for him to see Zac at all, never mind go to the movies," he said, rubbing his eyes stiffly.

"What does the council say in response to all these changes?" Hendrik fumed. "What does Visser say?"

"Ah, that reminds me!" Franck replied. "That's another new decree. The council will be the only Jewish organization legally allowed to represent us. All the other bodies are outlawed. Visser was the head of the JCC, which is banned now. He has no voice or influence. He refuses to collaborate with the council because he believes Asscher and Cohen are too compliant with the Nazis.

"Beaches and swimming pools are also going to be segregated. There may be other regulations I've forgotten, but the *Jewish Weekly* will give details in its next edition. It's never-ending," he sighed. "My head is spinning."

"It's been less than a year since the invasion," Elizabeth said. "We all used to get along under the old government. Now it's all gone to shit."

Franck was momentarily stunned. He could not recall the last occasion he had heard his wife swear.

"This Nazi-run government's a sham," Hendrik said, looking earnestly at his father, who was staring into his coffee cup. "It's a means for them to achieve their goals in the most efficient way possible."

"And yet, they tell us we should thank our lucky stars we aren't treated like the Polish Jews, who are governed severely by an SS-dominated administration," his father said.

"We can't trust the Nazis," Hendrik said firmly. "We never could."

"It's confusing. The Germans are logical people, and Hitler was so complimentary about our country. I thought they would listen to us and work with us. Not all this violence and segregation."

"Hitler's only been complimentary because he believes this country's people possess Aryan characteristics, but when it comes to Jews, his hatred knows no boundaries."

"But the country relies upon Aryans and non-Aryans alike. Without us, it isn't the same place at all!" his father protested.

"So what can we do now?" Elizabeth inquired.

They looked at each other until Franck beckoned his son to speak.

"There are a few options open to us," he said. "Firstly, we could do nothing. Do nothing and let events unfold as they may. Or we resist and frustrate the Nazis. Or we openly collaborate with them in the hope it may save our skins."

"Perhaps there's another option," Franck suggested. "Delay."

"What do you mean by delay, darling?" Elizabeth asked, a rare glimmer of hope in her eyes.

"Well, we run the council to give the impression that we're cooperating with the Nazis while hindering and delaying the introduction of their measures at every turn in the hope they'll soon lose the war, and we'll be liberated. The Russians, the British, or even the French may be marching through our streets later this year or early next."

"The Russians have an awfully long way to travel to reach us here," Hendrik said. "That leaves a great responsibility for the British and French. A strategy based on delaying the Nazis is a high-risk option."

Franck glanced at his wristwatch, then stood up and walked over to the wireless set, turning it on in anticipation of the BBC's daily broadcast of Radio Orange by the government-in-exile, fifteen minutes a day that provided a glimpse of the world beyond.

"How will you ever give up your beloved wireless, Father?" Hendrik asked.

"I'll give up *a* wireless set," his father replied.

"What do you mean?"

"A couple of the council members work for Philips. Apparently, there are mountains of old wireless sets and spare parts lying around in their factories. They can provide hundreds of radio sets for us to surrender to the Nazis," Franck answered, smiling. "The Nazis will never find out, and I'll be able to keep my set here."

"You're becoming a bit of a rebel in your old age, Papa!"

"Not so much a rebel. Perhaps more of a delayer."

Franck carefully turned the dial on the radio set to find the correct frequency. The three of them gathered closely around to listen.

FOURTEEN

The Hague – February 20, 1941

"Are you in control of the situation in Amsterdam?" Rauter asked.

"Excuse me?" the commissioner answered, trembling with rage. Rauter had succeeded in angering him with the very first words he had uttered.

"Well, you've only just introduced a Jewish Council to bring them under control and we've had murders of WA members, spraying of poison gas, and defiance of instructions to hand in all weapons. It doesn't sound like control to me," the soldier mocked.

The arrogance of this man sitting in my office! "Well, to start with, there was one murder, not plural," Seyss-Inquart replied. "And although Hendrik Kost died on Monday, he was actually injured during the February eleven riot—before the council was even formed. Your so-called poison gas was simply a bottle of ammonia that was accidentally spilled. The deadline for the surrender of weapons was only yesterday." He paused to gather himself and added coldly, "In any case, I seem to recall the formation of the Jewish Council was your idea."

"And do we know the results of our instruction to surrender weapons?" Rauter continued, holding a single leaf of paper in his hands like a magician before his reveal.

"I'm assuming you do?" Seyss-Inquart countered with undisguised animosity.

"Not good. Not good at all."

"I'm not even sure the Jews have any weapons to surrender."

"Perhaps. Perhaps not." Rauter seemed to relish every word. "They certainly haven't handed any in."

"Our agreed approach has always been a combination of velvet glove and iron fist."

"Now's the time for the iron fist."

Seyss-Inquart was uncertain whether this was a statement or a question. "Agreed. We must reassert our authority."

"Some real iron fist! At last!" Mussert exclaimed, leaning forward in his chair. "My men have been waiting for this!"

"This task's not for you and the unprofessional and erratic WA," Rauter scoffed in reply. "This action is for the German SS."

"I also believe it's for the SS," Seyss-Inquart added, watching Rauter to ascertain if he was going to speak further.

Mussert slumped back in his chair.

"We need to teach these radical and disruptive Jews a lesson they'll not forget," the Austrian continued. "They're influenced by the Communists, and we must remove them from the streets, where they can harm us." He pondered for several moments. "I suggest we take hostages and detain them until the Jewish community has carried out our instructions."

"Mauthausen's where we send dissenters," Rauter said. "That would certainly clean up the streets."

"Mauthausen," Seyss-Inquart repeated. "Taking hostages is temporary. Sending them to Mauthausen is permanent. Are these men communists or merely youngsters spoiling for a fight?"

"You just agreed to an iron fist," Rauter stressed. "Are you backtracking already? We must bring the Jews under control. The SS is satisfied for the government to work in conjunction with the Jews. But make no mistake, the SS will take over, should the relationship become ineffective. Remember, Nazification and dealing with the Jewish problem are cast iron objectives for the Führer and the German Reich. A strong message must be sent to keep us on track."

"Okay, a few hundred men will be taken hostage, selected by the Jewish Council," the commissioner suggested.

"Selection by the council will take far too long," Rauter interrupted. "I strongly advise that the SS starts to round up Jews at random. Tomorrow's Saturday, and there'll be many people out in public. We'll seize young men. They're usually the troublemakers. The SS will be fast and effective. I'll arrange an SS squad. Don't inform Asscher and Cohen. This action must be a surprise."

"Of course, of course. Nazification's our first and only priority," the Austrian agreed. "But at random? Whether they're troublemakers or not?"

"A Jew's a Jew," Rauter said with a shrug.

The commissioner paused.

Rauter rose to his feet and nodded curtly at his colleague.

"Is there anything…is there anything I can do?" Mussert asked nervously.

"As we've made abundantly clear, this isn't a task for the NSB or WA," Rauter replied.

The two visitors made their way out of the office.

Seyss-Inquart looked down at the pile of papers awaiting his signature. Ingrid was highly professional in her dealings with him, yet even she had raised an eyebrow when she had seen the bulk of these new decrees. Asscher and Cohen's leadership would be vigorously tested over the coming weeks, but he would not tell them today. They were going to have a surprise tomorrow in any case. He would wait until Monday to sign the decrees and then issue a communication. It was fine for Rauter to insist on the iron fist, but it was the commissioner who had to sugar-coat the messages and keep the Jewish Council cooperating.

He opened his desk drawer and retrieved a bottle of Scotch and a glass, rummaging around a little longer without success. He had no cigars left. His beloved Humidors were becoming less easy to procure. The local economy was weakening, which meant that the German economy was in the same predicament.

Suddenly, he raised his finger in the air. "Aha!"

He had an idea to sugar-coat the pill. He would have tomorrow's hostages shipped to Kamp Schoorl. Admittedly, it was a concentration camp, but it was known for maintaining bearable conditions for inmates. There was plenty of food and no hard labor, and it was well known to the general populace. He would inform the chairmen, and they would communicate this in a special edition of the *Jewish Weekly*. Once the hostages were in Schoorl, he would wait a while and then quietly move them on to Mauthausen. But not straight away. He would send them to Buchenwald first. That would further obscure the trail to the hard labor camp.

He smiled at his ingenuity and wished Rauter had been present. He poured the Scotch, took a swig from the glass and, humming contentedly, picked up his pen and started writing.

FIFTEEN

Amsterdam – February 21, 1941

Jonas Daniel Meyer Square was on the edge of the Jewish Quarter, wedged between the Plantage Park and Waterlooplein, with the twin towers of the Moses and Aaron Church looming above. The Portuguese synagogue, built in the seventeenth century, was also located there. The square was named after the man who, at the end of the eighteenth century, became the first Jew in the country to be formally registered as a lawyer.

On that Saturday morning, the sun was hidden behind banks of dark, forbidding clouds. The snow of the previous weeks had melted, leaving patches of water and mud scattered across the ground. Despite the dull weather, people were out in numbers to enjoy a day away from work. Some visited one of the three synagogues that were within easy walking distance, many chose not to.

Suddenly, at exactly ten o'clock, a group of fifty SS soldiers stormed into the square, immediately splitting into two groups and forming lines along its western and eastern perimeters. With the Keizersgracht and Herengracht canals to the north and south, the entry and exit points of the square were blocked within seconds.

The morning walkers were confronted by well-drilled soldiers wearing smart, clean uniforms, and each carrying a pristine Kar98k rifle. The contrast between the NSB and WA was striking.

"Nobody move!" an SS officer ordered. The terrified citizens did not dare. They outnumbered the soldiers by perhaps ten to one, but the rifles were levelled and pointed straight at them. As the SS edged inward in unison, the Jews slowly shrank back to the center of the square, like water draining down a plughole.

A young Jew in his early twenties, wearing a light-brown jacket and a black cap, ran out from the crowd to goad the soldiers. He was laughing and waving his cap around. It looked for all the world as if any one of the SS men would shoot him dead there and then. Instead, three soldiers broke ranks, surrounded the man and, with rifles still trained on him, marshaled him to a nearby curbside. A soldier approached from behind and brought him to his knees with a firm strike to the neck with his rifle butt. The trio returned to the SS formation surrounding the crowd before subjecting another Jew to the same treatment.

This process continued unabated. At the beginning, the soldiers were also checking the ID cards of the detainees, but the number of captives grew so quickly that this became impracticable, so they concentrated just on rounding the men up and keeping them on their knees.

Faced with loaded rifles at close range, most of the young men complied without objection and in silence. A few of them were surrounded by a protective cordon of family and friends while others made their own way to the center of the crowd, an area less accessible to the SS.

"Keep away, Nazi scum!" somebody in the crowd shouted. The soldiers remained impassive.

Others continued to foolishly taunt and dare the SS to take them. They were invariably captured—and swiftly. Like wild animals stalking their prey, the soldiers sought out their targets in the herd. Those at the margins of the crowd were easy pickings.

At one o'clock, the SS stopped. In three hours, they had taken around two hundred hostages, all on their knees, arranged in neat, straight rows, like an unwilling congregation. Then the soldiers surrounded their prisoners, motioned them to stand up, and escorted them across the square and out of sight.

The square was left in silence, stunned by the shocking events of the last few hours. And then, as if suddenly aware of the horror that had befallen them, some in the crowd began to wail, a lamentation that grew louder and constant like a storm wind, filling the square and blowing into every home in the Jewish Quarter.

*

The following morning, the Jews gathered in the square to discuss the events of the previous day in an attempt to discover the whereabouts of their loved ones and to ask the Jewish Council what was going on. There was no representative of the council in attendance; only a brief message had been sent, confirming that the co-chairmen were in direct contact with the Nazi leadership, and the next publication of the *Jewish Weekly* would provide a full explanation.

Many of the younger citizens vociferously condemned the council for its inactivity. Most of the rest begrudgingly accepted the situation and went about their everyday lives, milling around the elm trees and sitting on benches to talk with friends.

Nobody had thought about it. It seemed inconceivable. Yet at ten o'clock, the crowds looked up to see fully armed SS soldiers marching into the square, taking up positions along its western and eastern perimeters.

And the wailing began once more.

SIXTEEN

Amsterdam – February 24, 1941

It was two o'clock in the morning, and the night was dark and still. A thick blanket of cloud obscured the moon and sprayed icy rain on the roofs and streets below. The streetlights had been switched off, leaving the city a collage of shades of gray.

In Lombokstraat, the wind was whistling in from the nearby dockyards. A keen observer might have noticed two figures darting in and out of the shadows of the trees and buildings. They might also have spotted a routine in their behavior. One figure would move briskly out of the shadows, appearing to wipe their hand against the outside of the nearest lamppost before plunging back into the darkness. No sooner had their hand left the lamppost than the second figure would move swiftly forward and seemingly repeat the process on the same lamppost. The whole activity would only last a few seconds before the scene was cast back into stillness. When the operation had been repeated for each of the remaining lampposts, the pair moved on to the adjoining street.

The pair wore black coats and hats pulled down over their brows. Their physiques and the way they moved intimated that the first one was female, the second male. Beyond that, they revealed no defining characteristics. Nonetheless, they moved with an ease and speed that indicated this drill was well practiced. Only a flashlight and much closer proximity would have enabled anybody to identify Hendrik Kisch and Jacoba Veltman.

During the previous morning, there had been much discussion in the coffeehouses and workplaces of the Jews about the excessive reprisals that had been meted out by the SS on February 21 and 22.

At around six p.m. the same day, around three hundred people had gathered in the North Market to attend a meeting called by the trade unions. Feelings were running high. Representatives of the unions, the Dutch Communist Party (known as the DCP) and the Marxist Front were in attendance. Piet Nak of the DCP demanded a general strike—an extreme measure but one to bring the occupiers to their senses.

"We're all Amsterdammers! We're all Dutch!" Nak had shouted. "We must fight—and fight together against all oppressors in our country! If we don't respond, the Nazis will see that we're weak, and their actions will reach greater and greater extremes!"

Jacoba Veltman was present, wearing a dark coat and a black beret that sat on top of her eye-catching blond hair. Her piercing blue eyes gave her pretty face a serious, determined expression. Even without makeup, her lips formed a striking dark-pink border around her mouth.

Her father had been a printer by trade, and when he had died and his business was sold, she had retained one small printing press hidden in her basement. Almost nobody knew of its existence. At that time, it was being utilized to produce communications for the DCP, at considerable risk to Jacoba herself since the organization had been outlawed by Seyss-Inquart in 1940.

She walked among the crowds, handing out posters advocating an immediate general strike and asking for them to be widely distributed across the city for workers to see as they left their homes the following morning.

This was how Jacoba came to be with Hendrik. With a small paintbrush, she was applying a film of glue to the lampposts from a pot hidden inside her coat while he was following immediately behind to affix the posters themselves.

When they had run out of posters, the couple stood in an alleyway on Javastraat for a few minutes. He offered her a cigarette, which she accepted. The smoke drifted slowly upward, a pale, gray smudge against the night sky. The burning cigarettes created two tiny, bright-red dots against a sheet of black. When they had finished, the two briefly embraced and departed in opposite directions, both staying in the shadows.

Now it was a question of what would happen in the morning, when a great many of Amsterdam's workers would be greeted by lamppost leaflets with the message writ large in black ink:

STRIKE! STRIKE! STRIKE! Shut down the whole of Amsterdam for a day! TODAY!

*

"There are no trams in Amsterdam today!" Rauter exclaimed, walking into Seyss-Inquart's office without bothering to knock.

"What do you mean, no trams?" he replied, taken off guard.

"All the tram drivers have disappeared! None of them turned up for work this morning." Rauter explained. "Any communication from our Jewish Council? Or Mussert's NSB? They must've had a sniff of this."

"Ingrid! Ingrid!" the commissioner shouted. His secretary immediately scurried into his office.

"Yes, sir?"

"Please find Mussert or Asscher or Cohen on the telephone as soon as possible. It's of the utmost urgency."

Ingrid dashed out as quickly as she had arrived.

"She's a pretty young thing, that secretary of yours," Rauter said.

"She's…a very proficient secretary."

"Aryan or Jew?"

He was still considering a reply when the telephone rang.

"Seyss-Inquart here," he said, listening for a few seconds. "Stop there, Mussert! This isn't the time for pleasantries. What the hell's going on with the tram drivers in Amsterdam this morning?" His voice was booming, and his lips touched the telephone receiver, almost as if he was about to swallow it.

He continued to listen, nodding, then shaking his head. He rose from his chair, then sat back down. He tapped his pen on the desk.

"Calm down, Mussert!" Seyss-Inquart urged, back on his feet and pacing up and down as far as the telephone cable would allow. "Just to be sure, what you're saying is that the city's more or less shut down? Tram drivers, dock workers, factory and office workers have all stopped work? Jews and non-Jews. You're absolutely sure that non-Jews are also on strike?" He paused to listen. "You're telling me there have been posters and workers being approached in the streets. And you had absolutely no idea that this was being planned?" he demanded incredulously, looking at Rauter, who shrugged.

"No reports of similar action in other cities? But on the basis that you had no idea about this strike, then there could be plans afoot for nationwide action?" he asked. "Call me back in an hour and give me an update and your proposals for addressing this!" He threw the phone down.

The two men watched each other from their respective sides of the desk like proud but wary lions eying each other up.

"To bring everything to a standstill, there has to be many non-Jews taking part," Rauter remarked. "This can't be viewed as a purely Jewish insurrection. It's much wider. And what happens in Amsterdam today will be common knowledge throughout the country by tomorrow morning."

"Our worst nightmare is that we have continued widespread civil disobedience across the whole of the country in support of a paltry hundred thousand Jews," the Austrian said.

"More iron fist is required," Rauter agreed.

"It's all iron fist from now on. The velvet glove can be put in a drawer. It's not coming out again." The commissioner slammed his fist on the desk to make the point.

The soldier, unmoved, raised his eyebrows.

"Of course, we'll tell the council that it's still velvet glove," Seyss-Inquart added.

"Either Asscher and Cohen weren't aware of this strike or didn't inform us," Rauter said. "Whichever it was, they haven't served us well. You can do what you wish to them, but we do need to go in exceptionally hard after this strike today. The entire population must be deterred from thoughts of further activity."

"Let's agree on our next steps now. First, I'll tell the council that they must unequivocally demand an end to all strike action with immediate effect, otherwise there'll be severe and violent repercussions. I'll threaten to sack the chairmen straight away. Self-preservation should harden their resolve. Meanwhile, can you arrange a vigorous SS-led response to the strike in order to end it as soon as possible?"

"No further instruction is required," Rauter replied. "My men will make sure these people think twice before calling another strike. We believe we know who the leaders of the Communists and trade unions are, and their details are on file. They're sure to be involved. We'll get them off the streets once and for all. Do we need to do something to quell the rebellious spirit of the non-Jews as well?"

"I wonder if we should sack the whole of Amsterdam City Council, both Aryans and Jews?" Seyss-Inquart pondered aloud. "That will permit us to appoint our own people to senior posts. They're too soft toward the locals. Especially the police. Our man being put in charge of the police would certainly grant us more control."

"You know, I think that's a good idea," Rauter replied, almost surprised.

Ingrid appeared at the doorway. "Mr. Asscher's on the telephone, sir."

Seyss-Inquart snatched up the phone and spoke.

"Asscher, the Jewish Council's in huge trouble. You and Cohen are the chairmen and bear ultimate responsibility for its actions. You're not controlling your people, and I've received instructions from the highest authority to quell these strikes by whatever means necessary. If you can't do it, then I'll sack the lot of you, send you all to Mauthausen and appoint a whole new council. Is that understood?"

There was no time for Asscher to respond before Seyss-Inquart slammed the phone down.

*

By the end of the following day, the strike was effectively over. The Jewish Council published a special edition of the *Jewish Weekly* to instruct its readership to desist with immediate effect, this being the only way to avoid much more significant reprisals from the SS.

Rauter gave the SS orders to inflict severe sanctions. Those believed to have been involved, or even suspected of being involved in the strike, were to be arrested. Even before the SS could be seen, Amsterdam rang with the crack of rifles being fired.

The offices of the trade unions were ransacked. The Communist Party of the Netherlands was already an outlawed organization and as such did not have an office. However, the SS had the names and addresses of those most likely to be involved. After a couple of hours, they had rounded up and detained twenty of the strike leaders. Half of these were executed within the next few days. The remainder were transferred to Mauthausen.

Later in the week, Seyss-Inquart sacked the entire Amsterdam City Council and, in its place, appointed citizens with a strong allegiance to Nazi ideology, including the head of the police force.

SEVENTEEN

Westerbork – March 1941

"I can't believe that we're building a stage for plays and musical performances—like a real theater! In a refugee camp!"

Leo put down his saw and wiped the sweat from his brow. Although it was still early spring, the temperature in the barracks had been rising throughout the morning and had created an uncomfortably warm atmosphere for the men laboring there. Even so, they had worked well, and the stage was nearing completion. It was around a yard high, ten long paces wide, and in a semicircular shape. They were now sawing the timber for constructing two sets of steps, one on either side of the stage. If they finished by early afternoon, Schol had promised them the rest of the day at leisure.

"I know, it's unbelievable! Apparently, Schol has managed to conjure up a violin because one of the orchestra players had left his in Amsterdam," Jakob added.

"He's exempted all the orchestra members from any labor that might cause them an injury and restrict their ability to play. The musicians are being cosseted, just like they are in real life!" Leo laughed.

The two men were resting on the stage, legs dangling over its edge.

"I can't believe how pleasant it is in Westerbork," Jakob remarked. "I've heard about other camps—barbed-wire fences, dreadful sanitation, hard labor, people crammed into ramshackle barracks."

"I suppose we should keep our heads down and work hard," Leo said. "And keep our fingers crossed."

"I agree, but I'm not so sure what's going to happen next. Almost nobody has left the camp for weeks. Refugees aren't being moved on. They're being held. What will happen if new refugees continue to arrive?"

"There's not a lot of space here, but additional barracks could be built," Leo said.

"Who can predict what might happen? All I know is that today, the sun's shining and my belly's full. And I can travel outside the camp because I'm on the bread detail. Freshly baked bread and a trip into the village in the spring sunshine can't be such a bad thing."

Jakob paused for a moment, and when his friend looked at him, he stared back earnestly. "Given that there are no fences surrounding the camp, I've been considering whether I should try to escape," he whispered. "Not yet. It's not worthwhile at this point. However, if it does look as if conditions will worsen, then perhaps escaping might be an option."

"Whoa!" Leo answered. "Be careful! Escaping's easy. What's much more difficult is staying hidden and free. Even by Dutch standards, this region's flat. There're no hills, no woodland—no cover at all. There's nowhere to hide once you're on the run. A successful escape must include transport. And where will you find transport? My recommendation is to dismiss all thoughts of escape. Let's enjoy freshly baked bread and listen to the orchestra performing on a stage that we've built with our own bare hands.

"I understand that Schol has given permission for Mendelssohn to be played at the first concert. Camp Westerbork must be the only place in the whole of the Reich that's playing works by a Jewish composer!"

Leo wiped his brow with his sleeve and picked up his saw.

"Anyway, we'd best get back to work or the orchestra will have no stage to sit on, and we won't get our afternoon of leisure in the sunshine."

Jakob shrugged, then he too picked up his saw.

EIGHTEEN

Mauthausen – April 1941

Ziereis was rarely nervous. During his career, he had led and participated in many large and important projects. He was especially proud of his achievements at Mauthausen, where he had succeeded in adding a sub-camp in Gusen. Built in a matter of months with forced labor, it was already achieving its output targets and contributing healthy profits. Moreover, he had successfully managed the number of inmates, balancing the continuous stream of new arrivals with the death tolls. The population in the main camp was hovering around the two-thousand mark.

He was confident of profitably expanding the network of camps still farther and undertaking more complicated manufacturing activities. Over recent weeks, he had been evaluating the feasibility of a subterranean facility where work could be undertaken out of sight and protected from potential enemy bombardment.

However, today Himmler was paying a visit. These visits were infrequent and usually characterized by a short barrage of questions in relation to efficiencies, followed by the setting of demanding objectives that could not be challenged. Objectives set by the second most powerful man in the Reich.

He reassured himself with the knowledge that Himmler had a reputation for not outstaying his welcome and would usually arrive on site, hurry through the items on his agenda, then promptly depart. Ziereis admired the head of the SS for his ideology and had so far successfully carried out all the tasks that had been assigned to him. However, he could not help feeling fearful of a man who wielded so much power and influence.

Himmler was due to arrive at eleven o'clock, and exactly on time, three black Mercedes limousines pulled up outside the factory offices. Himmler and his entourage of eight SS officers walked briskly toward the waiting camp commander.

After a series of introductory salutes, Ziereis made as if to open the front door of the building, but his superior immediately said, "Let's go and take a look at the quarry." He led the party across the roll-call yard and out of the rear of the camp. There were no prisoners working the quarry at that moment, and a dull stillness hung in the air.

"Show me the so-called Stairs of Death," Himmler demanded.

"Of course, sir," he said.

As they walked to the base of the steps, Himmler asked questions in relation to the outputs from the quarry and what could be done to increase productivity.

"It all depends upon the effective management of labor, sir," Ziereis said. "Now that we're being sent increased numbers of Poles, we actually have too much manpower, so we need to resort to other options available to us, such as building extensions here in Mauthausen, working them in the Gusen camps, or on local farms. We've run out of space, so the prisoners now need to be worked to death.

"Some of the soldiers aren't keen on killing inmates directly, so we try to create situations whereby prisoners die of their own accord, so to speak. In midwinter, we're helped by the freezing weather. In high summer, they'll often buckle in the heat. It's unfortunate at the moment because the spring weather is neither one nor the other. But the stairs do cause many to succumb to physical exhaustion. If we must administer a solution that involves a bullet in the back of the head, then we tend to leave that to a small group of specialist soldiers with strong mental resilience."

"That's good," Himmler replied. "Yes, it can be psychologically troublesome to have to shoot prisoners, even if they're Jews. We're investigating ways of alleviating the problem. To protect the mental well-being of our men."

"I'm sure you're aware, sir," Ziereis interjected carefully, "but we've been utilizing a poison-gas truck. We had a group of Dutch Jews sent to us recently and we subjected them to a gas trial. The results were pleasingly positive. It was quick and efficient, and we used other prisoners to dispose of the bodies. Our men only really needed to supervise, which was much less distressing."

By now, the group was marching across the quarry. Ziereis noticed a body partly hidden behind one of the large boulders scattered across the area. Himmler also spotted it and inquisitively sauntered over, the camp commander following closely behind.

"How did this one die? The stairs?" Himmler asked.

"Possibly, sir. They usually die on the stairs themselves, but it's conceivable that this man struggled a short distance away and then dropped dead right here without anybody noticing. I'll get it cleared away." He made a mental note to punish the officer who had been responsible for tidying up the quarry that morning.

Himmler turned away, no emotion showing on his face. "Now let's get up these steps!" he said energetically.

From a distance, the 186 steps appeared to be uniform in shape and size, rising evenly from the base of the quarry to the upper dispatch area. Yet close up, they were quite different. They were made from roughly hewn slabs of stone that had not been mortared together. As a result, they were uneven and loose, meaning the rise from one to the next was never the same. Many of the steps wobbled as the group made its way up. Ziereis could well imagine the difficulties encountered by a prisoner with a fifty-pound block of granite on his back and wooden clogs on his feet.

The approach to the summit was clear, all discarded granite blocks and dead bodies having been removed earlier. The only evidence of the violent events that had taken place there was a smattering of dried pools of blood where prisoners had been beaten or shot. These were never washed away at the end of a shift but left as a caution to the others.

"How many prisoners die here each day?" Himmler asked.

"On average, between ten and twenty," Ziereis replied. "We'd much rather the granite blocks were lifted right to the top level. It impedes progress if anybody dies partway up.

"Of course, it's different if the camps are overcrowded," he continued. "If we cannot deploy all the prisoners, we have to introduce a target of perhaps fifty stair deaths per day. We hold a roll call every morning, so we know how many inmates have arrived and how many have died, then we can calculate our exact needs on a daily basis. We'll increase the number of lifts required per shift to improve the death rate. Even then, we prefer to extract the weaker inmates after they've reached the top of the stairs."

"So tell me more about these gas trucks," Himmler requested, looking downward as he cautiously scaled the final few steps.

"Well, we're using converted Magirus furniture vans, which can accommodate up to fifty prisoners at a time. What we've learnt so far is to make sure that the prisoners take their clothes off beforehand so that it's easier to remove their jewelry afterward. It takes a few minutes to herd the men into the wagon and seal it up. Fifty's a tight squeeze, but it's the same volume of air shared among more people, so the gassing only takes between ten and fifteen minutes. It's a relatively cheap process because we're using the carbon monoxide fumes from the vehicle engine. To keep the activity discreet, we park the truck beyond the roll-call yard where nobody can see it. When the work's done, the driver takes the truck off-site where we make other prisoners dig a mass grave and then remove and bury the bodies. This all reduces the discomfort for our men.

"There's one issue for our men who are supervising this process," Ziereis continued. "The truck's made of steel and isn't soundproofed, and there's a lot of screaming and banging for the first five minutes or so. Fifty dying men can make a hell of a racket. When we need gassing supervisors, we only accept volunteers. It's not compulsory. We've ended up with a few zealous and enthusiastic participants."

He looked across at Himmler, who had withdrawn a notepad from his uniform pocket and was scribbling notes intently.

"Very good," Himmler said, still writing. "These camps are operating extremely well. Please be prepared for a lot more prisoners and a lot more work in the near future. And please continue to send me detailed updates on the gas trucks."

"Thank you, sir. We'll be ready for whatever the Reich requires."

"One hundred and eighty-six steps aren't easy to climb, even without a heavy piece of granite," Himmler remarked, panting.

The entourage laughed.

Within ten minutes, the SS leader had gone, and within twenty, he was back in his office with a Scotch and cigar, very much looking forward to giving Pohl a debriefing.

NINETEEN

Amsterdam – June 1941

"There are people refusing to have the J stamped on their ID cards," Hendrik said animatedly.

The Kisch family was sitting at the dining table, eating their evening meal. They were all present, albeit Rachael had arrived thirty minutes late. The dwindling supplies of food that they had experienced over recent weeks meant their plates were soon empty.

"And who are these people?" Franck asked his son. "Radicals? Nameless communists?"

"You know, it's not possible for me to mention names, Papa," he replied. "To reveal any names would be extremely dangerous for them, for us, for me."

"What happens if somebody refuses to have a J on their ID card?" Hannes asked. "Will I need to have a J on mine?"

"Well, it's fine for you," his father answered. "You're too young for an ID card. You'll not need one for a while."

"And what about adults?" Elizabeth inquired softly. "What happens if they refuse?"

"It's illegal," came the blunt answer. "If you're caught without the J, then you'll be arrested and imprisoned or deported. It's as simple as that. If you're not caught, you'll spend all your days and nights worried sick that you will be. To make matters worse, the ID card system's exceptionally efficient. It's one of the best in the world. There's a replica of every card stored in the civil service offices, so the Nazis already have a copy. The council's recommending we submit our ID cards for stamping."

"There is another option," Hendrik countered. "Some of us are choosing to go into hiding. There have been so many discriminatory regulations from the Nazis, and the J stamp is the last straw. We consider the risks of going into hiding are much lower than allowing them to take more and more away from us."

"What about these exemptions I've been hearing about?" Elizabeth asked.

"Yes, that's true," Franck said. "The council has agreed with the government that those people who are integral to the maintenance and support of our community will be given an exemption from deportation."

"As a member of the council, you must be able to obtain an exemption for us?" she said, partly asking, partly demanding.

"Why should I be treated any differently?" Hendrik protested.

"Because you're our son!"

"But the exemptions will have to be approved by Seyss-Inquart, and he'll grant as few as possible, certainly far fewer than the council requests," her son dismissed. "Anyway, why should I take an exemption from somebody who may be more deserving than myself?"

"Franck, talk to your son! And please get him an exemption!" she begged, wringing her hands.

"Hendrik, it's honorable of you to refuse an exemption." Franck said. "The council intends to inundate the administration with exemption requests. They'll receive so many that it will take years to deal with them, whether he approves them or not. And we intend to challenge every request he declines. We've already drawn up a list of twenty-five thousand names, and there're plenty more to come.

"Whether you want it or not, you'll be granted an exemption, anyway. Members of the Jewish Council and their immediate families have already been approved."

"And how long will it last for?" Elizabeth persisted.

"*Bis auf weiteres*," Hendrik replied in a mocking tone.

"What does that mean?" she asked.

"It's 'for the time being' in German. The Nazis can remove an exemption at any time."

"There is an alternative interpretation of this," Franck reasoned. "The council agreed with the commissioner that *bis auf weiteres* means that every person who has an exemption will continue to enjoy it unless it's specifically withdrawn, and he needs a lot of Jews to make his life easier. We'll disrupt the process so much that most of us will remain exempt for a few years, by which time the war will hopefully be over. It's the strategy of delay again."

"But who really knows how long he'll continue to need us?" his son asked. "I can understand why some would prefer to go into hiding."

There was quiet around the table until Hannes spoke.

"So does that mean we're safe, Papa?"

Franck forced a smile as he looked at his son. "Yes, for the time being."

TWENTY

The Hague – June 1941

Seyss-Inquart was still disappointed with his office. He had been in this post for longer than a year and had no excuse for the slow pace of improvements.

He had added a silver-framed photograph of himself with Himmler, placing it on his desk in a position where Rauter could easily see it from his usual chair. This had been done purely to annoy his rival yet had backfired badly when the SS soldier had smugly confirmed that he too had one, but his had been signed by the SS leader. To make matters worse, it had not been feasible for him to subsequently remove the picture, because Rauter would certainly have noticed it and condemned the action as demonstrating a lack of loyalty or commitment.

Due to an administrative error, the report on the Merwedeplein roundup had been sent to Rauter first, and now the commissioner had to wait in his office to receive a briefing. The first roundup had led directly to the general strike, but he had been assured there would be no repeat. Having been informed that some 300,000 people had taken part in the strike, he needed to be certain.

At eleven o'clock, the intended time of their meeting, Seyss-Inquart heard Rauter outside his office talking to Ingrid. He remained seated at his desk, signing a pile of documents in the expectation of his colleague's imminent arrival. It was a full quarter of an hour later that he finally came through the door.

"You're late," the Austrian snapped. "I hope this report's worth the wait." He knew the answer as soon as he saw the smirk on the other man's face.

"We took them completely by surprise," Rauter replied. "There were absolutely no casualties on our side. We arrested about three hundred Jews, mostly young men. We were finished in a couple of hours. Asscher and Cohen were sat drinking coffee in the police station as all this was going on. Completely oblivious."

"That's good news," Seyss-Inquart replied begrudgingly.

"We had Mussert keep his ear to the ground for any grumblings from the trade unions or the commies. He heard nothing. I posted four extra night patrols as well, and there was no unusual activity reported. From the first tram to run and the first container to be unloaded at the docks, it was a normal working day. I think it's fair to say the appetite of the Aryan population to support the Jews has dissipated. The general strike was indeed a one-off. We've no fear of a repetition."

"I've seen a number of obituaries published in the newspapers for men who were in the first deportation to Mauthausen," Seyss-Inquart said. "Why was this done and why wasn't I consulted?"

"I apologize. I thought I'd communicated this," Rauter replied unconvincingly. "Himmler approved it, so I assumed you'd agree. The Jews must understand that the camp's a hell on earth. A place of no return. It's a highly effective deterrent. The message is strong. Misbehave and you go to Mauthausen and die. Behave and you go to a labor camp and survive. And I suspect the whole population has now received the message loud and clear."

"I'll speak to Asscher and Cohen in the morning," the commissioner said. "They must tell their people to choose the lesser of two evils."

"If you wish to reinforce the message, that's fine by me."

The Austrian disliked Rauter's offhand attitude, regarding it as yet another manifestation of his lack of respect. However, he thought that he might well be able to catch him off guard for a change. He drew a deep breath and spoke in a casual tone. "Of course, I can also inform the council about tomorrow's announcement." He watched as the soldier's head shot up, and their eyes met.

"I assume you're aware of this?" he continued, finding it difficult to suppress a grin. "It carries the highest degree of secrecy. Maybe the most confidential since the start of the war."

He watched the other man squirm in his chair.

"I'm sorry, I thought Himmler would've told you." He could almost feel the knife in his hand as it twisted in Rauter's guts. "I can trust you to maintain complete confidentiality on this, can't I?"

"Of course you can!"

"Of course I can. Tomorrow's the start of Operation Barbarossa."

Rauter looked blank.

He was thrilled that the SS soldier was sufficiently divorced from the highest echelons of the Nazi Party that he had not been privy to this top-secret operation.

"Barbarossa. The invasion of Russia," he continued.

"The invasion of Russia?" Rauter repeated with incredulity. "We haven't fully overcome the West yet. Surely, we can't be invading a huge country like Russia so soon?"

"Are you doubting decisions made by the Führer?" he asked earnestly.

"No, no! Of course not!" came the indignant response. "I'd heard…I'd thought…it would've been later."

"Russia's a long way from here, but there'll still be a significant impact on us. The army will need more conscripts to support the Eastern Front as well as additional weapons and ammunition. That'll create significant gaps in the German manufacturing workforce, which will have to be filled by the able-bodied populations of our recently conquered territories.

Far greater than could be satisfied by the number of available Jews. It's going to be essential to deploy non-Jews as well."

"Have you been told how many?"

"Eichmann's produced another one of his lists. He's demanding half a million people from the Netherlands to work in Germany." Adolf Eichmann was an Austro-German who joined the Nazi Party and SS in 1932, where he gained a reputation as an expert in Zionist and Jewish matters. From late 1939, he took on responsibility for the emigration of all Jews from the Reich. This was achieved through forced deportations.

"Fucking hell! That's a lot!" the soldier exclaimed. "The total population of the country's less than nine million. At a guess, there may be two to three million suitable men and women. That could be one in four required for forced labor!"

"Guesswork won't be enough. We'll need exact numbers and names. As ever, the civil service's record keeping will be exemplary, and I'm sure we'll access this information quickly. I'll engage them later this week. Meanwhile, I don't think a written decree on its own will suffice. We'll need some effective propaganda—and a rally as well." The commissioner paused to think. "We must have a Dutch speaker for a Dutch audience, so, in the absence of anything better, I suggest we use Mussert. He can arrange another NSB event, but with an open invitation to the public. Amsterdam's the biggest population center, so we'll have the rally there. I've already started making the arrangements," he concluded, smiling.

"We'll do what must be done," the soldier said, rubbing his forehead. "Trying to manage a hundred thousand Jews is tricky, but this'll impact the whole population. It's on a completely different scale."

"We do whatever's required for the betterment of Germany."

"Of course we do."

Rauter picked up his cap, gave a cursory nod, and left the room.

TWENTY-ONE

Amsterdam – August 1941

Although Rachael had been close friends with Jacoba Veltman at secondary school, they had lost touch soon after leaving. There had been no particular reason for this, so it was with genuine surprise and pleasure that they had recently chanced upon each other in Dam Square. As they were both on their way to appointments and had little opportunity to engage in conversation, they agreed to meet up for a drink the following weekend.

It was ten o'clock in the evening when Rachael walked into Café Alcazar to be greeted by the rumble of voices and the clinking of glasses. Plumes of cigarette smoke billowed across the room, obscuring its art deco furnishing. The bar was packed, and it took a couple of minutes for her to catch sight of Jacoba's striking blond hair, brighter still in the darkness of a booth against the far wall.

After the two women embraced, Rachael sat down on the padded leather seat and ordered a glass of wine from a passing waiter.

They spoke fondly about their lives since school and exchanged news of their respective families. Jacoba talked about the death of her father, of a life curtailed by a particularly aggressive cancer. Then, lightening the mood, she asked teasingly, "And what about a man in your life?"

"Not for me!" Rachael replied, laughing. "I'm far too busy for boys! What about you? You used to attract them like bees to a honeypot!"

"Well, actually..." She smiled mischievously. "There is a boy I'm seeing. You can vet him if you want. He's meeting me here tonight."

They enjoyed another glass of wine while they continued their conversation. Jacoba explained that she had studied chemistry at Utrecht University and then returned to Amsterdam to work in her father's printing business. Immediately prior to his death, the business had been sold, and she had taken a job as an office manager. Rachael told her that she had attended the University of Amsterdam and her degree in German had led to a career in teaching.

Suddenly, Jacoba's attention was attracted by something behind her friend, and she started to wave enthusiastically.

Rachael turned her head and watched as her brother emerged from the wall of smoke and approached the booth.

"Hendrik?"

"Hi, Rachael."

"Is he...?" she said, looking inquiringly at her blonde friend.

Jacoba and Hendrik hugged and kissed, then he sat down beside her. His sister noticed that their fingers remained intertwined on the seat between them.

"Is he not a little younger than you?" Rachael asked half-jokingly.

"He's growing up quickly!" Jacoba laughed back, looking up at his face. "You're a teacher, so you know it's very rewarding when you've got a willing student!"

Hendrik squirmed in his seat, hailing a waiter to divert attention away from his embarrassment.

A glass of wine soon arrived, and he took a long, deep gulp. He glanced at his girlfriend; as if this were a pre-arranged signal, her lighthearted demeanor immediately grew serious, and the topic of conversation moved on to current events.

"Six and a quarter has now banned the Jews from the beaches and the sea!" He scoffed.

"Sorry?" his sister interrupted. "What does six and a quarter mean?"

"It's a nickname," he replied, smiling. "Seyss-Inquart, when pronounced in German, sounds like six and a quarter." He paused. "And a quarter's less than a whole, which refers to his crippled leg!"

"Come on!" Jacoba chastised him. "Less of the nicknames and more of the facts."

"We've been forbidden to open our shops and businesses on Sundays," he continued, "and given that they're already shut on Saturdays for shabbat, they're going to be closed for the whole weekend. The busiest time of the week. It's a joke! Legally, we're not even supposed to be here in this non-Jewish bar."

"Shhhh!" his girlfriend insisted, placing her forefinger on his lips. "Young people are rarely snitches, but you still don't want to speak too loudly about your background."

She placed her elbows on the table in front of her and leaned forward. Rachael had never seen such a serious expression on her face.

"Ultimately, the point isn't about the regulations," Jacoba continued. "It's what we do in response that's important."

"Exactly!" Hendrik agreed enthusiastically. "Perhaps we should organize another general strike!"

"What are you saying?" his sister asked, shocked and indignant.

"You sound like Father! Always the one who argues himself into such a confusion that he ends up thinking doing nothing's the best solution."

"In his defense, he's only trying to keep us safe."

"We aren't contemplating a general strike," Jacoba said. "More like something on a smaller scale, but still of the utmost importance." She took a sip of wine and placed her glass down slowly and carefully. "More people are going into hiding as each new regulation's announced. To make good their escape, they all need forged papers."

She paused as the waiter deposited another three glasses of wine on the table. "I've discovered a technique on my printing press to replicate the watermark on the paper used to make ID cards. It's taken hours of experimentation and testing of different papers and inks. It's not perfect, but I'm confident it will be difficult for the SS or police to tell the difference.

"I can't be at my press twenty-four hours a day, and there are many times when there's so much work I can't keep up. So, I urgently require people who know how to operate the press when I can't. They must be smart enough to learn the watermarking technique quickly. The press is in my basement. It goes without saying that we need people who can be completely and unequivocally trusted." She paused. "If the Nazis find the press, I'll be a goner."

"Are you using this as a way to lure me into your house?" Hendrik replied, his smile dying on his lips when he saw her face.

"Grow up!" his sister admonished, understanding the seriousness of the conversation. "There's a time for joking, and it's not now!"

Suitably chastised, he addressed his girlfriend. "Of course I'll do whatever is requested of me."

"Thank you," she said in a tone that was serious yet warm. She took another long, slow gulp from her glass and continued,

"And once printed, we need somebody to deliver the paper to the forgers."

She turned her head toward Rachael.

"What's up?" her friend asked.

Realizing that both of them were staring impassively at her, Rachael was overcome by a sudden nervousness. The smoke in the room began to sting her eyes and clog her throat. She tried to pick up her wineglass but fumbled it and thought better of the idea.

"Would you be willing to deliver some of this printed paper?" Jacoba asked solemnly. "It would be an immense help to the Resistance. It would save lives for certain."

The word *resistance* made Rachael shiver. The enterprise became markedly more perilous and uncertain with the introduction of that one word.

"Me?" she asked.

"Women are much less likely than men to have their papers checked," Jacoba explained. "Most of the Nazis are lecherous pigs. Show a little cleavage or wiggle your ass, and they let you pass unchallenged. And between the three of us, it should be easier to transfer the paper from the printing press to the forgers."

They sat in silence.

Rachael was bemused. A few minutes ago, she had been talking to an old friend she had met by chance, and now she was being asked to participate in Resistance activities. Had it even been a chance meeting in Dam Square? Or part of a more elaborate plan? Had her young and impetuous brother recommended her as competent and trustworthy enough to carry out this work?

Jacoba added, "The ultimate beneficiaries will be Jewish men, women and children."

Rachael, drawing deeply on her cigarette, replied, "I'll do it." She was mildly surprised at herself, even as she spoke.

"Good on you, sis." Hendrik beamed.

All three raised their glasses and drank.

Rachael's wine flooded her throat, its aroma filling her nostrils and seeming to smother her breath. She felt dizzy, fearful, and excited all at once. Most importantly, she felt ready.

TWENTY-TWO

Amsterdam – October 1941

It is an unusually cool fall morning when Rachael leaves the day care center. It is shortly after six o'clock, and the city is barely stirring. Brooding gray clouds blanket the sky.

She has dressed to blend in with the bleak environment, wearing a dark-gray overcoat and with her hair tucked inside a headscarf of the same color. Pushing the four-wheeled pram through the open door, out into Middenlaan and west toward Waterlooplein, she walks briskly to overcome the morning chill.

As she presses on, she considers the changes that have occurred over recent months. She had been a teacher at the J.F. Krop primary school, where everything had seemed so straightforward. She had met Henriette and started to tutor the children at the center. Then, in the wake of the attestations, when the authorities had begun the segregation of Jews and non-Jews in the field of education, the school had been forced to reorganize, and she had lost her job. However, almost immediately, Henriette had offered her paid hours at the center looking after babies and young children.

Anyway, she loves working with children, and in the current circumstances, a job's a job. Whenever she leaves the center, the one thing that she always brings with her is her ID card with the word *exempted* and the letter *J* stamped upon it.

Toby is a well-behaved child. At two years old, he possesses a calm temperament and is rarely emotional or upset. He is also an excellent and deep sleeper. All these attributes have led to him being chosen to travel in the pram that morning, even if he is a little large for it. If one were to look carefully, it would be evident that both the top of his head and soles of his feet are regularly rubbing against its padded sides.

The distance to the Jewish Council offices is a brisk, fifteen-minute walk. And briskly is how she walks, but not so fast that she might draw unnecessary attention upon herself.

The roads remain almost deserted. It is only as she is approaching the end of Weesperstraat that she notices two SS soldiers ahead of her. She carries on walking toward them.

Leaning on the side of a building, their appearance is relaxed, almost slouching against the wall. Both are smoking cigarettes and casually flicking ash onto the pavement. Even from a distance, she hears their voices, punctuated by occasional burst of laughter.

She makes every effort to continue as naturally as possible, holding her head up and forcing herself to make eye contact with them. She has been advised that coyness might create suspicion. She should exude confidence.

She draws level with the soldiers without their paying the slightest attention and takes a couple of paces past them before one of them addresses her.

"Good morning, Fräulein," the soldier on the right-hand side of the two speaks in German.

She stops, turns, and looks directly at them. The speaker has a round face and sports a pair of spectacles with strong lenses that make his pupils look like marbles. She thinks his expression is pleasant, unlike the cruel aggression of most SS soldiers.

"Good morning, officer," she replies.

"You're out exceedingly early this morning. What brings you here at such an unearthly hour?"

"I work at the day-care center on Middenlaan. Quite often, the babies are distressed when dropped off by their parents. I take them for a ride in the pram, and they almost always fall asleep."

"And where are you going?" the first soldier continues.

"Nowhere in particular," she responds. "I walk out of the front door of the center in any direction. It's totally random. Toby doesn't care." She smiles down at the sleeping child.

Observing no animosity in the soldier's expression, she takes a step away. However, the second SS soldier, who appeared to be paying no attention, suddenly flicks his unfinished cigarette into the open street and lazily pushes himself away from the wall.

She is struck by his narrow, gaunt face and his cold, calculating eyes. Her heart is beating so hard and so loudly she thinks the soldiers must be able to hear it.

"What's in the pram?" the second soldier asks.

"A baby!" she says, immediately regretting her flippant reply and the nervousness it may betray.

"Very funny," he replies. "What's in the metal basket?"

"Baby things." Her mind is whirring, she can barely coordinate her words, but she recovers before he can speak again. "Diapers, blankets, some milk." She bends down to show them the contents of the wire basket, which is fixed to the wheel chassis beneath the cot.

"Whoa, stop!" the second soldier shouts. "Let me look." There is a harshness in his voice that makes her catch her breath.

He stoops and casually, disdainfully, rummages among the items in the basket, not bothering to keep them tidy.

She breathes in deeply but silently through her nose, trying to concentrate, to forget the thumping of her heart and the cloying dryness of her mouth.

"Please don't raise your voice. You'll wake the baby," she says. She wonders whether her voice is back under control or whether it is betraying her fear.

The second soldier stares, his cold and suspicious gaze locked onto her.

She scrabbles in her bag, withdraws her ID card, and waves it in front of the second soldier's face, partly to show it to him but also to break his intrusive stare. He pays no attention.

"Come on, Wolfgang, let's leave this. It's close to the end of our shift, it's not worth it," the first soldier remarks. "And I'm chilled to the bone."

The second soldier narrows his eyes, still studying her face. He looks her up and down, like a doctor examining a patient. "I look forward to seeing you again," he says.

The two soldiers move off, and she walks in the opposite direction, toward the river. Even though this is a detour, she wants to put as much distance as she can between her and them. She has only just recovered her breath and composure by the time she reaches the council offices.

*

The Jewish Council had only been in its Waterlooplein offices for a few months. The rent was not as favorable as they had been led to believe, and the chairmen had needed to make an additional request for funds from the Lippmann Rosenthal bank to pay for the hefty deposit. However, the location was advantageous, and the building consisted of open areas that could be quickly populated with desks, chairs, and filing cabinets to serve the considerable number of new employees.

As Rachael peered through the ground-floor windows, it seemed to be a work in progress. Desks were covered with untidy piles of paper, while filing cabinets were scattered across the floor with gaping, empty drawers. It was early, but a few employees were already darting around urgently.

She remained standing outside, gently rocking the pram back and forth. She was beginning to think that nobody would notice her presence when a young man in his mid-twenties appeared. He had long, curly brown hair, dark, piercing eyes, and olive skin.

Only the most observant onlooker would have noticed that this man had not exited the council office at Waterlooplein 117 but had, in fact, come through the adjacent door of 115.

"Hi, Rachael," he said, looking to his left and right. "I hope you've had a pleasant walk this morning."

"Thank you, Ruud," she replied quietly. "I was stopped by a couple of SS soldiers."

"Really?" he said, concerned. "Do we need to change our routines at all?"

"Maybe. One of them was suspicious. He searched the pram and found nothing, but he didn't seem satisfied. We could consider some variations. Different times, different routes. Different carers. I'll discuss it with Henriette."

"You have some blankets for me?" he asked.

"Indeed, I do." Leaning inside the cot, she gently rolled the child over and withdrew the blankets on which he had been lying. "As requested."

"And here are the replacements," he said, offering her a neatly folded pile of blankets identical in size and color to the ones she held.

The pair exchanged their bundles, and she gently slid the replacements underneath the child. He barely stirred.

"Thanks, Rachael. It's a busy time, so we may need more blankets later in the week. We'll be in touch. Goodbye. Stay safe and be careful." He patted the blankets and smiled, then, calmly studying his surroundings until he was satisfied he could see no unfamiliar faces, returned to the door of 115.

As he pushed the door open, she caught a fleeting glimpse of the inside of the building. There, at the very first table inside the doorway, was her brother, head down, reading studiously, pencil poised in his hand. She smiled.

Hendrik had started early that morning, as there were several leaflets that needed to be proofread before being sent for printing. He found it easier to concentrate with fewer distractions. There was only Ruud present that morning. The curtains were closed, and he could enjoy total privacy.

Over recent weeks, he had become accustomed to the fear triggered by the slightest unexpected sound or movement. He immediately looked up when the door opened, but relaxed when he saw Ruud, cradling the blankets containing the newly printed pamphlets.

There was a moment prior to the door closing when Hendrik glimpsed the square beyond. A woman was standing there, gently rocking a pram. Even when wrapped tightly in a dark coat and headscarf, there was no doubt. It was his sister, looking straight at him. He returned her smile.

And then the door was shut, and she was gone.

TWENTY-THREE

Amsterdam – December 1941

The men waited in silence.

Typical, Walter Sueskind thought, only Asscher could be late for a meeting held in his own factory.

The Asscher diamond factory was situated on Tolstraat to the south of the city center. Walter had been surprised at the size of the building, having a preconceived notion that this type of business would not require much space. As it was, the factory was a four-level edifice occupying a large corner plot. He had learned from the receptionist that the Asscher family owned the largest diamond enterprise in Europe, boasting a large sales showroom that covered most of the first floor and contained several discreet side rooms to provide esteemed clients with more privacy. The second floor accommodated the employees who traded the diamonds, the administrators who managed the operations, and the accountants who counted the profits.

The third floor was heavily fortified, as it was there that the diamonds were stored and shaped by a team of highly trained cutters. There were steel bars on all the external and internal doors and windows, and security guards positioned at the exits. There were also supervised changing rooms where staff would put on their work clothes, a standard blue coverall with no pockets or linings where stones could be hidden.

The fourth floor was reserved for the exclusive use of the company directors. Judging by this spacious meeting room, he could only guess how big Asscher's personal office might be. A large photograph of two sailboats on a glistening sea hung on one wall, with a five-foot-long oar mounted opposite.

As he had made his way through the building, Walter could not help but contrast the clean, organized sense of wealth that pervaded here with the chaotic and impecunious life of the Jews beyond the bars.

*

The members of the council waited quietly, not wishing to broach any council matters in the absence of Asscher. They had tried to do so at a previous meeting, but Cohen had conducted proceedings so awkwardly that no one had made another attempt.

Asscher breezed into the room at around eleven-thirty, thirty minutes after the scheduled start. He made his way to the head of the long, rectangular table, which was covered in a jet-black cloth that would have undoubtedly displayed sparkling diamonds to stunning effect. Cohen, even as joint chairman, had left the head of the table empty for his colleague.

"Right, gentlemen, to business." Asscher began to speak before he had fully settled into his chair. "We've got a lot to cover, and time is short. We've received several new government regulations."

"More regulations! Will they ever stop?" Franck Kisch, sitting next to Walter, muttered, but not loudly enough to draw Asscher's attention.

"Regulation VO211/1941 relates to the Chamber for Culture. Jews will no longer be able to obtain membership of the chamber." Asscher read from a sheet of paper in front of him.

"Does that mean new memberships?" Walter asked.

"That means all Jews will be excluded from the chamber, including those who currently hold membership."

"But membership's the only way that artists, writers, musicians, and actors can legitimately work!" Judge van Lier protested.

Walter had regularly seen the judge attending the Royal Concert Hall for a recital or opera performance. Twenty percent of the Royal Concert Orchestra was Jewish, and Walter tried to imagine a recital where one in five chairs was empty. The Nazis were supposedly lovers of culture, but excluding the Jews would only diminish the arts. It proved how strong their allegiance to Nazi ideology must be if they were prepared to implement this regulation, he thought.

"We've been informed of another measure that will be introduced early in 1942," Asscher continued, glancing at Cohen as he did so.

Asscher drew long and hard on his cigarette. Walter could not recall seeing Asscher without a cigarette in his hand. The smoke billowed and drifted toward Cohen. From where Walter was sitting, the co-chairmen looked like ambiguous shapes shrouded in a thick fog.

"Well," Asscher continued, "unemployment is rampant among our fellow Jews. To be honest, it's a drain on our scarce resources to have to support men who aren't earning income. At the same time, in Germany, many able-bodied men have left their employment to join the armed forces. This has created thousands of unfilled jobs in their economy. It makes sense for our unemployed Jews to be carrying out those jobs. In Germany. It's simple supply and demand."

"In Germany? So men would be separated from their families?" van Lier asked.

"Any family members who are fit enough to work can accompany their men," Asscher replied.

"And the old and the young will be abandoned here?" the judge continued.

"If they're able to work, they can accompany the men," the diamond merchant repeated, shrugging. "If not, they can't."

"And could our people be working in armament factories that supply the German army?" van Lier pushed on. "Guns and weapons that could be used against the Netherlands and its allies?"

"I don't know. Maybe. That's outside our control."

"But surely, our community will lose many of its strongest and fittest people," Bernie Krouwer said.

Krouwer was a butcher, the only member of the council who was not a judge, lawyer, doctor, or senior businessman. He never wore a tie and was the only person sitting around the table without a jacket. He wore his dark-brown, scuffed work boots for these meetings and possessed unusually large hands, which now lay on the table, fingers splayed.

Asscher made as if to speak but stopped as Krouwer slapped his hand on the table.

"It's no wonder there are so many unemployed Jews," he said. "It's because the Nazis have deprived us of work. We aren't allowed to work for non-Jewish organizations or even trade with them." He wiped his brow with the back of his hand. "We should be protecting jobs in this country, not somebody else's!"

The co-chairman remained upright in his chair.

"If only it were that easy, Krouwer," he replied in a tone which Walter thought patronizing. "There's an irrefutable logic in using freely available labor. A Jew working for the Germans is in a much better situation than one deemed surplus to requirements. The alternative, as Rauter and Seyss-Inquart have relentlessly told us, is roundups in the dead of night and transportation to Mauthausen. Therefore, we propose that the next edition of the *Jewish Weekly* will include a request for able-bodied, unemployed Jews to make themselves available for work in Germany." He paused and looked intently at Cohen, not removing his gaze until the professor nodded slowly, without expression.

"How many do they intend to transport?" Walter asked.

"One thousand four hundred," he answered. "And please do *not* use the word transport. Can I ask you all to refer to this as *working in Germany*?"

A stunned silence fell upon the group.

"If we don't have enough people coming forward, Professor Cohen and I will make the selection on behalf of the council," he added, "to shield you from this unpleasant task."

Walter looked around the table and noticed several of the other members nodding.

The rest of the meeting passed him by like the blur of a passing express train. He had arrived feeling low, and these announcements dragged him farther down into a darker, sadder place.

"I believe that's everything," Asscher said finally, rising from his chair. "Unless there are any other comments?" He was already gathering up his papers and moving away from the table as he spoke.

And then he was gone.

For a moment, Walter thought it was a magic trick. One moment, the co-chairman was there, and the next, there was a puff of smoke and only an empty chair remained. And a stack of new and onerous regulations.

He decided to walk down the stairs rather than take the elevator and found himself accompanied by Franck Kisch.

"Have you seen the latest article in *De Vonk*?" Walter asked warily, pausing on a stairwell.

"*De Vonk*'s an illegal communist newspaper, a useless rag full of articles fomenting revolution, devoid of any factual evidence to support its views," the professor replied.

"Have you read it recently?"

"Er, no."

"I don't believe it's purely pro-communist anymore. It's more anti-Nazi. It contains several articles criticizing and challenging their repressive practices and their persecution of the Jews and other minorities. They were instrumental in the general strike."

"Anyway, what does this *De Vonk* article say?" the professor asked doubtfully.

"It says that the work camps are an elaborate hoax. The Nazis insist the Jews *are* being sent to work camps, but in reality, they're merely staging points. They're going to send us onward to the east..." He dropped his voice, so it was barely audible. "...to extermination camps where we'll all be killed. Hitler wants to wipe us out."

"Everybody knows there are camps to the east," Franck replied. "But there's no proof of extermination camps."

"But there's no disproof either."

"The burden of proof—"

"Forget the legal reasoning!" he interrupted. "You're not arguing in a court of law. This concerns the lives of you and your family! All of us! What if it *is* true?"

"The Germans are pragmatic people. Like Asscher says, why kill us when we can be put to useful work?"

"I agree that Germans are pragmatic, but Nazis are evil," Walter replied. "What about children, old people, the infirm? They can't work, so why bother feeding them?"

Franck shook his head. "But surely, the Allies would know of such camps. It would be on the front page of the *Times* of London or on the BBC, not just *De Vonk*."

"The eastern part of the Reich is completely cut off," Walter insisted. "None of the Allies know what's really going on out there. How come we've heard so little news coming back from the east?"

Franck's head seemed to tremble, wavering between a shake and a nod. "I don't know," he mumbled. "It's so difficult." He worked his gold fountain pen fretfully between his fingers.

"You can see as clearly as the rest of the council," Walter urged, grasping his coat sleeve. "As each month of 1941 has gone by, the Nazis have introduced more severe regulations. If the article in *De Vonk* is right, we as members of the Jewish Council are helping to send our brothers and sisters to their demise! Don't let it happen to your family!" Walter pleaded, firmly squeezing his friend's arm.

With that, he turned around and slowly descended the stairs. He glanced back to see Franck standing in the stairwell above, motionless except for his left hand, which was still fidgeting with his pen, and lost in thought.

TWENTY-FOUR

Germany – January 1942

Germany had experienced particularly poor harvests in 1940 and 1941. A sizeable proportion of the agricultural workforce had been redeployed in the manufacture of armaments and other war-related materials. By the second half of 1941, it had also become clear to the government that there was going to be insufficient food to satisfy the needs of the population and its armed forces. Without the certainty of food supplies, the Nazi leadership decided it would address the problem of excess demand by reducing the number of hungry mouths in Europe. Their objective to annihilate European Jewry remained. However, now the imperative was to accomplish this as quickly as possible.

In July 1941, Hermann Goering wrote to SS-Obergruppenführer Reinhard Heydrich commissioning him to devise a plan to deal with the *Jewish question*. Since seizing power in 1933, the Nazi Party had introduced many laws and decrees to persecute the Jews in Germany. Heydrich's focus now lay upon the Jews living elsewhere in Europe.

His initial plan entailed deporting five million Jews to Siberia. In addition, he intended to starve to death approximately thirty million Jews and other undesirables in Russia and Eastern Europe, thereby freeing up food supplies for German consumption.

In Russia, the Jews were sparsely distributed among many small villages in exceptionally large regions, unlike most other countries where they were concentrated in the bigger cities. Consequently, it had proved difficult to gather them together in big enough groups for economical deportation to camps. As a result, the so-called Einsatzgruppen were established to kill the Jews in situ, in the towns and villages where they lived.

The Einsatzgruppen were selected from the ranks of the SS and were mobile killing squads. They followed the German army into villages that had recently been conquered and killed all Jews who remained alive there. These squads were quick moving and traveled light. Pistols, rifles, and spades for digging mass graves were standard equipment for them.

Although Jews formed the vast majority of victims of the Einsatzgruppen, the undesirables included communists, priests, those with mental or physical disabilities, partisans, Romani and other ethnic minorities, prisoners of war, suspected radicals, and homosexuals. Women and children were not spared.

The squads murdered hundreds of thousands of people in Poland, Russia, and Serbia during the six months after the start of Operation Barbarossa. One squad of 1,700 SS soldiers killed 137,000 Russians in this same period.

However, Himmler recognized the mental stress caused to the SS soldiers in this wholesale shooting of men, women, and children. As a result, he actively pursued poison gas as a more efficient and less stressful way of killing Jews in large numbers.

On December 7, 1941, the Japanese bombing of Pearl Harbor led to the United States entering the war. This eliminated any lingering hopes the Germans held that the war would be ended sooner rather than later.

Heydrich's initial plan was undermined. Since there was neither enough time, food, nor infrastructure to transport millions of people across an active war zone to reach Siberia, the Nazi leadership agreed to his revised plan to deal with the Jewish question—the mass extermination of Jews in camps in Eastern Europe. This approach became known as the *Final Solution*.

In December 1941, Heydrich communicated this plan to senior members of the Nazi government. He then invited fourteen second-level government and SS functionaries to a meeting which took place at a villa on the outskirts of Berlin. Apart from Heydrich and Eichmann, none of the top ranks of the Nazi government or the SS attended.

The SS leadership had purchased the villa as a conference center, and it enjoyed stunning, unbroken views across Wannsee, a picturesque lake to the west of Berlin.

The meeting took place on January 20, 1942. Heydrich spoke for approximately sixty minutes, explaining the *Final Solution*. He solicited the cooperation of the attendees to ensure transport of the Jews to the camps. Once there, responsibility for the Jews would transfer solely to the SS. Government officials arranged the transport, the SS arranged the killing.

The deputy Reichsführer presented a document produced by Eichmann, which estimated of the number of European Jews to be transported and exterminated. This list was divided by country, whether within or outside German control.

While the meeting was formal in tone and content, the attendees were able to engage in relaxed conversation afterward. They enjoyed cognac and cigars on the terrace overlooking the lake and held open discussions about how the objectives could be met. Some attendees showed greater enthusiasm for the *Final Solution* than others, but everybody understood and accepted the need to implement it.

This meeting became known as the Wannsee Conference and is regarded as the first event that formally outlined and authorized the *Final Solution*.

The list provided by Eichmann showed 160,800 Jews living in the Netherlands, all of whom had been identified for extermination in camps in Eastern Europe with poison gas as the chosen method of killing.

TWENTY-FIVE

Amsterdam – March 1942

Even from a distance, Hannes knew there was something amiss. Isaac was sitting on the stone edge of the Keizergracht canal, not moving, his head and shoulders slumped forward, staring into the waters below.

"Zac, where's your bike?"

There was no reply. Hannes jumped off his bike and sat down next to his friend.

"Is there something wrong with your bike?" he asked. "It's a sunny day. We could go on a long ride!" he added enthusiastically.

There was still no reply. He leaned forward and bent his neck so that he could see his friend's face. He noticed the quick, shallow breaths that made Isaac's shoulders shudder. A tear coursed down his cheek, forming a droplet, which fell into the gray water.

"What's wrong?" Hannes inquired once more, placing his left hand on his friend's shoulder, squeezing lightly.

"We can't see each other anymore," Isaac sobbed. "The Nazis have forbidden it!"

"Of course we can. We see each other all the time. We're best friends. They can't keep us apart. Who cares what the crazy Nazis say? They'll see us riding our bikes and think we're two brothers out playing. They'll never suspect I'm Jewish."

"I'm sorry," Isaac cried. "I can't. My papa won't let me. He says that he can't put me in danger. And my playing with you could put me and the rest of the family at risk. They could send us away. To a horrible prison or camp. I don't want any of my family going to prison, Han. I'm sorry."

"It's crazy," Hannes argued. "What's so different now that wasn't true last week?"

"I think it's the badge," Isaac responded. "You're going to have to wear a badge."

"What do you mean, a badge?"

"Haven't you heard today's news?"

"Heard what? I woke up late and dashed straight out of the house to make sure I got here on time. What badge?"

"All Jews must wear a badge every time they're out in public. It's a yellow star with the word Jew written in the middle."

"It's okay, those things are for grown-ups. They're not for children," Hannes insisted.

"This one is!" Isaac cried. "I checked with my papa. Every Jew over six years old has to wear the yellow star badge. Including you!"

"Well," he said defiantly, "I'll simply take off my yellow star whenever we meet."

"It's crazy, but it's the law! We shouldn't break the law," his friend added, the tears flowing readily down his cheeks now.

"But it's a crazy law from the stupid Nazis! Any law that keeps friends apart must be stupid. And we should ignore those laws! So, go and get your bike, and let's be off!" Hannes cried, his enthusiasm tinged with desperation.

Isaac shook his head, slowly and solemnly, and with that, he swung his legs around and stood up, making sure to keep his back turned to his friend.

"I'm sorry, Han. Goodbye," he mumbled, then walked away.

Hannes remained, watching the gentle rippling of the canal. His mind had been thrown into confusion. He felt angry with the Nazis and their yellow star badge. He almost felt angry with Zac and his dad for allowing the badge to come between them. But, beyond that, he felt an emptiness in his stomach that would not shift. An emptiness that weighed him down and had started the moment his best friend had uttered the word goodbye.

*

It was some time before Hannes returned home. In an act of defiance, he had ridden his bike slowly around the perimeter of the Jewish Quarter, but riding his bike in such pleasant weather and without his best friend served to darken his mood.

It was a quiet morning. He did chance upon a couple of policemen on Kerkstraat, then a small group of SS soldiers who sat outside a café on Prinsengracht, drinking coffee and laughing loudly. He gazed at them as he passed, but they either did not see him or ignored him. Crazy Nazis and silly stars, he thought.

It took half an hour or so to cycle around the perimeter. By then, boredom had started to set in. The sunshine and fresh air had partially dissipated his rage, leaving a residual indignation in the pit of his stomach. He was fairly sure he would not cry again, so he decided to make his way home.

When he entered the living room, his mama was sitting at the dining table, sewing. Her face was a study in concentration, expressionless and focused. He watched in admiration as she looped stitch after stitch, the needle thrusting in and out of the cloth at a speed he could hardly follow. As the light caught the darting needle, it would glint before disappearing on its next loop.

His mother was concentrating so hard on her work that she appeared not to notice the presence of her son. After a few moments, she stopped sewing, placed her work on the table, traced the line of stitching with her index finger, then raised her head and looked at him.

She smiled weakly, and he smiled back. The knot in his belly stirred.

She picked up the clothing and hung it on the back of a chair. He recognized the dark-gray jacket that his father wore when working at the university, and over the left-hand breast pocket he could see the results of her handiwork, a six-pointed yellow star with the word Jew at its center, stitched with black thread.

The boy had imagined that the badges would be pinned onto clothes like a medal, to be taken on and off as required. It now dawned on him that these simple patches of material were permanent. His heart sank.

A pile of patches rested on the edge of the table next to his mother. He guessed there must have been twenty or so. Without a word, without a change of expression, she picked up another item of clothing and raised her needle to recommence her work. He recognized his school blazer.

"Do I need a yellow star badge?" he asked, fearful that he knew the answer.

His mother did not raise her head to acknowledge his words but drove the point of her needle through the badge and into the fabric of his blazer, drawing it back to complete the first stitch.

"Mama, don't!" he shouted. "If I wear a yellow star badge, I can't play with Zac anymore! It's all gone crazy!"

Unmoved, his mother continued to stitch.

"No!" he exclaimed frantically, running over and placing his hand over the partly sewn badge.

This did prompt his mother to respond. She raised her head and looked him squarely in the eyes.

"I'm sorry, but all Jews have to wear the yellow star. Not only here but in the whole of the country. It's a measure the Nazis have already introduced in Germany. There have been no exceptions there, and there'll be no exceptions here. It's illegal not to wear it," she said before repeating, "I'm sorry."

"But it's a stupid badge!" he yelled. "There's no difference between me and Zac, so I don't need to wear it! It makes no sense."

She placed her arms around her son and drew him close, squeezing him tightly. Her eyes were moist, but he could not see them. She blinked hard and, without releasing him, muttered in his ear.

"You're right. It doesn't make sense. But the Nazis think that there *is* a difference between you and Zac. You're a Jew and Zac isn't. The Nazis hate all Jews. Even you, my beautiful son."

She sensed his warm breath against her shoulder and knew from his flickering eyelids that he, too, was crying.

"It's so unfair!" he said, his words muffled against her now-damp blouse.

"I know," she replied. "I know."

They remained together for a few minutes before his mother gently pushed him away.

"You'll be eight years old in a few weeks. You're getting to be a big boy and need to behave like one. Life with the Nazis may get worse before it gets better. Do you understand?"

He stared back at her.

"Do you understand?" she repeated.

"It's crazy, but I understand," he said. "I need to be a big boy now."

TWENTY-SIX

Amsterdam – May 1942

The city had been so quiet since the introduction of the curfew that Franck Kisch woke up as soon as he heard the commotion in the street below. He scrambled out of bed, resisting the temptation to turn on a light, and found his way to the bedroom window. Very carefully, he drew the curtain, creating a narrow slit through which he could see the events unfolding in the street below.

Directly opposite, there were around ten soldiers outside Albert Prins's house. One of them was banging loudly on the door and shouting, "Open up! Open up in the name of the government!"

Four houses farther up the street, Franck saw that another group of soldiers had entered the property, and he heard muffled screaming and shouting emanating from within. Looking in the other direction, he could see a third group of men marching. The lead soldier held a piece of paper in his hand and was looking back and forth between the paper and the properties they were passing, evidently searching for a particular house.

He was dumbfounded. There had been plenty of raids across the city, but this was the first time he had actually seen one taking place, in the dead of night and outside his own home. The aggressive shouting of the soldiers cut through the silence like a jagged knife. He had not looked at his bedside clock, but he guessed it must be between one and two o'clock in the morning. He tried to imagine the fear Prins must have felt on hearing the shouting and banging on his door.

A member of the council had told him that some Jews had become blasé about these surprise raids. They recognized that eventually they would be certain to become victims themselves, and with that inevitability came a sense of calm. Franck could not feel that way. He was constantly terrified of being raided and separated from his family.

Although he could see little more than shadows, the family up the street started to file out of the house. He supposed it was Hans Meijer, the baker, and his wife and two sons. They were laden with bags and suitcases, which they deposited on the roadside when an SS soldier barked at them. Another soldier struck Meijer with the butt of his rifle. The baker stumbled but managed to walk on.

Franck could make out Hans and Elizabeth Meijer and their son Jacob, who was slightly younger than Hannes, but there was no sign of their older son, Joshua, who was in his early twenties. The professor knew Joshua still lived with his parents, and he had seen him earlier that day. He wondered where he was at that moment. The baker's son had been lucky.

The Meijer family shuffled silently past the front of his house. Hemmed in by heavily armed soldiers, they looked small, fragile, and insignificant. Meijer was walking with his head held high, but his wife's head was bowed, and she was dabbing her tears away with a handkerchief. Jacob, holding his mother's hand, glanced around in a state of bewilderment. Watching them, Franck felt a tremendous sadness but one tempered with relief that it had not been his home the SS had visited.

By the time the Meijers had passed, the front door to the property opposite had been opened, and the soldiers barged in. This time, he could decipher the words spoken by the SS soldier.

"Everybody in the house needs to come now," he shouted. "You're being taken to a work camp in Germany, where you'll be working in a factory to support the war effort. The work will be hard, but you'll be housed and well fed. I've got five people listed for this household. You may take one suitcase with you. If you have any other suitcases or belongings, these must be left outside your house and will be forwarded to you later. Write your name and address on each case you leave. There's a train waiting at the station, so please hurry up! There's no time to waste."

"But my father's eighty-four years old and ill! He's bedridden!" Franck recognized the shrill, desperate voice of Marianne Prins.

"Arthur Weismann, aged eighty-four years," the soldier replied. "He's on the list. Please get him out of bed. Immediately!"

"You can't!" she shouted.

"Trust me, Jew," the soldier warned. "It's going to be much better for your father to come with you now. Otherwise, he'll be arrested and sent to Mauthausen."

"He's too sick to go!" she implored. "He'll die!"

No reply came.

The third group of soldiers was now rapping on the door of the Schrijvers' home.

Franck let the curtain close. He breathed deeply, shook his head, and wiped his sweaty palm on his nightshirt. His wife lay in bed, her back to him. He thought of his son in the adjoining room. He had just observed three sets of SS soldiers, only yards from his own door. With disgust, he recalled the words of Asscher at the last council meeting and repeated in the *Jewish Weekly* that morning: *No further raids are envisaged for the time being.*

The Nazis had never been trusted, but these were downright lies that they weren't even attempting to disguise. He wondered how long his exemption would keep the SS away.

He returned to bed and quietly slid beneath the covers, thankful his wife had not woken and had avoided being upset.

Elizabeth lay with her back to him. She heard the rustle of the sheets. She had barely slept for days. She had lain, eyes wide open, dreading every noise outside. And fearing every silence in between.

*

The Hague – May 1942

"So, how do you assess last night's raids?" Seyss-Inquart asked Rauter.

"Well, they were undoubtedly successful. We rounded up four hundred Jews," the soldier answered. "And with almost no objection or resistance. They seem to be accepting of their fate. They surely can't trust the council anymore, yet they still appear to."

"The additional trains arrived at the station on time," the Reichskommissar said. "Once again, the Dutch railways did what they were asked. And there were no leaks out into the community."

"We do have a logistical issue," Rauter said. "The raids take place at different times, each with a few arrests, so the Jews arrive at the station in a somewhat chaotic, uncoordinated manner. We'd benefit from a holding facility to bring them to. Then we could take them to the station later. In one go, so to speak."

"When Eichmann last visited us, he was insistent that we increase the number of deportations. Yet one week, he may ask for no trains, then the very next one, there's a huge requirement. With such uncertainty over supply and demand, a holding facility would make sense," the commissioner admitted begrudgingly.

"Well, I may have just the solution for you," Rauter said. "The Jewish Theater. It's only used by Jewish actors and artists, so it's about time we closed it down anyway. The auditorium and the other rooms dotted around the building should provide enough space to hold the Jews and allow us to send consistent numbers to the station."

"That's a good idea," Seyss-Inquart agreed. "I'll deal with the paperwork straight away. We may need to deploy additional manpower to set this up swiftly."

"But don't use valuable Aryan resources," Rauter said. "The council employs thousands. Let the Jews set up and run it. We'll only need a small number of SS soldiers to supervise."

"Asscher and Cohen can print a notice in the *Jewish Weekly*. This must be in place by the end of July, or we'll have Eichmann breathing down our necks."

TWENTY-SEVEN

Westerbork – June 1942

Leo Blumensohn was practicing with the choir outside barracks 87 when a builder's wagon pulled into view. It was fully loaded, which explained its slow and deliberate progress to the eastern side of the camp. He was not unduly concerned, as there had been regular construction works taking place since he had arrived, and he recognized the name *Robben* painted on the side of the vehicle, the name of the preferred building company.

However, his attention was certainly grabbed when a second, similarly laden vehicle trundled into view, coming to a halt by the side of the first. Within ten minutes, there were four wagons in a row. The choir had ceased singing, and its members were whispering to one another.

Leo had been the primary contact among the inmates whenever Robben's workmen had been there, and he had always been informed of oncoming projects in advance. His working life in Germany had given him experience within the construction industry, and he was young, strong, and able to participate in any manual labor required. The Robben management had passed excellent reports about him to Schol, which had led to him developing a reasonable relationship with the commandant.

The unexpected arrival of these wagons prompted Leo to seek out Schol. After all, the proposed works would certainly require him to provide camp labor to assist. He had spotted a substantial amount of timber loaded on the back of the vehicles, which suggested to him that additional barracks were being planned.

The commandant's office was on the western edge of the camp, just beyond the barbed wire. Leo walked along the gravel path that constituted the only road and ran through the camp's center. By the time he had reached the modest wooden hut, a further four wagons had passed him. Standing by the side of the road, he could inspect the contents of the passing vehicles. There were even more timber planks of various lengths and thicknesses, and he spotted a large quantity of thin lengths of steel.

As he reached the commandant's office, a gray Mercedes pulled away. He recognized it as Schol's, so he started to run, waving his arms furiously and shouting after the vehicle, "Hey! Stop!" The car continued and disappeared behind a sandstorm of yellow dust thrown up by its wheels.

He was about to return to the choir when he noticed another Mercedes parked behind the hut. He wondered if Schol had changed cars and was at his desk after all. As he approached the office, his spirits rose when he heard voices from within. Striding confidently up its wooden steps, he knocked on the door and waited.

"Enter!"

He gently turned the doorknob and walked in.

The office was full of soldiers. He recognized the gray service uniforms of the SS. Six of them were gathered around a surveyor's drawing laid out on Schol's desk; sitting in the commandant's chair was not Schol but an SS officer in his mid-thirties, a mop of curly blonde hair giving him a boyish look. He wore a conciliatory expression. His mouth, even in a neutral position, appeared to form a smile.

"Come closer!" the officer said enthusiastically, waving his hand in Leo's direction. "How can I help you?"

"Well, sir," Leo answered, perturbed by the aggressive stares of the other soldiers. "I couldn't help noticing the arrival of several Robben vehicles, and I wanted to ask Commandant Schol whether he needs me to set up any construction teams."

"Perfect timing!" the gentle-faced soldier replied, gesturing to the document on the table. "We were reviewing the plans as you knocked. Come here, and I'll gladly show you what's been proposed."

He suddenly stood up. "I'm forgetting myself! We haven't made formal introductions. Please accept my apologies." He spoke in a tone that Leo thought was genuinely contrite. "My name is SS-Obersturmführer Gemmeker. I'm the new Westerbork commandant. And these are the SS officers who are going to manage the camp from now on."

Leo approached the desk and leaned over the drawing. He looked at it, tilting his head quizzically from side to side.

"And you?" Gemmeker asked pleasantly. "What's your name?"

"My name's Leo Blumensohn, sir."

"Well, I'm sure that with the new camp management, you'll continue to play a positive and influential role." Gemmeker smiled. "Let me show you." He then drew a line with his finger, outlining the rectangular camp perimeter.

"And these?" Leo asked, pointing to what appeared to be barracks in the northern, eastern, and southern areas of the camp.

"That's the reason for the wagons," Gemmeker said. "We're going to build an additional twenty-four barracks plus a number of smaller outbuildings, including a prison."

"Well, by my reckoning, that's an extra two to three thousand inmates," Leo said.

"Your sums are wrong," the commandant replied. "We expect between two hundred and fifty and three hundred Jews per barracks. That's between six and seven thousand."

"But the camp is home to eleven hundred refugees at the moment and can cater for eighteen hundred at most." Leo sounded dumbstruck.

"Orders are orders," Gemmeker said. "Former Commandant Schol told me the work ethic of the inmates is of the highest order. I'm sure this will continue."

Leo opened his mouth to speak, but Gemmeker preempted him.

"Former Commandant Schol did a fine job but wasn't the right man for the camp's next stages. Now it's a task for the German SS."

"Schol was too lenient with you lot," a gruff voice growled in the background. "The camp needs much better management and efficiency."

"This project is urgent," the new commandant said. "The twenty-four new barracks are to be erected by the end of July."

"Unfortunately, it's not going to be possible to build them to the same standard in that timescale," Leo replied.

Gemmeker raised his eyebrows. "The materials we've purchased will allow us to complete the project on time."

"Do you mind if I ask another question about the plans, Commandant?"

"Of course not. Ask away!"

"For these barracks to hold seven thousand people, do you intend to have them equipped with three-tiered sleeping bunks?"

Gemmeker paused a moment before grinning. "Well done, Blumensohn! Very well worked out."

"And where will these additional refugees come from?" he ventured.

"Right, we really must get on!" Gemmeker replied, his amicable tone vanishing.

"Yes, sir," Leo took the hint, turning on his heels and making his way toward the door.

"Blumensohn!" Gemmeker said.

"Yes, sir?"

"We'll be running a much tighter ship than you've been accustomed to. As a start, make sure all inmates are aware that whenever you address me or the other SS officers, you must salute. Failure to salute is an offense punishable by a spell in the prison block. Is that understood?"

"Yes, sir!" he replied, saluting. A prison block was not an addition Schol would have countenanced, he thought. He fumbled nervously behind his back to find the door, leaning on it to steady himself. There had been a menace in the commandant's words that belied his genial appearance.

As he made his way back, Leo tried to imagine how these new barracks might be squeezed in and contemplated why a camp that had housed a thousand inmates for almost three years was suddenly expected to accommodate seven thousand. He thought of the choir, whose pure singing could be heard drifting in the summer air; the schoolchildren studying in their classrooms where only the scratching of pencils could be heard; the performers rehearsing on the stage that he had helped to build; and then the new barracks, each crammed with three hundred refugees, stacked in bunks three high. And a dirty, rat-infested prison block.

TWENTY-EIGHT

Amsterdam – July 1942

Franck Kisch was studying the edge of the dining table, passing his finger over an indentation in the wood that had been made years earlier by a dropped casserole dish and rubbed smooth over time.

He spoke without lifting his head.

"Events have taken another turn for the worse. Nazi persecution has continued to rise sharply. Now, we're seeing large-scale transportations to work camps, which may continue until there are none of us left."

He rubbed the table edge again and slowly looked up. He saw his wife at the opposite end of the table, his daughter on his right, and his sons on the left. He tried to force a smile.

"We still have exemption from deportation," he continued. "I don't know how long it'll last, nobody does, but it could end soon. So we must take decisions and start planning straight away."

The room was bathed in the bright, ethereal light of the evening sun.

"The Nazis have ordered all Jews to transfer their savings to the puppet bank Lippmann, Rosenthal & Co. This puts the SS in charge, which means we'll lose control of our money. Perhaps forever. Fortunately, several weeks ago, I visited my bank and withdrew my cash. It's here in the house, stashed away in several hiding places."

"What can we do with guilders, Father?" Hendrik asked.

"People generally like hard cash, and the Nazis are no different. Whatever rules and regulations are in existence, some will bend or break them in exchange for cash. The Dutch are the same. It's probably human nature."

"Bribery?" his son inquired with incredulity. These were actions he never thought his father would consider.

"Yes," Franck replied. He looked around the table. Elizabeth was watching him expectantly while Rachael's demeanor was calm. Hannes was looking on intently, although his vacant expression showed he did not really understand. Hendrik was leaning forward attentively, his elbows on the table and his chin resting on his clenched fists.

"So we've decisions to make. And we've got money to help us. Let's discuss our options," Franck said gravely.

"The Westerweel group is smuggling Jews out of the country," his son said. "Through Belgium, then down to the south of France, beyond the clutches of the Nazis."

"And how would they feel about smuggling a family of five?" Elizabeth asked tentatively.

"That's a difficult one, Mama. They only take one or two people at a time because a group of three or more can look conspicuous. Especially traveling over that sort of distance."

"We can't let the family be split up!" she pleaded, wringing her hands.

"If that's the case, then the Palestine Pioneers may not be an option," Franck said.

"What about going into hiding?" Rachael asked. "If we've got money, we can pay our way to a safe house."

"You're right," Hendrik said. "The Nazis are transferring Jews living in other parts of the country to Amsterdam. As the Jews are moved out of an area, so is the Nazi infrastructure. They relocate their soldiers and close down the local Jewish Council. That area then becomes a safer place to hide.

"The Nazis want to fill their deportation quotas. Raiding Amsterdam streets is much more fruitful than traveling into the countryside to arrest small pockets of Jews. Going into hiding in the countryside could be a good option."

"If we did wish to consider going into hiding, I'll make contact with some of my sources," Hendrik said with reticence.

"Please, could you do that?" Franck requested. "See if they can find a suitable hiding place for five."

Hendrik looked directly into his father's eyes. He swallowed hard before proceeding.

"They'd be hiding four," he replied.

"What do you mean, four?" Elizabeth shrieked.

"I'll be staying here. There are things to do."

"What things? What could be more important than family?"

"The Nazi regime's a plague, Mama. All over Europe, decent people are fighting to stop them from spreading their evil farther. I can't join an army, but I can fight them here in the Netherlands."

"Franck, please reason with your son!" Elizabeth urged.

The professor looked carefully at his son, licking his dry lips.

"Hendrik," Franck said. "I'm immensely proud of you. What you're proposing is enormously brave and noble. If you wish to remain here to fight the Nazis, then you have my blessing." He closed his eyes tightly, and a solitary tear squeezed out, running slowly down his cheek until he wiped it away with the back of his hand.

"Franck, are you mad?" his wife shouted, tearing at her hair. "He's twenty years old. He's still a boy!"

"Hendrik's right, my love," he said. "All over Europe, men are fighting the Nazis, some even younger than him. And with the Americans and Japanese also committed to the war, the whole world's involved. How can we prevent or even dissuade him from doing the same?"

Elizabeth looked from her husband to her eldest son. Her erratic breathing heaved her chest violently. She covered her face in her hands and moaned, a deep, long mournful moan, almost primordial.

"You promised to keep the family together!" she said, bitterly. "Now you've broken your word. You've betrayed the family."

"Father's not betraying anybody," her son interjected. "He's standing up for what's right. And I'm an adult able to make my own decisions. Some things are bigger than one family, Mama."

There was quiet around the table once more, save for Elizabeth's intermittent sobbing. Franck looked at his son and nodded in approval.

A cough broke the quiet. Rachael carefully tucked her hair behind her ears. "I'm not going to leave the children and babies behind," she said.

"Excuse me?" her father said. "Those children in the day-care center. They come and go all the time. How could you possibly have become so attached to them?"

"Irrespective of how well I know them, Papa, they're still children. And with all the raids and deportations, more and more children are at risk. They need protecting. How can we not help defenseless children? They're the next generation."

"So, you're going to put these children you hardly know ahead of your own flesh and blood?" her mother asked incredulously.

"I'm surprised you can even make the comparison," Rachael scolded her mother. "These children are just one signature away from being deported. I can help them."

"Well, it looks as if our family is shrinking by the minute," Elizabeth lamented. "It's not as if you're saving any of these children. You're only looking after them until they're deported!"

Rachael looked blankly at her mother. "Please, let's not argue about this. Hendrik will soon have to go into hiding anyway. He's young, fit, and strong, and the Nazis will want to send him to a labor camp. The moment there's a risk of me being taken by the Nazis, I'll join him. Until then, I'll continue to work at the center."

"So, you two have already discussed this?" Franck asked.

The siblings glanced at each other, then both nodded. Their father raised his eyebrows in surprise.

"In the beginning, the Nazis might have tolerated us," Hendrik said. "But now it's abundantly clear they'll treat the Dutch Jews in exactly the same way as those in Germany and Poland."

"But if we don't do what they ask, it'll be a lot worse," his father said. "Yesterday, they threatened to send seven hundred hostages to Mauthausen if we don't provide four thousand Jews for this week's transport. That would have been seven hundred lives on our conscience."

"For all we know," his son countered, "the Nazis are going to kill four thousand anyway, so it's just a question of timing.

It's seven hundred deaths now or four thousand deaths later on."

"We can't be one hundred percent sure that the four thousand will die," Franck argued. "So the valid comparison is seven hundred *certain* deaths versus four thousand *possible* deaths. Shouldn't we be trying to avoid the certain deaths? Also, I'll add that it's much easier to debate these matters around the dining table than it is with a list of potential deportees in your hand, some of whom are your personal friends."

Hendrik was tapping his fingers on the table. Rachael leaned over and gently placed her hand on top of his. He took a deep breath before continuing. "We mustn't fall out over this. Let's agree to differ. We'll make our own decisions based upon our respective opinions."

Franck looked at his son, who appeared resolute and calm but without the redness in his cheeks, which usually betrayed his frustration and anger. He recognized at this moment that the erratic youth had become an adult. His daughter's demeanor was similar, her hand still resting on that of her brother. He felt a surge of love and fear for them both.

Elizabeth had grown pale, her mouth drooping listlessly open, and the vacant look in her eyes made her appear almost comatose.

"Okay, we may be in disagreement in certain areas," the professor said, "but I think we can make some decisions. Rachael and Hendrik will stay behind. The others need to go into hiding." He turned toward his wife. "The council and the Nazis will notice my absence. Therefore, I suggest that you and Hannes depart first. I'll follow as soon as I'm sure the two of you are safe and in place."

"Are you abandoning us as well?" she asked.

"Not at all, my love. We'll make our escape plans together, and I promise I'll be with you soon after. The Nazis are raiding everywhere, so we need to act quickly and decisively."

Elizabeth's head sank to the tabletop, where she wept loudly and uncontrollably.

TWENTY-NINE

Amsterdam – August 1942

The facade of the Dutch Theater had remained unchanged since its construction in the late-nineteenth century. The ornate pediment, sitting on top of four Tuscan columns, was adorned with sculpted classical figures surrounded by cherubs. Its whitewashed exterior made it stand out against the surrounding dark, brick buildings.

It took Walter ten minutes to walk from his home on Prinsengracht to the theater. The council had appointed him as theater manager when it was selected as a holding site. One of the thousands of Jews who had fled Germany in the late-1930s, he could converse equally well in German and Dutch. He had a round, kindly face and a gentle disposition, with black hair of medium length. He smiled frequently, and even when not doing so, his expression was agreeable.

As he approached the theater, Walter could not avoid contrasting the original purpose of the building with its current use, packed with two thousand Jews awaiting deportation. He recalled how it had been before the Nazi occupation, when he and his wife, Johanna, would walk up from the tram stop and enjoy the evening sunshine for a while before entering the theater through its imposing frontage and walking into its dark oak paneled foyer. There, they might wait for their friends before going into the bar for preshow drinks. In those days, there had been no segregation between Jews and non-Jews, not in the audience, not among the performers, and not in the authorship of the works staged. He wished he had been the manager of the theater then rather than now.

How it had changed, and in such a short time. Against the backdrop of a bewildering bombardment of decrees and regulations, the Dutch Theater had become the Jewish Theater, and now not a theater at all. The Jews locked inside were like animals caged in a zoo, staring forlornly through glass doors and windows, yearning for freedom. The auditorium had been transformed into a refugee camp with families sheltering between the rows of seating, on the stage, or in the aisles.

"Sir," Walter said, nodding a greeting at the SS guard outside the front entrance. The soldier seemed uninterested, leaning against the wall, sheltering a cigarette with his hand.

Walter opened the door with his key, walked in, and locked it behind him. As soon as he turned around, his nostrils were filled with the fetid stench of people crammed together with too little space and limited access to hygiene facilities.

Walter himself attracted attention. As a member of the Jewish Council and a man with the front door key, he had an uncomfortable power among these people. Upon spotting him, they would frequently rush up and start bombarding him with their questions and entreaties. He found this incredibly distressing. There were so many plaintiffs talking at once that he could barely understand what any of them was saying. All he could see were their pleading, desperate faces. Yet even without hearing their words, he could guess what they were asking. They were inquiring about the whereabouts of loved ones, where they would be going, and when and how they could obtain an exemption.

Despite this, he would invariably stay awhile, listen as best he could, and attempt to ease their fears. He would give updates from the council or hand out copies of the *Jewish Weekly*. The chairmen had been insistent that whatever he communicated had to be aligned with their message.

Today, however, he could not afford to spend time in the foyer. He had an important meeting. He followed the signs to the stalls bar. The room had been emptied, leaving two simple rows of tables and chairs. New arrivals to the theater would be processed and registered here. Depending upon the numbers on any given day, there would be between two and eight registration clerks employed by the council, all of them paid for by the Lippmann Rosenthal bank out of funds stolen from the Jews' savings.

The clerks would record the details of each newcomer on numbered lists which, when complete, were signed off by an SS officer. These lists were used again when it came to selecting and sending Jews for transportation to camps. The clerks also created individual records, which were stored in one of four dark-green metal filing cabinets lined up against the wall.

In the corner of the room, away from the registration desks, Walter saw Henriette Pimentel. They greeted each other, and Walter led her back to the foyer, unlocking and relocking the front door and walking out to a bench located about halfway between the theater and the day-care center.

They did not attract the suspicions of the guards because they had been working closely together on the day-care center project. The severe overcrowding in the theater caused by the large numbers of people arrested during the recent raids had taken even the Nazis by surprise. It had been suggested that there was space in the day-care center to accommodate all the children younger than thirteen years old. They would be reunited with their parents when they were selected for transportation. This arrangement also meant that parents were extremely unlikely to try to escape from the theater because they would never countenance leaving their children behind in the center.

"I can't bear the prospect of these poor children being sent to camps," Henriette said.

"I appreciate what you're saying, but I'm not sure what we can do," Walter replied.

"I have a plan, but I'll need your help for it to succeed. It will be dangerous for both of us."

"The lives of children are potentially at stake. Their lives are more important than mine."

She smiled. "Well, I'm much older than you!"

"So tell me the plan."

Watching her, he noticed her gray hair and the tired expression on her face, but there was a steely determination in her manner.

"The SS guard standing outside the theater supervises the center as well. He watches every single person who goes in or out of either building, adult or child. But, as you know, the teacher training college is next door," she gestured to it, "and isn't supervised at all. It's a Protestant seminary, so nobody's expecting Jews there. Anybody going in or out does so without attracting the attention of the SS."

She drew a long breath and stood up to ease her aching limbs before sitting back down.

"The director of the college is called Johan van Hulst. He's a proper gentleman, hates what the Nazis have done to the Jews and, like us, cannot abide children being placed in harm's way.

"To the rear of the center there's a hedge. It's around six feet high and separates us from the college. It's completely out of sight. We can pass smaller, younger children over the hedge and into the college garden. Johan and a group of his teachers and students will keep them in the building for a night or two while forged papers are produced and an escape route planned. And then they'll take them, one by one, straight out of the front door of the college, without being challenged.

"A small child can be smuggled in a duffel bag or a shopping trolley or in a pannier attached to a bike. The children can be hidden in anything that's big enough to hold them. A child could even walk out in plain sight, holding the hand of a teacher pretending to be its parent. The children will then be escorted to safe houses across the city. In the following days, the Resistance will take them out of the city and into the countryside. As far away from here as possible," she concluded.

"That sounds like a splendid plan," Walter said. "But what's my role?"

"Well, every child's registered at the theater before being transferred over to the center. The names of the children we smuggle out will also be on the registration lists, and unless we do something, children who aren't physically here will be selected for deportation, and we'll be found out."

"Of course, I understand," Walter said thoughtfully. "Somehow, we need to erase every smuggled child from the theater registers."

"Exactly," Henriette replied. "And there's one more task for you. The parents must agree for us to smuggle their children. Otherwise, they'd report them missing.

"It's clear," she continued, shuffling on the bench, "that the Nazis have increased the frequency and size of the deportations. The deportations used to be well organized, but not so much now. They're rounding up Jews whenever and wherever they can. It's as if they've been given a target and can't keep up. We can only smuggle out a relatively small number of children on any given day, so we do need to start as soon as possible."

"Leave it with me," Walter said. "If you want to start tomorrow, then please give me the names of the first children in the morning. You make sure the children disappear from the center, and I'll make sure they disappear from the registers."

*

It was around noon the following day when Walter made his way into the theater auditorium. He thought it was desperately sad to see this once-lovely space converted into a grim and ugly refugee camp. Immediately after a deportation, this area might be almost empty of people, but today, there were over two thousand registered, stretched out across the crimson velvet seats and plush carpeted aisles. The stench was so strong that he was obliged to hold his breath as he passed one of the five public toilets that served both as sanitation and a supply of fresh water.

To prevent escapes, the SS had screwed the windows shut, meaning that the only source of fresh air was via the small courtyard to the rear of the building, to which access was severely restricted. Its high walls were topped with barbed wire.

Nobody had given him a description of Wilhelm and Anna Schrijvers, so his only option was to walk among the refugees asking if they knew the couple. After a while, he found somebody who not only knew them but could pinpoint their whereabouts, in the space between the stage and the first row of seats.

They were a young couple in their late twenties. He had black hair and a bushy, imposing beard flecked with gray. She had delicate features and striking, pale-blue eyes. According to the register, they and their two-year-old son had been rounded up two days ago, which explained why their clothing was relatively clean and their disposition positive.

"Wilhelm and Anna Schrijvers?" he asked as he approached.

"Yes," they replied together.

"Do you have a son called Willy?" he asked.

"Oh my God! What's happened to Willy?" the mother shrieked.

"It's fine, it's fine. There's nothing wrong with Willy." Walter raised his palms to calm them. "I need to speak with you. In complete confidence. You must promise not to talk to a living soul about what I'm going to tell you." He knew this was a promise very few people could realistically make. The SS had a nasty habit of making people divulge their secrets.

They nodded.

"I believe we can smuggle Willy out of the day-care center. To a safe house in the country."

"That's unbelievable news!" Anna said.

"To do this, I need your permission," he added. "We'll remove his name from the registration records and provide him with forged ID."

"Of course! Of course!" Wilhelm consented.

Walter sensed a cloying, tightening feeling in his guts. His heart was pounding so loudly that he thought it might echo around the auditorium.

"We must act quickly. This evening or tomorrow," he urged.

"So when do we leave?" Anna inquired.

"I'm afraid it's only Willy who will be able to leave." He grimaced. "We can help children escape from the day-care center, but not adults from the theater."

Walter watched as reality dawned on the young parents' faces, the transformation of their elation into disappointment, then despair.

"So we'll be forced to part from our beloved son, our only child?" she demanded, pausing as the truth dawned on her. "Perhaps forever? I can't do that!" She buried her head in her husband's jacket and sobbed violently.

"I appreciate your dilemma," Walter said gently, "but your son has much better prospects in hiding than he does with you in Westerbork. You might be listed for deportation at any time." He paused, turning his eyes away. "And I'm sorry you won't be able to say goodbye either. It's impossible to bring him back here, even for a few minutes."

"I'm never going to see my son again!" she cried, emitting a deep guttural moan that made Walter's skin crawl.

"An escape may give our son a decent and long life," Wilhelm said, placing his arm around his wife's shoulders. "With us, he'll share our fate. What bigger incentive could we have to survive this damned war than being able to see Willy again?"

"I know this is a tremendously tough question," Walter said, "but I really do need an answer. Do you give permission for us to smuggle your son out of the day-care center?"

Wilhelm nodded slowly. "I'd do anything for him, and this is his best opportunity." Although she was burrowed inside her husband's jacket, Walter could Anna's head nodding gently.

"Thank you both," he said. "Although I can't tell you where he'll be going, I'll let you know as soon as we've moved him. Remember! Please don't tell anybody! Not a word! His life and yours, and the lives of many others, are at stake."

THIRTY

Westerbork – August 1942

The new barracks had been built on time and, as expected, were of inferior quality. The cheap wood, together with the hasty construction, meant they provided barely any protection from the elements. August was especially hot and dry, and the scorching wind whipped the earth up into sandstorms that sped across the open heathland, lashing the new huts and leaving grains absolutely everywhere inside: on the floors, in the beds, on tables, on blankets, on the laundry hanging from makeshift clothes lines suspended from the ceilings. The sand fought for space with the lice on the skin of the multitudes of new inmates.

The first two thousand people to enter the camp during 1939 and 1940 had been Jewish refugees from Germany, and it was they who continued to inhabit the original sturdy and comfortable barracks. The Dutch almost exclusively occupied the new barracks. A sense of inequality and mutual antagonism grew between the Jews of the two countries, which occasionally almost equaled their animosity toward the SS.

Gemmeker had appointed Leo as the supervisor of the inmate construction teams, and he had been continuously acting as a referee between the two factions. He tried as much as possible to use Dutch and German laborers and insisted upon displaying no favoritism. In his mind, he could understand the perspective of the Dutch Jews. After all, the camp was located on their land.

A dislike for Kurt Schlesinger was one of the few things that both Dutch and German Jews had in common. A German Jew, he had arrived in the camp with his wife in March 1940 and subsequently been promoted to Chief Service Officer (CSO) of the Ordedienst (OD) in February 1942, a role which made him de facto camp manager.

The OD was an organization whose role was to keep the camp running smoothly. Taking its orders from the SS camp commandant, its members were selected from among the German Jewish inmates rather than from the ranks of the brutal SS soldiers.

Members of the OD wore an instantly recognizable uniform of green coveralls. Each one had two markers confirming their identity and authority, an armband around their right biceps, and a badge pinned to the left breast of their clothing. The presence of the badge particularly angered the other inmates because it covered their yellow star. This reinforced the distance between the OD and their fellow Jews.

The CSO leader selected OD members in his own image, meaning that they behaved as immorally and corruptly as he did and were despised almost as much as he was. Their allegiance did not lie with their fellow Jews but with themselves and the SS. They were not allowed to carry firearms but had permission to carry truncheons and sticks, which they deployed frequently, often without provocation. Their behavior was so merciless that the other refugees nicknamed them the *Dutch SS*.

Schlesinger regarded himself not as a German but a proud Prussian. To that end, whatever the weather, he always wore breeches, boots, a black leather coat and an officer's cap, adopting an attitude of superiority toward his fellow Jews. His thinning black hair was always oiled, and he wore a pencil mustache, also heavily oiled. He was sufficiently corrupt to accept bribes from anyone, provided that requests could be easily accommodated and kept hidden from the SS.

Leo was talking to one of the Robben contractors about repairs required in the kitchen block when he noticed the OD leader approaching, swinging his arms in a pompous, almost comical manner. He possessed the most insincere smile Leo had ever seen.

"You've done splendid work here," Schlesinger said.

Leo knew that a compliment from this man would often be followed by words that were much less pleasant.

"Thank you. What can I do for you?" he asked, his tone brusque.

"Of course, this request isn't from me." The OD leader smiled. "It's from our lords and masters, the SS. The hierarchy in Berlin is pushing Commandant Gemmeker to increase the deportation numbers. To do that, we're going to have to move a lot more refugees in and out of camp and, as ever, with the greatest efficiency."

Leo was keen to discover what the SS had in mind, but Schlesinger always played the performer, keeping his audience waiting. It was only when he picked up his hammer as if to start work again that the CSO got to the point.

"Listen," he said, "Hooghalen railway station's a good three miles away, so we're forever marching inmates back and forth. It's very time-consuming." He allowed himself a dramatic pause. "As a result, the SS have ordered us to extend the track from Hooghalen so the trains can be loaded and unloaded in the center of the camp. It's going to make the process much faster, and it will require fewer SS guards. This concept has been successfully implemented elsewhere in the Reich."

Leo put down his hammer to consider the implications of this statement. "And when will this work start?" he asked.

"The first shipments of gravel, timber sleepers, and steel track are already here, waiting at the station. The Dutch National Railways will take overall responsibility for building the extension, but we'll be using camp labor."

Leo enjoyed working on these sorts of projects; they distracted him from everything else that was going on around him. While they lasted, he was granted improved camp privileges and was exempt from transportation, but he felt as if he had been working day and night all year on building works. In addition, he had continued his association with the choir and assisted with the setup of the two school barracks. The laying of a railway extension would be yet another arduous, energy-sapping task, yet he knew the consequences of refusal, and being tired was better than being transported.

"Laying the track won't be a complicated project, as the land's flat. But we'll need plenty of manual labor," he said. "The more labor we have, the quicker the track goes down."

"Well, the good news for you is that you've got plenty of labor to choose from!" Schlesinger replied smugly. "In fact, I suspect you're going to get a lot more in the next few months. Just give me the names of the men you want, and you can start straight away."

The CSO started to move away before turning back. "By the way, you need to give me your list of laborers first thing in the morning. A surveyor from Dutch Railways will be on site tomorrow."

*

Leo provided the list as instructed. He wished to keep as many of the inmates occupied as possible, so they would be exempt from deportation. He thought it ironic that this project would delay deportations for some but speed them up for others.

Leo planned to start the extension job with one team and train them up before recruiting the next team. This process would continue until he had the crews he needed. He envisaged each team consisting of two men to lay and level out the gravel, four to carry and position the sleepers, and four to position the lengths of track and bolt them down. He then added another two men as cover. He would supervise the works under the direction of the Dutch Railways' surveyor and would be engaged in the most important activity, the exact positioning of the track prior to it being secured.

Two days after his discussion with Schlesinger, Leo and his team of workmen walked to the station early in the morning. It was a glorious day, as the summer sun rose above the horizon and quickly warmed the earth below. For a few minutes, outside of the perimeter fence, Leo felt free.

On arrival at the station, the team removed their shirts and set to work with Leo offering training at each stage. As midday approached, the scalding August heat slowed their progress. The men were dry-mouthed and gasping for water, gulping for air like drowning fish. The spades of gravel, the sledgehammers, the sleepers, and lengths of tracks that they had comfortably handled earlier now felt like they were made of lead.

Schlesinger had allocated two members of the OD to supervise for the railway laborers at Hooghalen station. They were standing in the shade of the platform.

"Any chance of a drop of water?" Leo asked the OD supervisors.

"What did you say?" replied the first supervisor, a thickset man with a bald head and a belly that looked much too large for the inmate of a camp suffering from food shortages. He spoke to Leo as if he were an unwelcome interruption to his conversation.

"Please, could we have some water?" he repeated. "The men are working hard and sweating like pigs. They're already dehydrated and won't be able to last until lunchtime at this rate."

"Lunchtime!" The bald man laughed loudly, wiping sweat from his forehead with his sleeve. "Do you think you're at the Ritz Hotel and are going to receive a nice plate of sandwiches with the crusts cut off? You're fucking laborers and you've only been going for a couple of hours. You haven't earned any water!" He turned back to his colleague and continued his conversation.

Leo realized that attempting a rational discussion with this man was futile, a waste of scarce breath. He would need to adopt a different approach to persuade him.

"CSO Schlesinger has ordered us to build this railway extension as quickly as possible," he said. "If he turns up and sees that workers are collapsing with exhaustion…well, you know what he's like." He paused to allow his words to sink in. "All we need is a little water. That will keep the men going."

The bald man grunted, edged out of the shade, and made his way into the station building, emerging minutes later carrying two metal jugs of water. He slammed them down on the concrete platform so aggressively that water slopped onto the scorching concrete and immediately fizzled away.

"Now drink quickly! There's to be no delay!" the OD man shouted.

The workers rushed over to the platform and started swigging directly from the metal jugs, being careful not to spill a drop and to leave enough to share around.

Leo waited for the others to drink first before taking his turn. He picked up the jug to take a gulp but felt an excruciating pain in his left hand as the bald man struck him viciously with his stick. The jug dropped to the ground, spilling the remaining water.

"You're not laboring!" the man sneered. "You're just supervising. And you're not getting any water!" Both OD men laughed.

The laboring team was granted another two jugs of water during the afternoon, but they again forbid Leo from partaking. As he trudged away after the last jug had been emptied, one of the team members approached. In his hand, he held an upturned metal box, the sort that was used to cover cable connections that ran alongside the railway tracks, about the size of two wine bottles. Fresh water lapped against its insides, which, to Leo at that moment, looked more beautiful than any sea or lake on Earth. Leo carefully took the container and greedily gulped the water down, ensuring that the guards did not spot this clandestine activity.

"Thank you, my friend," he said appreciatively.

The new team made slow progress, laying thirty yards of track during that first day. With three miles needed to reach the camp and a further five hundred yards to re-join the main line beyond, Leo and the surveyor from Dutch Railways had agreed that one hundred and fifty yards per day were required.

Later that day, Leo explained to Schlesinger that he would need a further two teams of laborers and he would supervise them all, with the assistance of Jakob.

"I don't care who you use or how many," the CSO replied. "They aren't going anywhere else."

"It's important to keep them all fit and healthy," Leo continued. "If a couple of men drop out, then the entire project might be delayed. Could I ask that we're permitted to take some bread, cheese, and water from the canteen? Is that something you could agree and clarify with the OD supervisors?"

"Just do it," the CSO said. "Tell the supervisors and the kitchen staff that I've approved it and I'll have them on the next transport if they slow the work down. That should be sufficient clarification for them."

For the remainder of the summer and into a mild September, the teams continued to make satisfactory progress. The weather turned in October, and the open plains whipped up a freezing wind that chilled the men's bones and slowed them down. In November, the track extension was finished, running from Hooghalen station in the west, through the center of the camp, re-joining the main line to the east.

THIRTY-ONE

Amsterdam – November 1942

Rachael is holding the boy's clammy hand. She soon realizes it's not his hand that's clammy, it's hers.

The entrance to the day-care center has double doors. Dottie, a member of staff, opens the right-hand door and pushes her pram into the street.

Rachael and the boy are standing behind the closed door.

She takes a glance outside and sees her colleague waiting, rocking her decoy pram gently back and forth. It's nine o'clock in the morning; on the opposite side of the street, she glimpses the Jewish Council employees arriving at the theater to start work and the SS guard on duty outside. She hopes that early in his shift, and with plenty of people around, he'll be paying little attention to the center. Still, she's terrified they'll be spotted.

She must keep a constant watch on Dottie; she cannot afford to lose sight of her for a second in case she misses the signal. In the distance, she hears the metallic screeching of brakes and the toot of a horn. Without removing her gaze, she speaks to the boy.

"Are you ready for a run, Karl? Just remember, we need to keep up with the tram. It's not far. A few hundred yards. You're a big, healthy boy. I'm sure you'll reach the stop before I do. What do you think?" Before she finishes speaking, Dottie turns the pram leftward, away from the city center.

The rumble of the tram is becoming louder. Rachael checks her watch. Tram 14 is right on time. "Ready?" she asks, pulling the boy close.

Suddenly, her colleague moves off, and a moment later, the tram emerges from the left, its front obscuring the entrance to the theater. She dashes through the doorway, dragging the boy behind her. She has been told by those with experience of the tram run that holding hands will slow them down, so after a few strides, she lets go of the boy and pushes him forward with the palm of her hand.

When they set foot in the street, they are so close to the tram cab that Rachael can see the profile of the driver's face. But the vehicle is moving faster than them, and soon she can only see the back of driver's capped head.

"Run, Karl!" she gasps, gulping air into her lungs. "Keep up with the tram! To the next stop. Not far."

She's pleased the boy is faster than her and is edging in front. He glances back and she sees a grin on his face. Thank goodness, she thinks, he doesn't appreciate the seriousness of what he's doing. To him, it's just a game. Karl is one of the older children who have been staying at the center, fourteen years old, taller than her, and running strongly.

She can't relax just yet, but she already senses the tram is no longer pulling ahead and it will shield them from the sight of the theater guard. The tram decelerates, and now she's sure they are going to succeed.

By the time they reach the tram stop, the two hundred yards from the center have taken them around a bend in the road and out of sight of the guard.

The pair climb on board. When she offers some coins to pay for tickets, the driver smiles and shakes his head.

The two of them sit together at the rear of the tram, her panting beginning to ease. He's still smiling proudly, barely out of breath. She stays silent until she catches her breath and can speak. She leans over and cups her hand around the boy's ear.

"Well done, Karl! That was great. Now you're going to have a day of adventure! And a trip to the countryside."

"It was easy, Miss Rachael!" he replies. She barely recognizes the diffident child she first met in classroom 3B.

*

Walter passed a cup of coffee to the SS guard, who took a sip and smiled as he felt the warmth of the brandy coursing down his throat.

It was midday, and the guard's shift was not yet half completed, but his feet ached and the knee that had been damaged by shrapnel during the war was starting to play up in the cold.

This was an undemanding job, the soldier thought. He did not like the Jews, but neither did he enjoy the prospect of battering down their house doors and rounding them up like cattle. Every day, there was a stream of Jews being taken in and out of the theater, and he was relieved this job never involved any of that.

"Nice coffee," he said, raising his metal cup.

"You're welcome, sir," Walter replied. "I chanced upon a bottle of brandy, so I thought I'd share it with you." He raised his own cup of coffee in response. His did not contain any alcohol; he wanted to keep his senses sharp. Also, when it came to obtaining favors from the guards, alcohol was almost as useful as hard cash or tobacco.

"I hear there's going to be more raids this evening," he said, looking directly at the guard. "Or is it just talk? It would be useful to know."

"Well," the guard replied, lowering his voice to a whisper. "I can neither confirm nor deny the rumors. However, it may be of benefit to us all if you brought in additional registration staff tonight and made sure the overflow area is set up."

The overflow registration area was a small courtyard to the rear of the theater, which was used whenever the number of Jews rounded up exceeded a thousand in a single night and the barroom could not cope.

"Thank you," Walter replied. "It makes the management of the building more straightforward with your help."

The SS guard leaned forward, close enough for Walter to smell the coffee and alcohol on his breath.

"You've certainly not heard this from me. Is that understood?" the guard said sternly.

"Of course! What you say is kept strictly between us, I swear."

"The word is that Eichmann has a shortage of French Jews to transport, and he's demanding Seyss-Inquart takes up the slack." The guard paused for a moment before continuing. "We're going to need a lot of Dutch Jews."

"More than the current average of a thousand per week?" Walter inquired.

"Of course, rumors can be passed on and exaggerated," the guard said. "But the SS officers have indicated it's in the region of ten thousand."

"Ten thousand! That's impossible!" Walter was unable to keep his voice down.

The soldier put his index finger to his mouth and glared at him.

"They don't care where the ten thousand come from," the guard continued. "They're bringing Jews from all over the place. Men or women, adults or children, healthy or ill, they'll take whoever they can, from wherever they can."

"They'll be sleeping standing up in the theater. There'll be so little room," Walter said. "Even if the SS took ten thousand prisoners, we'd have no space for them here or in Westerbork."

Suddenly, the soldier appeared to notice something over Walter's shoulder.

"That's strange," he said, looking puzzled.

"What is?" Walter asked.

"It's the girl with red hair."

"What do you mean?" Now the theater manager was starting to worry.

"Look, there's the girl with red hair returning to the center," the guard said. And indeed, as Walter turned round, he saw Rachael passing through its entrance.

"And?" Walter asked.

"Well, my eyesight isn't the best. I can't see faces from this distance, but she has very distinctive hair, and I often spot her coming and going."

"It's fine," Walter replied, aiming to make light of her appearance. "She's perfectly legitimate. She works for the Jewish Council and has an exemption because she's employed at the center."

The guard screwed up his face, unconvinced. "That's not the problem," he said. "You see, I saw her arriving this morning. And entering the center again just now." He paused and pointed across the road. "But I've not seen her leave. By my reckoning, you can't enter a building twice without leaving it once."

"It's impossible to keep track of every individual," Walter said, his mind racing. "With all the people coming and going around the center and theater, plus the pedestrians, and the trams passing…" He immediately regretted drawing attention to the trams. "It's easy to miss someone leaving."

"Perhaps you're right," the guard replied, but a trace of doubt lingered.

"Would you like another cup of my special coffee?" Walter asked.

"Don't mind if I do," the other man said.

Walter hoped that a further dose of caffeine and alcohol would distract the soldier from any more thoughts of the girl with red hair. He would speak to Rachael and warn her to be more careful in the future.

THIRTY-TWO

Amsterdam – January 1943

Hannes had been allowed to stay up late and play with his toy soldiers in his bedroom. The adults were in the living room, Franck fidgeting with his gold pen, Elizabeth fretting with a loose thread on the clean, white tablecloth, and Hendrik pacing up and down from the wall to the curtained window. Rachael was calm, sitting with her hands placed on the table, examining her fingernails.

Without speaking or prompting, the others joined her, taking their usual seats.

Franck looked at his son.

Hendrik put his hand into the inside pocket of his jacket and withdrew a battered brown envelope, which he opened and then removed three cards, setting them down side by side. He unfolded each one in turn to reveal three ID cards. He pushed them into the center of the table, and the others leaned forward to scrutinize them.

"The forger's very skillful," he explained. "He's been able to make the ID cards appear well-weathered. And look!" He raised one to the ceiling light. "The watermark's clearly visible. It's been glued between two wafer-thin sheets of paper. The glue dries hard to make it feel like cardboard."

Rachael picked up another card, rotating it in her fingers.

"It's a little stiff," she remarked, "and the watermark's a bit faint."

"We're never going to escape!" Elizabeth groaned. "We'll never get past the SS!"

Hendrik looked at his sister in admonishment, surprised at her lack of tact.

"It's fine, Mama!" he reassured their mother. "Keep touching the card, bending it, rubbing it, and it'll soon become softer. You'll mostly be traveling by night. If anybody checks the ID, they'll never notice the slight difference in the watermark by the light of a torch or a streetlamp. Don't worry, many other people have successfully escaped using cards like these."

Franck picked up the third card and swiftly placed it in his trouser pocket without looking.

"And there's something else," the young man added, rummaging in his coat pockets again and throwing some multicolored sheets onto the table.

"Ration cards!" Elizabeth exclaimed, recognizing the familiar colors: yellow for potatoes, pink for butter, blue for powdered milk, and green for general produce.

"You'll have no problems with forgeries here," he continued. "These are the real thing. Stolen from the government's central stores. They're untraceable. Completely risk-free."

His mother counted the sheets of ration cards and made as if to distribute them between the four of them.

"No, Mama," Hendrik said. "They're all for you and Hannes to use when you reach the hiding place. It's deep in the forest, but there'll be some friendly locals who'll use the ration cards on your behalf in the town."

The hidden village was a group of huts that had been built in the forest of Soerelse by the people of nearby Vierhouten. There were twelve huts with a total capacity of one hundred, located in the densest part of the forest, an area deemed too remote for the Nazis to even consider searching for absconded Jews.

Franck, who had remained silent for a while, now spoke. "It's time." His voice quivered. "Shall I go and fetch Hannes?"

"Let's go through the travel arrangements one more time," his elder son said. "Let him play for a few minutes more. Mama, it's absolutely vital you keep to the plan."

"I'm going to escort you for the first section," Rachael said. Their parents watched her intently.

"Vierhouten's to the east of the city," she continued, "so we'll start by crossing the park. It's usually locked at night, but Wim Kuijpers kept a key when he was sacked by the civil service, and he's opened it for us. There's no transportation tonight, so the streets should be relatively quiet. We'll stick close to the railway line for a couple of miles, then…" She paused. "Then I'll say goodbye, and Jacoba will take you to the city limits. There's a roadblock on the Ringweg, but we've bribed the SS soldier who's on duty. He's been bribed before, so we know he's trustworthy."

"A trustworthy crook!" her father scoffed.

"Beyond there, the coast should be clear," she said, ignoring her father's comment. "The Jewish graveyard's only a few hundred yards farther, where a car will be waiting outside the gate. Vierhouten's sixty miles away, so you should be there in around two hours. Is that clear, Mama? Do you have any questions?"

Elizabeth shook her head, holding back tears.

"You must stay strong for Hannes," Hendrik said.

Their mother nodded.

"I'll go fetch him now," Franck said, leaving the room and returning minutes later with his sleepy son.

Now it was Franck's turn to rummage in his pockets, withdrawing three pristine white envelopes. "Here's some cash for you," he said, handing an envelope to each of them. "Let's hope it's not needed, but it's there just in case."

He kneeled and embraced his young son, squeezing him as hard as he ever had. "Be a good boy for your mama," he murmured. "And I'll be with you soon. Do exactly as she says. Do you promise?"

"I promise," Hannes answered, still half asleep.

Rachael also stooped to embrace her little brother.

Hendrik tousled his brother's hair. "You be a big boy now, won't you? Until Papa arrives, you'll be the man in the family. Understood?"

Hannes nodded.

Hendrik and Rachael bade their mother farewell, by which time her tears had become a continuous stream, drenching her mascara and forming black rivulets, which snaked down her face like streets on a map.

Franck and Elizabeth approached each other slowly, almost fearfully. They embraced. With each breath, his arms clenched more tightly around her shoulders. He did not wish to release her and let her see his own tears.

"I'll be with you soon, my love," he whispered in her ear.

"We've never been apart!" she said.

"We've discussed this many times, my love." Burying his face in her hair, he inhaled the comforting lavender scent of her shampoo. "You and Hannes must go first, but I'll follow you. It'll only be a few weeks, I'm sure."

He raised his head to look at Rachael standing close by. He nodded. She took hold of her mother's arm and gently pulled her away.

"Come on, it's time to go," Rachael said. "Put on your coat. I'll carry your case."

All five members of the family made their way to the front door. Hendrik ventured outside to ensure the coast was clear. The street was empty and dark.

"Right, it's time to go!" he echoed the words of his sister, serious and emphatic. "Make no noise unless absolutely necessary. And listen to exactly what Rachael says. Now, both of you must be strong. At night, the city's the domain of the Nazis, Jews *must not* be caught out at night."

Almost brusquely, Rachael grabbed her mother's arm and moved out. Hannes, who was holding his mother's hand, was obliged to follow. Hendrik and Rachael exchanged some whispered words, hugged briefly, then he swiftly marched off while the others walked silently away in the opposite direction.

Franck remained standing in the doorway, hands in his pockets. In front of him lay the quiet, deserted city streets and behind him an equally quiet house. He could face the empty streets, but not the house.

He stood for a full fifteen minutes, hearing not a sound within or without. Finally, he turned and closed the door behind him.

Tears still welled in his eyes.

THIRTY-THREE

Apeldoorn – January 1943

The Apeldoornsche Bosch had been opened in 1909 as a psychiatric hospital for Jews and had been built in woodland on the edge of Apeldoorn, a small town about sixty miles south-east of Amsterdam. The property comprised four wide, two-storied pavilions, which accommodated most of the institution's patients and activities and were encircled by a looping road. Over time, several smaller buildings had been added close by, outside the loop but within the hospital's perimeter wall.

By 1939, there were separate sections for men, women, and children, and for those with particularly acute psychological problems. There were also buildings to house the facility director and most of the senior staff, a synagogue, a sports field, and areas dedicated to quiet and relaxing activities such as reading and meditation. All of these were nestled within an undisturbed, peaceful environment.

From the very start, the Bosch had embraced modern thinking in relation to the treatment of psychological disorders. Patients were encouraged to spend time outdoors with nature and to participate in sports and other games to ease their symptoms. The facility welcomed patients across the psychological spectrum, from those with mild anxiety to others with severe mental illness.

During the first two years following the Nazi invasion, the Bosch was relatively unaffected by the events taking place elsewhere in the Netherlands. However, from the spring of 1942, Seyss-Inquart's anti-Jewish measures and regulations started to take their toll. All the non-Jewish staff were forced to leave, albeit they were soon replaced by German Jews fleeing their homeland. The number of Jewish patients also increased significantly. By the end of 1942, there were approximately 1,200 patients (of whom 100 were children) and 350 staff employed there.

Dr. Jacques Lobstein was the director and senior medical officer of the Bosch. He was convinced that since there had been no direct Nazi intervention in the operation of the facility between May 1940 and December 1942, there was unlikely to be any in the future. But, irrespective of their indifference toward the Jewish patients and staff, parts of the Nazi organization were certainly interested in the buildings and their surroundings. In late December 1942, when Seyss-Inquart was assuring Dr. Lobstein that the facility would not be closed, he was also receiving requests from various departments within the SS organization to take it over.

Rauter personally made a full physical inspection of the facility on January 11, 1943. Rumors were rife that the facility was to be emptied, but Dr. Lobstein chose not to react.

*

The train journey from Amsterdam to Apeldoorn lasted little more than an hour, but it was a nerve-wracking experience for Hendrik.

It was not the train journey itself that was problematic because the route was never busy and ID papers were rarely checked on board. Firstly, Amsterdam station had been teeming with people and soldiers, and although his papers looked genuine enough, he could not shrug off the fear of being stopped and exposed. He was convinced that the dread of being caught would be reflected in his outward behavior and make him conspicuous to the SS and police.

Later, there was a change at Utrecht station, which made him feel physically ill. The station platform was sparsely populated compared to Amsterdam, and he promptly found an unoccupied bench where he could sit and read. However, two SS soldiers arrived on the platform soon afterward and, to his dismay, took up places right beside him.

His sweaty fingers stuck to the pages of his book as if it were fly paper. He felt almost paralyzed, ending up not turning the pages at all but simply glancing up and down the same lines repeatedly, terrified the soldiers would spot his awkwardness and follow him onto the train, disembark at Apeldoorn, and the mission would be terminated before it had even started.

Every time he caught one of their movements in his peripheral vision, he was certain it would be the precursor to a formal request to examine his papers.

When the Apeldoorn train finally approached the platform, he rose immediately and walked forward, thankful the SS soldiers had not pursued him.

"Hey, you!" a voice barked behind him, cold and clear across the wide concrete platform.

Hendrik did nothing, just stood waiting for the train to decelerate and come to a halt.

"Hey, you!" This time, the voice was louder, angry, competing with the sound of the train's squealing brakes. As the train slowed, Hendrik could make out the passengers in their compartments.

"Hey, you!" the voice came again. "Don't you ignore me. There's nobody else waiting for that damned train, so stop pretending I'm not talking to you!"

Hendrik glanced furtively to his left and right, and it was true. Nobody else was standing by the edge of the platform to board the train.

"You come here now because you certainly don't want me to come and fetch you." There was no mistaking the threat.

He turned slowly to face the soldiers for the first time. They looked to be around the same age as him, one with typical Aryan features of blond hair, fair skin, and cold blue eyes, the other brown-haired and with a darker complexion. Observing them sitting side by side, he wondered whether these Nazis genuinely believed they both belonged to the same race, a race superior to all the others.

"Come here!" the blond soldier demanded.

He walked forward, step by tentative step, coming to a standstill a couple of yards short of the bench.

"Pick it up, you littering Dutch scumbag!" the soldier barked.

Hendrik stood in bewildered silence, his eyes scanning the smooth concrete expanse between them.

"Are you blind as well as stupid and dirty?" the soldier asked, pointing.

There, on the platform, half in the shadow of the wooden slats of the bench, lay his leather bookmark. His brother had given it to him shortly before they had been separated.

"Pick it up!" the soldier shouted. "Don't think I'm going to do it for you, you lazy bastard."

Hendrik bent down to retrieve the bookmark, knowing he was only feet away from the soldiers. He flinched, expecting a blow.

"I could shoot you if I wanted to," the blond soldier said.

"Leave it," the darker soldier countered. "It's not worth all the paperwork we'd have to fill out."

"Do you hear that?" the blond soldier scoffed. "My colleague here thinks you're not even worth the paperwork."

"Let's go," the other soldier said, rising to his feet. "There's a bar on the far side of Station Square and it's open all day."

Hendrik thought he detected a mild insistence in the man's tone.

The blond soldier suddenly jerked his hand to his holster. Hendrik leaped backward. The air in his lungs seemed to be sucked from his chest, making him gasp. The soldier laughed, but realizing his colleague was walking away toward the exit stairway, he followed.

Hendrik stood motionless. It seemed as if a tremendous earthquake had shaken his whole being, tossing his insides around, and nothing was in the correct position anymore. His body felt alien. His head throbbed, and a sense of nausea swelled within him.

The sound of a whistle brought him back to reality, and the slow groaning of pistons reminded him that he had a train to catch. He ran the short distance to the nearest door, yanked it open and jumped inside as the train lurched forward, taking a place at the back of the carriage so he had a view of all the rows of seats in front. He took a deep breath and looked down at his clenched fists. As he unfurled his fingers, the bookmark was exposed. The worn, brown leather felt soft and warm to the touch. He teased its frayed edges and recalled the words of his brother when he had given it to him.

"Remember, look after it. You must give it back when we see each other again."

Hendrik closed his eyes and took several deep breaths. When he reopened them, the turmoil he had felt had begun to subside, like a runaway train coming to a gradual halt.

Carefully placing the bookmark in his trouser pocket, he clenched and unclenched his fist several times more. Now he was ready.

THIRTY-FOUR

Apeldoorn – January 1943

Hendrik could scarcely believe his eyes when he first walked through the imposing gateway of the Apeldoornsche Bosch. He proceeded along a short, straight asphalt roadway lined with lime trees before joining the loop. Within a few moments, the administration pavilion revealed itself from behind a coppice of trees, looking almost palatial, each floor of its wide facade possessing thirty large windows set against a brilliant white exterior. It was like something he had seen in pictures of French châteaux.

As he drew near, he understood why this location had been chosen for a psychiatric facility. In the afternoon sunlight, the buildings and their surroundings were quiet and serenely beautiful, no doubt able to soothe all but the most troubled of minds.

The impression created by the interior was the same. Its large and imposing entrance hall provided more than enough space for the staff and patients to move around without the sense of thronging commotion present in many hospitals. As one might expect in a clinical institution, it was clean but spartan. The staff wore pristine white uniforms. There was the general hum of people talking but none of the screaming and shouting sometimes associated with a psychiatric institution.

A member of staff welcomed him and was able to point out where Dr. Lobstein's office was situated—halfway along a nearby corridor on the ground floor.

The doctor was sitting at his desk with his head resting on his hands. He had been reading a clinical report from a colleague in Switzerland. To Hendrik, he looked like an archetypal medical professional. Wearing a white coat, Lobstein had thinning hair, a neatly trimmed gray beard and sharp, intelligent blue eyes behind the circular lenses of his gold-rimmed spectacles.

Hendrik did not waste any time.

"Dr. Lobstein, I've been sent here from Amsterdam," he said. "We have it on very good authority that the Nazis are going to empty this establishment. There are a number of SS and government departments that wish to occupy these buildings. They'll remove every single person—patients and staff. And they're coming tomorrow."

Lobstein paused, rubbing his beard. "And who are you?" he asked, realizing he did not even know the identity of the young man standing before him.

"My name's Hendrik and I'm with the Resistance. More than that, you don't need to know, but I've come here in person to make sure you understand what's going to happen to this facility."

"They're just rumors," the doctor replied casually. "In any case, they're already here and have done nothing of the sort."

"What do you mean already here?" he asked, baffled. The informant had definitely told them tomorrow.

"The commandant of Camp Westerbork arrived earlier today. His men were wearing green coveralls with the letters OD on them. He told me they're only passing through on their way back from training and they'll be leaving in the morning."

"Dr. Lobstein, please listen to me! They won't be leaving until they've purged this hospital. Believe me, my information originates from the highest levels of government."

"Why would the Reichskommissar and the commandant both lie to me?" Dr. Lobstein asked, a touch of arrogance in his voice.

"They'll lie to anybody. All over the country, the Nazis are indiscriminately rounding up Jews—men and women, children, and babies, old and young, healthy and sick."

"What are we to do?" Dr. Lobstein asked with a quiet desperation. "The OD men are overnighting in one of the outbuildings."

"I've no idea why they're here," Hendrik said. "We were told that the trains and lorries would be arriving later tonight and the raid will happen in the morning."

"But what are we to do?" the doctor repeated, staring vacantly around the room.

Hendrik thought it ironic that Dr. Lobstein, the director of a psychiatric hospital, seemed himself to be in a state of mental shock.

"I don't know why they've arrived today, but no matter. Please instruct all your staff not to turn up for work in the morning. If the Nazis *are* telling the truth and depart tomorrow, the staff can come back the day after. Otherwise, they stay away for good."

"What about the patients? Without the staff, what will they do?"

"If the Nazis remove all the patients, the hospital won't need staff."

"There'll be mayhem if they try to round up severely ill psychiatric patients with no clinical or support staff in attendance," Dr. Lobstein protested.

Hendrik shrugged. "How many staff do you have?"

"Approximately three hundred and fifty."

"If any of your staff wish to stay, they must understand that there's a risk of them being transported to Westerbork as well. What do you think is the minimum number of staff you'd require?"

"With basic treatment and medication, I'd estimate fifty."

"Okay, we can save two hundred and eighty of them," the young man spoke quickly but clearly. "Can you arrange for there to be only fifty staff on site tomorrow? All the others must stay away."

Dr. Lobstein looked bemused. "We've been treating a number of patients suffering from serious psychological problems for many years. We hold detailed records of every single one so that we, and the rest of medical science, can improve the future treatment of these illnesses. All that invaluable medication, therapy, and research for nothing! Research that will benefit Jews and non-Jews!"

"I'm sorry, Doctor," Hendrik said. "The Nazis will fill every square inch of space on the trains. I'm quite sure they'll take everybody they can. If you believe some of your patients are fit to leave the clinic tonight, then that's fine, but they must be gone before dawn!"

The doctor paused for a moment. Gradually, his face hardened, and his lips tightened to a thin, determined line. "Well then, young man! We'd best get started right away!" He took Hendrik by the arm and led him out of the office into the corridor.

Over the following hours, the two of them talked to the staff in all four main buildings, giving them the option to stay or leave. Those who wished to leave were asked to depart immediately and to each contact two or three of the remaining staff who were absent at that time, whether due to being on a different shift pattern, on vacation, or off sick, in order to explain the situation to them. They were advised to stay away for at least forty-eight hours.

The director retrieved a list of the current staff from a filing cabinet and wrote by the side of each name whether they were staying or leaving. By midnight, the exercise was complete. Of the 352 staff on the list, 192 had confirmed their desire to leave and 67 volunteered to stay behind with the patients; it had been impossible to contact the rest.

"The SS officers will have the OD men up by seven in the morning," Hendrik observed, "so we have less than seven hours."

"Seven hours to do what?" the doctor asked.

"To save as many patients as possible. They must leave in the dark. We'll have no chance moving anybody during daylight hours. Do you have any patients that require little supervision whom we could smuggle out tonight?"

"We have four categories of patient from mildly agitated to severely disturbed. I'll need to check my list, but it may be one or two hundred, I would estimate."

"Can we take them away now?" Hendrik could not believe how disengaged Dr. Lobstein was from the task. The doctor seemed to have fallen back into his melancholic state of earlier. Silent on the outside, bombs exploding on the inside. Unable to grasp that Jewish lives were at risk.

"We could do," the director replied.

"Then let's go through the list and identify them!" Hendrik urged. "They'll need to leave the site accompanied by members of staff until we can arrange for their relatives to collect them."

By three o'clock in the morning, they had evacuated twenty-seven children with mild conditions, each accompanied by a member of staff. That made another fifty-four escapees.

Hendrik himself could not risk being apprehended by the Nazis, so decided to make his exit before dawn. With the SS and OD in the vicinity, he planned to avoid the main entrance and the loop road. Before leaving, he agreed with the doctor for a further thirty-five patients and their carers to be smuggled out.

Among the trees, it was pitch-black. Hendrik could intermittently see his way but only whenever the moon broke free of the clouds. He could barely see his breath condensing in the bitterly cold air and struggled to keep his bearings. He decided to walk in as straight a line as possible, crossing the loop road and pressing on until he reached the perimeter wall. At that point, even if he were lost, he would at least be able to get off the site.

Once he had traversed the road, he guessed he was only a couple of hundred yards away from the wall. Foliage crunched unavoidably beneath his feet, every step sounding like a firecracker exploding. He proceeded slowly, flailing his arms to locate low-hanging branches. Looking up, he noticed a silver lining forming around the edge of the clouds, signifying the reappearance of the moon. This enabled him to observe the silhouettes of the trees around him and, a short distance to his right, a large dark bulk, which he guessed had to be one of the hospital outbuildings.

He entered a small clearing and, with the advantage of moonlight, increased his pace. Suddenly, a man appeared from behind a tree, his OD armband clearly visible. The two men stood and watched each other, only a few yards separating them. Hendrik surmised by the way the man was adjusting his trouser fly that he had been answering a call of nature.

The OD man belched loudly and swayed like a tall tree in a gale. His hands were patting his uniform in an unusual manner. Hendrik realized this nervous fumbling was the OD searching for a weapon about his person. The search proved fruitless.

He's unarmed and drunk, Hendrik thought. I can easily overpower him. However, the prospect of the man making an unholy din, if tackled, made him reconsider.

The OD man looked down at his empty hands and laughed. "No gun! No baton! It must be your lucky day!" He paused for a moment. "And if you've got a gun, then it's certainly not mine."

"It's not your lucky day," the young man replied, pulling his revolver from his coat pocket.

The OD guard raised his eyebrows. "Are you Dutch?"

Hendrik nodded.

"Look, we're both Dutch," he continued. "I'm a little drunk, and so are most of my colleagues. It's a miserable, bitter night. You're a young lad. Why you're here at this time of night, I've no idea, but it can't be legitimate. We don't want to be running around all night chasing after you when it's warm inside." He belched once more. "So why don't you leave now, and we'll never see each other again."

Hendrik weighed up his options. Whether drunk or not, a gang of OD men on his trail was the worst possible scenario. This man, in his condition and in this light, would surely have little chance of remembering his face come sober morning.

Without another word, he simply turned and ran. He ran quickly and without hesitation. The trees and low-hanging branches surged into his line of sight, and he was barely able to avoid them. Once, his forehead crashed into a tree branch, but he was lucky it was only thin, scratching his face and knocking him off his stride.

Blindly, he rushed on until he spotted the perimeter wall standing just ahead. Lobstein had told him that the psychiatric facility was a healing institute and they did not treat patients like prisoners, so he was relieved to see the wall was a low brick construction, about five feet high with no barbed wire or shards of glasses along its top.

He grabbed the top of the wall and glanced over his shoulder. The scene was surreal. The moon illuminated the clearing where he had been standing earlier, yet the surrounding area was still cast in dark shadows. Although it felt as if he had been running for an age, it lay only a short distance away. He could pick out the individual trees that encircled the clearing like rows of well-trained soldiers.

And then he noticed the OD man, standing by a tree, hand resting on its trunk. Relieving himself.

Hendrik tightened his grip and nimbly pulled himself over the wall. He took the decision to walk along the railway track until he reached the next station, in case there were OD or SS men in Apeldoorn.

THIRTY-FIVE

Apeldoorn – January 1943

Dr. Lobstein did not go to bed that night but stayed in his office, either pacing up and down or sitting slumped at his desk. His sixty-year-old bones ached, and he had never felt so tired, but he knew he could not sleep.

As the sun rose and daylight crept into his office, his mood began to lift. At nine o'clock, he donned his coat and started his daily rounds as usual. Staff numbers were low but adequate, and his usual team accompanied him. By midday, he felt hungry and, having not eaten for a considerable time, went to the canteen. Most of the kitchen staff had left and not returned, so he had to be satisfied with some cold meat he found in the refrigerator.

He was beginning to relax and could barely comprehend the events of the previous night, wondering if he had imagined the entire episode. He had been informed that the OD contingent had departed early in the morning. On several occasions, he picked up the telephone to start calling the staff to return but stopped short of dialing. He spent the afternoon writing up the notes from his observations of a young patient with schizophrenia. He had observed an improvement that morning and was keen to share his thoughts with the Medical Institute of Vienna.

At eight o'clock in the evening, the director heard a banging on the front door. He waited for an administrator to deal with it but soon remembered none was present. Kurt Hazes had decided to take flight yesterday.

He rose from his desk and made his way toward the entrance. The banging grew louder, and he could hear shouting. "Open up in the name of the government!"

A distinguished-looking soldier in a smart gray uniform stood at the glass door. Dr. Lobstein recognized the commandant from the previous day. He shuddered when his gaze strayed beyond Gemmeker. The OD guards had evidently not traveled back to Amsterdam after all because forty or fifty of them were lined up in the courtyard.

As he unlocked the door, he saw and heard a convoy of trucks appearing one by one around the loop road. The hope that had slowly grown in him during the day evaporated in a second. The young man had been right.

"I have orders to remove all Jews from these premises." Gemmeker waved a piece of paper in the doctor's face.

"I'm afraid we're severely short-staffed today," Lobstein responded, holding the door slightly ajar. "And many of our patients need special treatment. It will take a considerable time for us to move them. It would be better to come back tomorrow."

The commandant leaned in close, so close that the doctor could smell stale coffee on his breath. With a polite grin and no trace of emotion, Gemmeker said, "There's a train with thirty carriages waiting at the station, enough for a thousand passengers. I understand you have approximately a thousand patients here. The numbers match nicely, don't you think?

"You can see behind me the trucks that will carry the patients to the railway station. The train will leave at seven o'clock in the morning. Its destination will be the transit camp at Westerbork. And it must be full and ready to go by seven. Is that abundantly clear?"

"I'm really not sure we have enough qualified staff to do that," Lobstein insisted.

"Do you have a conference room where we can gather the staff together?" the SS officer asked, barging through the door.

"Yes, directly behind me, there's the lecture theater, but I'm sure the staff will confirm my view."

"Please gather all the staff there. Immediately."

It took fifteen minutes or so for the employees to assemble. In the meantime, Lobstein had managed to brief some of his senior team. He would allow the commandant to speak first, then they would provide a robust vindication of his position, substantiated by medical facts.

Gemmeker coughed to gain the audience's attention, and when silence reigned, he spoke. "I've been given orders to remove the patients from this establishment. Here's the signed decree." He brandished the piece of paper once more. "Dr. Lobstein informs me that you can't move them all in time. I'm sure he's right. So, I'll save you the distress of fulfilling this task. The OD officials who've accompanied me will do it themselves. You'll wait in this room while our work is in progress." He started walking toward the exit. "There'll be guards posted at the door. Anybody trying to escape from this room will be shot." He nodded his head and walked out, to be replaced by a guard carrying a machine gun.

The theater hummed with voices. The doctor stood in embarrassed silence. He had prepared the arguments so well, producing a compelling argument. But he had now learned that the Nazis did not care; they were going to remove everybody, irrespective of any resultant distress caused.

In time, the room fell still. There were no windows, and the only connection with the hospital outside came from the hollow noises that rang through the surrounding halls and corridors. The cold, tiled floors echoed and amplified every sound. The thumping of the OD men's boots became an army of a thousand soldiers, and the banging of truncheons on bedroom doors, the explosion of bombs.

Dr. Lobstein heard the shouts of the soldiers, at first distant, then becoming nearer and louder, until they were directly outside in the entrance hall. He thought he heard a truck revving its engine.

For reasons of safety for themselves and others, the patients with severe mental illnesses were housed separately on the upper floor. The OD men had now arrived. And then came the screaming.

When he closed his eyes, the doctor imagined the OD bursting into their rooms. He knew the patients individually, and his mind conjured up their terrified faces as the bright lights were switched on and strangers appeared before them. Some patients might not have set eyes on an unfamiliar face for years.

Shouting at them. Pulling them out of bed. Treatment routines that had been established with careful deliberation by the clinical team over a long period were being destroyed in a few turbulent and frightening minutes.

The staff in the theater cowered while the screaming and beseeching grew louder as the patients were herded nearer. Many shuddered when the cries seemed to be right outside.

Then the door opened, and Gemmeker walked back in.

"We need twenty of you to accompany the seriously ill patients to Westerbork. Otherwise, it'll be a traumatic journey for them. Do we have any volunteers, or shall I choose twenty at random? We've no time to waste."

Several of the skilled nursing staff stepped forward, and this prompted others to follow suit, but not twenty.

The commandant strolled around the theater, pointing. "You can go. You. You. You can go…" He finally stopped. "That's it. Twenty. Follow me now!" He looked at Dr. Lobstein, who had himself stepped forward. "You're in charge of the hospital, so you stay. Like the captain of the ship."

He escorted the twenty members of staff out of the lecture theater. Over the next few hours, the remaining staff sat in silence, listening as each truck growled its departure.

When the noises had finally died away, the door was opened once more, and the commandant reentered. "You! Come with me!" he barked, signaling to the director.

An empty entrance hall greeted Lobstein, cast in eerie silence. He followed the SS officer outside.

"Dr. Lobstein, there's been a miscalculation, and the train's already full," the commandant explained, turning back to face the building. "There are patients still in their beds. We didn't have enough room for them. You and the rest of your staff and patients will soon be able to join them in Westerbork. We'll need to requisition another train. In the meantime, you must stay here and wait, and we'll arrange for your collection in due course. Is that clear?"

"Yes," the doctor replied. As the number of staff and patients in the facility had shrunk, the last vestiges of his hope had trickled away.

"I've just noticed those words," Gemmeker said, pointing at the arch that spanned the building entrance. "What language is it and what does it say?" There was a message chiseled out of the stonework, illuminated by a single spotlight from above.

"It's in Hebrew," Lobstein replied. "It means *Care of the Soul, God heal the Soul*. It's been the motto of this institution from its inception."

Gemmeker opened the door of his Mercedes, which was parked nearby, and turned to speak.

"Dr. Lobstein, I certainly hope your God's able to heal you."

*

In the second week of February 1943, a small group of OD guards arrived at the Bosch. They collected the remaining patients and staff, including the director, and took them to Westerbork on a regular passenger train.

Upon arrival in camp, Dr. Lobstein inquired after the colleagues and patients that had preceded him. None of them had been seen. In exchange for a full packet of cigarettes, an OD guard made inquiries of the SS officers and was able to discover their whereabouts. The earlier train transporting just over a thousand patients and staff had never been destined for Westerbork. It had traveled directly to Auschwitz.

THIRTY-SIX

Vierhouten – February 1943

Elizabeth awoke and, for the briefest moment, did not recognize her surroundings. The gloomy, enclosed space soon brought her to her senses. No matter the weather, the sickly smell of damp, fetid wood was pervasive and made her queasy.

She lay on the bed and allowed her eyes to become accustomed to the darkness within the hut. The low roof trusses, which always seemed to hover directly above their heads, emerged from the shadows like prison bars. Each hut had been built within a cutting dug out of the forest floor, with a sloping roof covered with moss and grass. From a distance, each looked like an innocuous mound.

She heard the slow, heavy breathing of Ruud, asleep in the next bed, with Anneliese. The other occupants of the hut had been subjected to their continuous bickering, which, in this confined existence, Elizabeth had found almost unbearable.

Why argue? she thought. At least you have each other. You're lucky. My family has been torn apart.

They had been told only to venture outdoors after dark. Although the twelve wooden huts were located among the dense pines of the forest, there was still substantial activity from both the Dutch and German SS in and around the town of Vierhouten during the day. However, the Resistance had advised them that, as more and more Jews were transferred to Amsterdam, the SS presence would shrink.

She looked toward the door and saw a faint sliver of daylight peeking through. It was mid-afternoon, not time to rise yet. The refugees moved during the hours of dark, like ghosts drifting among the trees.

She turned on her side to make herself comfortable, laying her arm on the bed beside her.

"Hannes?" she murmured, her arm patting the bedclothes. "Hannes?" she repeated more loudly. There was no reply.

She fumbled in the dark, bumping into objects and people as she did so. "Hannes! Have you seen my son?" There were no affirmative replies.

"Don't make so much noise, for God's sake!" somebody muttered. "He's probably gone to the toilet."

Yes, the toilet, she thought, opening the door and allowing daylight to stream inside.

She made her way to the rudimentary pit they used as a latrine. To reduce both the stink and the risk of being discovered, a new latrine was dug out every week with the old one being filled in. However, there was no sign of him. She visited the site of the previous week's pit, just in case, but he was not there either.

"Hannes!" she called, running back, looking urgently in all directions.

By now, there were people milling around outside, some arriving from the next hut, which was located a hundred yards or so farther on.

"Hannes!" she cried once more.

"Quiet, woman!" a man scolded her.

"She's lost her son!" one of the women replied. "Have you no pity?"

"We'll all be lost if the Nazis hear her racket!"

The hut dwellers silently spread out across the forest in search of the boy.

*

Fritz Schreiber and Albrecht Lahm enjoyed being members of the SS. Although they had been kept relatively busy with their duties, being stationed in the rural heart of the country had left them with a surprising amount of free time.

The two men had known each other since they were children, both living on farms near Hamburg, and had learned to hunt from an early age, when their respective parents had first placed a rifle in their hands. They had joined the SS together in the middle of 1942 when the Nazi Party had demanded that all able-bodied Germans join the struggle against the Jews and communists.

Hunting had been an integral part of their upbringing, and the nearby forest had been too great a temptation. They had started to sneak off at regular intervals. Their gray-green SS field uniforms provided good camouflage among the trees and bushes, and their Mauser Kar98k rifles were well maintained and accurate. Any animals or birds they were able to shoot would be left hidden at the edge of the forest and collected later, when they would build a fire and cook a meal in the open air.

From their previous hunting trips, they had learned that few animals braved the sparse open landscape on the outskirts of the forest, and the denser inner areas were almost impossible for the soldiers to penetrate quietly enough to obtain a clear shot at their prey. So, they settled upon the areas where the pine trees were thinly spread and animals would cautiously venture out. There, they had successfully shot and killed numerous rabbits and a few roe deer.

The soldiers were of similar stature, strong and muscular, another consequence of their agricultural roots. As they walked through the forest or crept through the undergrowth in their SS uniforms, it was only Lahm's jet-black hair that distinguished him from his brown-haired friend.

"Shh…" Lahm whispered, pointing to a line of shrubs to their right. "I can hear something!"

The two men crouched down. There was a distinct rustling emanating from behind the bushes twenty or so yards distant, with clear, open space in between. Instinctively, the men raised their rifles.

The dark-haired soldier closed his eyes and took a deep breath to steady himself. Upon reopening them, he glanced at his neighbor, who was scanning the narrow stretch of bushes to their right.

The rustling stopped briefly, then restarted. Lahm was convinced it was growing louder. His finger was poised on the trigger, waiting for the moment when the animal broke into the clearing.

He was taken completely by surprise when a flash of white appeared before him. He jerked his weapon; his finger twitched and sent a shot into the air, high and wide of its target.

"What the hell!" Schreiber shouted. "What was that?"

"Listen!" Lahm insisted.

They heard a pounding in the undergrowth.

Lahm made as if to follow in pursuit.

"Wait!" the other man warned.

The two men stood up and listened intently.

The sound of the trampling of vegetation grew fainter until, moments before it disappeared, they heard another sound.

"Mama! Mama!"

They looked at one another.

"Sounded like a boy's voice," Lahm said. "It must have been his white shirt that caught me off guard. A child can't be on its own in the forest. There must be others."

"We don't know how many of them there are," Schreiber replied. "We should go back and muster reinforcements! The forest's too big for us to find them on our own."

"Agreed. Let's hope this hunt has a successful ending. We might bag ourselves some human beings!"

The SS soldiers slung their rifles over their shoulders and rushed out of the forest toward their barracks at the edge of the village.

*

"Mama! Mama!"

Elizabeth heard her son before he burst through the undergrowth and into the clearing that ringed their hut. He dashed toward her, arms outstretched.

"Mama! Mama!" he repeated, collapsing into her embrace.

"Hannes!" she answered, surprised and relieved. "What have you been up to?" His clean shirt was covered in twigs and thorns and speckled with spots of blood where his skin had been pierced.

He kept his head buried in her chest, catching his breath.

"You know you shouldn't leave the hut during the day!" she admonished him.

The boy mumbled some words into her chest.

"What did you say?" his mother asked.

"Soldiers!" he said, then repeated clearly and loudly, "Soldiers!" and pointed over his shoulder into the dense thicket.

Some of the other refugees who had witnessed the boy's sudden arrival gathered around.

"What did you say, boy?" a gray-haired man asked.

"Soldiers in the woods," he stammered.

"Did they see you?" the man insisted.

He stared, wide-eyed, at the man first, then at his mother, who smiled weakly at him.

He nodded at the man. "Possibly."

"We must tell the other huts at once!" the man shouted. "We've been discovered!"

Immediately, with an almost military precision, those in the vicinity moved off, some inside their nearby huts, the others beyond the clearing to where the remaining huts were located.

Mother and son stayed for a few moments.

"We've only just got here!" she cried forlornly, clutching him by the hand and leading him into their hut. "And how will Papa find us if we've left?" Her question hung in the air, unanswered.

She pulled their suitcase from under the bed and flipped it open, revealing it to be already half full. They had been warned they may need to evacuate at short notice. She leaned over to the inverted wooden crate that served as a nightstand and swept up her hairbrush and the last remnants of her makeup, arranging them quickly but carefully inside the case.

"Quick!" the gray-haired man called from the doorway. "The SS could be here at any moment!"

Ruud and Anneliese rushed out of the hut without speaking.

Elizabeth led her son outside. It was eerily quiet. Even the forest birds were silent. There was the distant sound of people thrashing through the undergrowth, but nothing more.

"Come on!" she urged, plowing straight into the knee-high thicket that bordered the hut. Thorns immediately shredded her last pair of stockings while Hannes bare legs were pierced by scores of tiny barbs, his steps hampered by the labyrinth of roots across the forest floor.

"Ouch!" he exclaimed as another thorn embedded itself in his flesh. Brushing it off, he didn't notice his mother stumble and fall behind him. When he did, he looked up to see her lying on the ground, propped up on an elbow, her face frozen in horror. In fear and trepidation, he followed the direction of her gaze, down her legs to her feet. He tilted his head to the side, but whichever way he looked, her right foot was pointing at an impossible angle, like a broken matchstick.

"Mama?" he asked.

She continued to stare at her foot, tears now rolling down her cheeks.

"Mama?"

She forced herself to look him straight in the eyes.

"You must run!" she instructed him slowly and deliberately. "Hurry and catch up with the others! Remember to follow the tall tree!" She pointed into the distance at the peak of a huge pine tree, which jutted out above the forest canopy and was the marker for their escape route.

He held out his hand to his mother.

"No! You must go without me. My ankle's broken. I can't go on."

"I'll carry you," the boy replied.

She laughed despite her pain.

He stretched his hand out farther. This time, she took hold of it and pulled him to her. He fell to his knees and hugged her; she reciprocated with her free arm.

With all her determination, she grabbed the back of his shirt and tried to pull him away. He reacted by embracing her more tightly.

"Hannes, you must go!" she insisted. Without looking at him, she continued, "I'll catch you up later when the doctor's set my ankle straight." She tugged at his shirt again.

He shook his head resolutely. She let go of her son's shirt, placed her hand on his chest, and pushed him firmly but gently away.

"I love you so much," she said. "I want nothing more than to go with you, but I can't. And you can't stay with me. You must run as fast as you can to catch up with the others. Do you understand?"

She turned her face to his.

"You must go now!" As she spoke, she gathered her strength and pushed his chest, this time with force, until her fingertips lost contact with the soft cotton of his shirt.

"Run as fast as you can, my sweet boy!" she implored, her upper body collapsing back to the ground as the pain in her ankle surged like storm waves crashing into the shore. She raised her unsteady arm and gestured toward the trees. "Run!" she repeated. "I'll be with you soon!"

"Promise?" he begged.

"I promise," she replied, her voice full of sadness.

He watched his mother for a moment, lying motionless, staring blankly at the tree canopy above. He followed the direction of his mother's pointing finger and started running. He ran quickly, a whirlwind of flailing limbs, numb to the thorns scratching at his legs. The density of the forest frequently hid the top of the big pine, but he did not stop running, hoping upon hope that it would come back into view each time. And it did.

He kept running until he almost collided with the gray-haired man, who was making his own escape through the undergrowth.

*

Elizabeth listened until the sound of her son bursting through the forest had died out completely. The agony surged through her leg once more, and she was forced to bite hard on her lip until the pain subsided. She lay there, waiting with dread for it to rise up again.

She was almost relieved when she heard, then saw, a line of gray-uniformed SS soldiers coming through the trees. The nearest one approached her.

"Stand up!" he ordered.

She saw his polished boots and well-ironed breaches but could hardly see his face, which seemed to be far above her.

"Stand up," the soldier repeated, "and put your hands up!"

"I need a doctor," she replied, gesturing at her leg. "I think my ankle's broken."

The soldier looked at her misshapen foot.

She was beginning to feel giddy with pain.

Another soldier walked up to where she lay. The tone of his voice and the way the other man shrank back gave her the impression that he was an officer.

"What's going on here?" he barked. "What's the holdup?"

"We've caught this woman, but she can't move, sir," the soldier replied, pointing at her leg. "I'm sure it's broken, so we'll need to take her to a doctor."

"We've neither the time nor the resources to take her anywhere!" the officer growled. "We've already discovered four huts, and there may well be more. There's likely to be an entire group of Jews at large right now. We've got to catch them before they go too far or we'll lose the light. There's no time to waste." He put his hand on his holster.

"But sir!" the soldier replied hesitantly.

"Look, these hut dwellers, once caught, are likely to be executed in the morning in any case," the officer said, his tone emotionless.

A single shot rang out like the crisp crack of a whip, and the leaves in the canopy above crashed noisily as birds squawked and took to the air, as if unable to watch.

The SS soldiers moved onward.

THIRTY-SEVEN

Westerbork – February 14, 1943

It was Sunday evening, and Gemmeker had summoned Schlesinger to the entertainment barracks. A rehearsal for the upcoming revue show was underway. He was sitting in the front row, the only spectator. He was gently tapping his feet and playing a pretend piano on his thigh.

The commandant had seen the OD leader enter but raised his hand, not permitting the other man to approach until the song was finished, at which point he beckoned him over. Gemmeker might pass his congratulations to performers face-to-face, but he would never show open appreciation of Jewish achievements in a public forum.

"We've received notification from The Hague of the deportation numbers for this coming Tuesday," the commandant said, still looking toward the stage. "It's on the desk in my office. I can't recall the exact number, but it's about the same as usual. The register of inmates is also there. I thought you could take them and make a start on selection." His fingers continued to tap on his leg, although the music had stopped. "And a sign has arrived for the railway platform. It's been manufactured by the Dutch National Railways to their standard specification. Please make sure it's put in position before Tuesday's transport."

Gemmeker then dismissed the CSO with the same airy wave of the hand with which he had summoned him.

The CSO resented the fact that the commandant seemed to consider the revue show more important than the OD leader. Sometimes he felt like an errand boy, fetching documents and sorting out camp trivia. Yet it was he, Kurt Schlesinger, who would take a piece of paper and ensure it was converted into a definitive list of names for transportation.

It usually took him around five minutes to walk to the commandant's office from there, but he had no enthusiasm to hurry. He made his way slowly along the pathway running through the camp, which the inmates had nicknamed the Boulevard of Misery because it ran alongside the railway line, the scene of the deportations. But this thin strip of gravel was the only place in camp not submerged in thick, sticky mud.

As he walked, he watched young lovers giggling or kissing, families laughing, groups discussing politics or other issues of the day that had been communicated by the latest *Jewish Weekly*. It could have been a clear, cool evening in any town or city, except that, strolling in the last sunlight of the day, he wondered how many of them would still be there by Tuesday afternoon.

There were six thousand names in the register, of which about one thousand would usually be transported. One in every six, he thought. As he proceeded along the Boulevard, he noted every sixth person and imagined it would be them going this week. For a fleeting moment, he thought of their family and friends who would be left behind, and how utterly random this entire process was.

It makes no difference in the end, he reminded himself. They'll all be going eventually. He was only doing his job. If he didn't, then somebody else would have to and he'd be on the train instead.

He quickly located the papers on Gemmeker's desk and picked them up. The single sheet from the Sicherheitsdienst (Security Service) in The Hague showed the required number to be deported—1,100. He made a note of the number and replaced the sheet on the desk before taking the register, which listed the 6,000 current inmates by barracks and date of arrival.

His next task was to inform the prominents, a small group of inmates who claimed to represent the interests of the rest of the camp and took decisions on their behalf. As it was Schlesinger's job to select the prominents, they were invariably like-minded and German. As a result, Dutch citizens were nearly always first on the list when it came to selecting deportees from the register.

There were around two thousand German inmates in the camp at that point, living in the original barracks and cottages, which provided a good standard of living. They mostly had jobs and were exempt from deportation. On the other hand, the Dutch were housed in the larger, flimsier barracks and were obliged to endure an appreciably lower standard of living. They were rarely granted exemptions and often employed in menial, laborious jobs.

To the CSO, the affluent Dutch made the ideal inmates. They were more likely to be chosen for deportation but had the means to procure an exemption for themselves and their families. In the past, he had been offered (and had accepted) cash, jewelry, stock certificates, and even sexual favors.

While returning to his cottage, Schlesinger knocked on the door of each of the prominents, telling them to meet at eight o'clock in the morning to agree the names. Before going to bed, he skimmed through the last pages of the register where the most recent arrivals were recorded. There were no names he recognized. Most of these people had been placed in five of the new barracks. He quickly determined that these inmates alone could form the majority of the deportees for the week. This would make the discussion in the morning much more straightforward. He had no patience for the monotony of going through the register line by line, bickering about who should go and who should stay.

*

Westerbork – February 15, 1943

Bad news travels fast, and everybody in camp knew by Sunday evening that there would be deportations on Tuesday morning. Though expected, this nonetheless threw the inmates into a state of fear and uncertainty. Even those with the relative security of a job and an exemption never felt completely secure, knowing that a word from Schlesinger or Gemmeker, or indeed any other senior SS official, might still lead to expulsion.

Inmates would try to lead their lives as normally as possible on Monday mornings. The children attended the school barracks, while the employed adults went to work in the hospital or on construction projects. Those who were unemployed, and most likely to be listed, would gather in small groups to chatter, inadvertently increasing their anxiety.

The selection process took place in the canteen barracks and was straightforward, as the CSO had anticipated. He chaired the meeting with six of the prominents. The Nazis sought no involvement in this process, except the commandant had given the instruction that no revue performers were to be listed.

The meeting of February 15 passed quickly. They examined the latter pages of the register and transferred names onto handwritten lists, ordered by barracks number. From time to time, a prominent would suggest a name he felt should not be transported. The CSO did not really care, so he permitted some exemptions to ensure the prominents at least felt they had genuine influence over the selection process.

The definitive list of deportees was drawn from five new barracks, the majority of whom were recent arrivals. The lists were then typed up before the OD leader summoned his supervisors to the canteen and gave each his list.

At ten-thirty that morning, the door to the canteen opened and the OD supervisors walked purposefully out. Five of them carried sheets of paper, the rest did not.

A crowd had gathered outside the canteen. There was immediate relief for those who saw that the supervisor responsible for their barracks was empty-handed. In contrast, the others watched their supervisor and felt a crushing dread. They turned and made their way back to their barracks, maybe running, maybe meandering, maybe even walking as if nothing momentous was happening at all.

Barracks 72, the last one to have been built, had been more or less emptied by each of the last seven deportations. Its current occupants were waiting in silence as the OD came through the door.

The supervisor for barracks 72 was Wilhelm Hofmaier, a fifty-year-old German Jew, a refugee from Hamburg who had been in camp since 1940. He lacked the gravitas and appearance of a professional official. His hair was unkempt, and he looked as if he had not shaved for several days. His bulging belly spilled over the top of his trousers, in stark contrast with the near emaciation of those around him.

"Listen up, everybody!" Hofmaier demanded. "This is the list of people who'll be going on tomorrow's train. As usual, I'll be reading the list in alphabetical order. If I call out your name, come forward so I can tick you off, then go and pack your things. Remember, only one suitcase is allowed, plus one bundled blanket. There'll be an early start in the morning. Five o'clock. If you've got questions or requests for exemptions, they're none of my business. Go and see Oberdienstleiter Schlesinger in the canteen barracks. He'll be dealing with all queries. Good luck trying." He paused for a moment. "There are two hundred and forty names on today's list from this barracks."

There was a concerned murmuring from the inmates. In the region of three-quarters of them were going to be deported in the morning.

"I can't pronounce all these names, so I'll spell them out," the supervisor continued. "It's a long list, five pages, so I'll not accept any interruptions."

He took a deep breath. It seemed as if the whole barracks breathed in at the same time. "A-S-S-E-R. Asser Israel, Asser Lena, Asser Joseph and Asser Matilda," he shouted to ensure his voice carried to the farthest bunks. "Come forward now. No dawdling!"

Somewhere near the back of the wooden building, Dr. Johannes Arons, a former colleague of Professor Kisch, closed his eyes in relief. Arons was prior to Asser in the alphabet, meaning his family was safe for at least another week. He had so wanted to smile at his wife. But how could he? Not when so many of those around him still awaited their fate. He was thankful his name was Arons; for better or for worse, he would always be one of the first to learn the news. For people whose names began with Y or Z, it was a hellish torture, he thought. Waiting and not knowing.

*

Leo looked down at the weighty metal sign in his hands. The black lettering against a yellow background was the color scheme he recognized from every other railway platform sign.

Schlesinger had insisted he erected the sign on Monday, and it had to be prominently displayed. The railway platform was sparsely furnished and not intended to provide any comfort to passengers but to create an open space for efficient loading and unloading.

He found a place where the platform narrowed, squeezed between the kitchen and maintenance blocks on either side. He decided to hang the sign on the outside wall of the maintenance block. It had pre-drilled holes, so it took barely five minutes for him to put it up. He stood back to check it was straight.

"It's only half right," a man's voice spoke behind him.

"Excuse me?" he answered, without turning.

"That sign's only half right," the voice repeated. "The top half says *Westerbork to Auschwitz*. That's fine, we've seen lots of folk going from here to Auschwitz. But the bottom half says

Auschwitz to Westerbork. I don't know about you, but I've never heard of a single soul making the journey back."

"Why would anybody need to come back?" he asked tentatively.

"Not one person, for any reason?" the man asked. "Why bother making a nice new, shiny sign like that? We've no choice about where or when we go. It's not as if we can choose to go to Paris or Madrid. Auschwitz on a Tuesday morning is the only time and destination. That sign's just another example of Nazi kidology and deception. Put up a convincing and realistic sign, making Westerbork station look as normal as any other, taking happy and gullible passengers from A to B. Nothing could be farther from the truth. There are no return tickets from Auschwitz."

Leo stared at the sign. How many trains had left Westerbork? Perhaps eighteen or twenty? Not one person had returned, not one single letter received. Was that credible? Was it the logical result of the disruption of wartime? And how could the very young, the old, and infirm contribute to a work camp? Perhaps they were given light duties. His head was spinning with uncertainty and contradictions. The Nazis had always talked about the work camps in the east being required to support struggling German industries. The Nazis were very pragmatic people, and the Jews would be more useful to them in Westerbork than in a work camp like Auschwitz.

He turned to reply to the man, but there was nobody there.

THIRTY-EIGHT

Westerbork – February 16, 1943

At five o'clock on Tuesday morning, the silence was suddenly broken by the banging of fists on the doors of the five barracks. The supervisors were returning with their deportation lists. Despite the early hour, it seemed as if most people were already waiting, and as the doors opened, they promptly started to file out, each holding one suitcase and a bundle.

One wet and cold winter, followed by a hot and dry summer, had left the poor-quality timber used to construct the new barracks warped or disintegrating. The door to barracks 72 was scarred with holes as if pounded by a machine gun.

"Come on! There are two hundred and forty on the list," Hofmaier shouted as he entered the barracks. "For every person who doesn't come forward in one minute, I'll seize five others instead. One way or another, at least two hundred and forty of you are leaving this morning!"

There was a tense murmuring among the tight rows of bunk beds, but almost immediately more people started to shuffle forward. Like a receding tide, the inmates who weren't being deported stepped back and allowed the others to pass.

The supervisor made his way back outside the door and waited, his deportation list in one hand and a pencil in the other. Without lifting his head, he continued, "Form three lines. Three straight lines. Three lines is the best way to approach and load the train." He paused for a moment. "Let me remind you, everybody not on the list must stay in the barracks! There's no chance for tearful goodbyes on the platform. Bid your farewells here and now. And make it quick! Remember, you'll see each other again soon at the work camp."

A woman stepped out through the doorway, holding a baby close to her chest with one hand, a suitcase with the other. A small boy of three or four years accompanied her, heaving a suitcase he could barely lift.

"Name!" the supervisor barked.

"Dukker Elsje," the woman replied quietly. For an inexplicable reason, when she observed this man's blue eyes, it reminded her of her brother. She wondered what had become of him and if he could have undertaken the role of an OD supervisor, herding fellow Jews into cattle trucks.

Hofmaier scanned the page with his finger, halting part way down.

"Dukker Elsje, date of birth May 22, 1918. Dukker David, date of birth July 16, 1938." He looked up to study the woman and baby. "The baby's not on the list."

"My daughter was born while I've been here," Elsje answered.

"Shouldn't make any difference," he answered dismissively. "The hospital's responsible for registering all births. It's vital to keep the register up to date. I'll have to take this up with CSO Schlesinger."

"But what about my baby?" she inquired nervously.

"Your baby's not on the list." He remained expressionless. "You want to take your baby with you to the work camp?"

"Yes, of course!" she confirmed.

"Okay. If that's what you want. Under no circumstances tell anybody about this huge favor I'm doing for you! The SS don't like bending the rules. Especially for that," he added, nodding at the baby.

As she walked past, he stepped forward so she could not avoid brushing against his coveralls. He leered at her.

It took the best part of an hour for all the deportees from barracks 72 to be accounted for, at which point the supervisor instructed the three lines to move forward in the direction of the Boulevard of Misery and the waiting train. Every thirty yards or so, they would pass an OD guard whose task was to make sure there were no attempts at escape or other form of disruption.

As they drew closer to the train, other groups of deportees converged upon each other, adding to the congestion. An old lady was pushed past on a wooden cart with two large wheels, causing gridlock.

At the train side, there was a desperate clamor. The OD men were brandishing their sticks indiscriminately as terrified deportees hurried to embark. There was a narrow set of wooden steps by each cattle truck, which the elderly, infirm, or young could use for boarding, but the more energetic would simply lever themselves up with their arms. Some remained standing on the platform to help the less able to reach the straw-lined floors of the trucks.

CSO Schlesinger was enjoying this morning. The preparations had gone well, and the cattle trucks were filling up quickly and with no interruptions. The train would easily depart prior to its eleven o'clock target. He could never understand why the Nazis were so obsessed with the departure time. He had spoken to plenty of the train drivers, and each had said that the journey was over eleven hundred miles and would stretch over at least three days and two nights. There were persistent delays as trains full of soldiers and armaments going westward shared the same tracks as those full of Jews traveling eastward. What difference would a delay of an hour or two out of Westerbork make?

However, the commandant was certainly fixated on the right number of deportees departing at the right time. He was standing at the rear of the railway platform, his uniform clean, pressed, and with shining regalia, a contrast with the mud and dirt that surrounded him. His hands were clasped casually behind his back. His entire entourage adopted the same stance.

His entourage consisted of four SS officers and his chief medical officer, Dr. Fritz Spanier. They looked as if they were casually talking about the weather while ambling around Alexanderplatz in Berlin on a sunny Sunday afternoon rather than overseeing the transportation of more than a thousand Jews. The commandant was accompanied by his pet beagle, Heinrich, who darted in and out of the queues, sniffing around curiously. The men talked and smoked cigarettes continuously.

Gemmeker insisted that, as each cattle truck was filled and shut, the supervisor had to sign the list and pass it to him for countersigning. Schlesinger was in the habit of making an extra copy for himself on the previous evening, so he could better manage the operation. He knew that underfilling the transports was strictly forbidden, so he always made sure he had a reserve list of twenty names in case of a shortfall. He encouraged the OD supervisors to overload rather than underload the wagons. Sixty adults in a cattle truck was a tight squeeze, he knew, but sixty-five could hardly make it much worse and gave him some leeway on numbers.

"Hey, you!" the CSO shouted, pointing at an OD guard pushing a wooden trolley that carried several barrels. The man stopped. "You've missed out one of the wagons!" he continued, edging forward and pointing. "Remember! Every wagon needs two barrels, one full of water to drink, the other empty to piss and shit in."

"Yes, sir," the man bowed toward his superior and heaved his trolley back to the wagon he had overlooked.

Then the doors began to close.

Each cattle truck had one sliding door on each side. Their runners were invariably so rusty that two OD guards were frequently required to pull or push them shut, which made a sound like the screeching of a thousand cats. Eventually, each door would close with a hollow, metallic clang, the supervisor would drop the door's metal locking arm into place and, with a piece of white chalk, scrawl on the outside of the door the number of deportees held within.

The OD leader always paid close attention to the chalk marks. One time, he had seen the number 82. Even with a high proportion of children, it was a seriously overcrowded wagon. With one small barred and unglazed window for ventilation and one barrel of water for sustenance, it was hardly surprising that the weakest rarely survived the journey.

The CSO remained well back on the platform, close to the commandant's group, watching.

When all the cattle trucks had been filled and locked, the supervisors brought the final deportation summary to Schlesinger for review prior to passing to Gemmeker. By then, the platform was quiet, save for the OD and SS men standing around chatting in their respective groups. He glanced up and down from one end of the train to the other, then scrutinized the piece of paper in his hand, smiling at the grand total of 1,125 names. Another successful day.

He was about to hand the summary to his boss when he noticed that the sliding door of a nearby cattle truck was still ajar by about a foot. It was difficult to spot on this dark winter's morning; the sides of the truck were filthy, and the gap itself was a sliver of profound emptiness. As the weak sun moved from behind the clouds, a few rays touched the sides of the cattle truck like exploring fingers. The gap remained consumed by blackness, but as the creeping rays moved gradually across, they revealed a white face peering out.

The boy must have been in his mid-to-late teens. The angle of the sun meant it was only his face that was illuminated, like the moon in a dark sky. His visage was unwavering, and the CSO was struck by the equanimity of his expression. In the midst of the traumas of an overcrowded camp and deportation, the boy possessed a look of innocent serenity.

For a fleeting moment, Schlesinger had an irresistible urge to rush forward and drag the boy from the cattle truck, but his thoughts were broken by commandant's voice beside him. "Do you have the final paperwork so this train can go and we can get on with the day?"

"Yes, sir," he replied. "One thousand one hundred requested. One thousand one hundred and twenty-five deportees loaded."

"Well done!" the commandant praised. "As ever, a very orderly process. Let's get this show on the road, shall we?" He paused. "On the subject of shows, the revue's being performed tomorrow evening. Will you be attending?"

"Of course, sir. I'm very much looking forward to it." The CSO forced himself to display enthusiasm for something he had never liked nor watched during peacetime and despised even more now, sat among the inmates, their hateful stares boring into him.

The commandant signed the summary sheet and waved his arm in the air until the train driver had reciprocated in acknowledgement. The train's doleful whistle pierced the air, signifying another week of respite for the remaining inmates and an unknown future for those departing.

Schlesinger glanced back at the door of the truck. The sun had passed, obliterated by winter clouds, and the boy's face had disappeared too like the flame of an extinguished candle, and the sliver of darkness had returned.

The train lurched forward.

"You two!" he shouted, pointing at some nearby OD guards. "That truck door's still open! Close it at once before the train goes, or I'll make sure you'll be on the other side of a door exactly like it come next Tuesday!" The men frantically dashed to the truck and managed to slide the door shut before the train gathered speed.

He hoped the commandant had seen his display of authority, but on turning, he saw that Gemmeker was already walking off, deep in conversation with Dr. Spanier.

Gemmeker's dog had found a child's doll in the mud and was flaunting it proudly in its mouth.

The CSO followed, several paces behind, doing his best to keep his boots free of mud and dirt and quietly congratulating himself on another successful transportation.

THIRTY-NINE

Amsterdam – March 1943

"Let me look at yesterday's registration list," the SS guard requested impatiently.

"Yesterday's list, sir?" Walter replied.

"Yes. I can't remember signing yesterday's list."

"No problem, sir. Let me go and get it for you."

Walter made his way from the theater foyer up to the administration room to retrieve the list from the filing cabinet.

The SS guard had turned up at the entrance, demanding to see him at once. He guessed straight away why he had been summoned and kept his fingers crossed that the guard would not uncover his deception. It was too soon for him to be caught; they still had so many more opportunities to smuggle children out.

By SS standards, this soldier was relatively elderly. To Walter, many of the SS seemed young and inexperienced. This man, Fischer, had wisps of gray hair poking from under his cap, and his wrinkles showed as thick shadows across his face and forehead.

Walter returned to the foyer and passed the single sheet of paper to Fischer, who examined both sides.

"I'm sure that's not my signature!" he exclaimed.

Walter mouthed some words in reply.

"What did you say?"

Walter spoke quietly, as if imparting a secret. "You did have a little bit to drink last night, sir."

"Let's go outside where we can discuss this without interruption," the soldier said less forcefully, pulling one of the entrance doors open and allowing it to slam shut before the theater manager had passed through.

Outside, the two men were alone, save for the guard responsible for watching the entrances to the theater and the day-care center. The SS man moved several yards farther away.

"Talk discreetly," the SS man warned, looking at the list. "That really doesn't look like my signature. Even after a couple of drinks."

"They were quite big drinks, sir," Walter replied. "The bottle of Scotch was emptied. Glenlivet—it's your favorite, I believe? The empty bottle's still in the bin upstairs if you want me to fetch it?"

"No, no, no!" the SS man exhorted. "No need to fetch it!" He paused again to consider the sheet. "I recall a couple of late roundups and eighty-six registrations last night. This says sixty-eight. It doesn't feel right."

"Are you sure, sir?" he asked. "Eight six compared to six eight. Are you sure you haven't simply mixed the numbers up? It's the sort of mistake anybody could make. I've only got sixty-eight names, so if it was eighty-six, we'd be missing eighteen people, vanished into thin air!" He made his best effort to laugh, although his tongue seemed to be glued to the dry roof of his mouth. Changing eighty-six to sixty-eight had seemed such an easy and clever ruse at the time, but it was looking much riskier now.

"Of course, you're right," Fischer replied. "There are so many Jews being rounded up these days, it's only human to get a little confused."

"You can trust me and my team," Walter said.

"I believe I can," the SS man replied. "Oh, and Sueskind?"

"Yes, sir?"

"That empty Scotch bottle…best dispose of it."

"Of course, sir."

"And Sueskind…that Glenlivet's exceptionally good. Might you be able to procure another bottle?"

"I'll do my very best, sir."

He started walking away, crossing the road toward the day-care center and taking in several gulps of cool, fresh air to calm himself down. He would have to be even more vigilant in the future. Nonetheless, he was excited. He was about to tell Henriette she could smuggle a further eighteen children out, their very existence having been erased from the theater records.

*

This was not the time Johan van Hulst wanted an inspector from the Ministry of Education to visit the teacher training college, but he knew that raising any form of objection would have been counterproductive, merely creating suspicion.

He had not previously met the inspector, Gezina de Wolf. The children were hidden in the only classroom on the fourth floor of the college, and he needed to shield them from her. He decided that he would attempt to persuade her to participate in a cursory tour of the premises, thus making sure she spent most of her time in his office, preoccupied with mountains of paperwork.

He checked his appearance in the mirror. His smart suit and tie, his circular, black-framed glasses, and his serious expression belied the fact that he was only thirty-two years old and the principal of a college. He was a devout Christian, and the college was funded by the Reformed Church, which bolstered his confidence in his position and helped to reduce his nervousness about the imminent inspection. If the children were discovered, then not only the college but also the day-care center would be exposed.

De Wolf arrived precisely on time at eleven o'clock. He guessed she was in her mid-forties, with a cheery face framed by shoulder-length, light-brown hair. He immediately felt at ease in her presence, especially as she acquiesced to his proposal of the shortened tour.

When he realized how quiet the college was, he did start to feel on edge. There were students on site that day, but they were all in classrooms, and the hard, wooden floors amplified every step van Hulst and de Wolf took and echoed right around the building. He found himself talking in an unnaturally loud voice in an attempt to drown out any potential background noises, but these actions merely served to exaggerate the inevitable periods of silence in between.

By the time they reached the third floor, his heart was pounding so hard he thought his ribcage might explode. If they walked along the full length of the corridor, she could not fail to see the stairway to the fourth level. He had already decided that, should she ask, he would explain that the room was locked and the key had been mislaid. It was an incredibly weak excuse.

He looked down at his watch and seized his opportunity.

"Good grief! It's midday," he exclaimed. "The third floor's very much like the second and first, so I suggest we go downstairs now. We can have lunch and you can inspect our records."

He turned around, and to his tremendous relief, the inspector followed suit. A weight was lifted off him.

De Wolf took one step forward, then paused.

"Is there something wrong?" the principal asked cautiously.

The inspector's brow was knitted, her head cocked on one side.

"We always get noises in this building," he explained nervously. "It's old and cavernous. There are hundreds of creaking floorboards!"

She remained quite still. "I can hear somebody crying," she said. "A baby or young child."

Van Hulst had previously handled several tricky episodes with the Nazi government and SS officials. He had a filing cabinet full of falsified documents which had permitted Jewish students to avoid transportation, and he had successfully withstood the most intense SS questioning. His hatred for the Nazis and their ideology was so vehement that he had convinced them that this devout Protestant could not conceivably be aiding Jews.

The inspector took a couple of steps away from the principal. She paused and listened once more. She slowly turned to face him.

"Meneer van Hulst," she said. "Please, can you explain why there are children in this college?"

"Mevrouw de Wolf. Please don't oblige me to answer that question," he replied. "They're babies and kids. All younger than twelve. Innocent children shouldn't be caught up in all of this!" He spread his arms wide.

She seemed to consider his comments for an age, and her expression gave no hint of her thoughts. Finally, she approached him and spoke softly but clearly.

"You're doing a great service. The Nazis are increasing their efforts to deport Jews as quickly as possible. We must react with the same speed and save as many children as we can. Before it's too late."

His jaw dropped in shock. She ignored his surprise.

"I'm in direct contact with most of the Resistance organizations operating in this country and its neighbors—the NV Group, Amsterdam Students, both Touw and Westerweel Groups. With the concentration of Jews and the SS here in Amsterdam, we now have more opportunities to hide people elsewhere. Let's continue this in your office, and we can discuss how I might help."

Before he could recover enough to speak, the inspector continued, "Also, if you're planning any escapes today, don't postpone them because of my presence. Keep them going. Every child counts."

His sense of relief was so strong he felt almost euphoric. Tears welled in his eyes, and he thanked God for his good fortune.

*

At three-thirty that afternoon, at the end of the academic day, a steady flow of teachers and students left the college, exiting through the doorway at the front of the building. A number departed on bicycles, two of which were equipped with an oversized pannier, each containing a baby shrouded in a blanket. Two of the walking students carried rucksacks containing tiny human cargoes. Two teachers departed holding the hands of eight-year-old children (who were not their children). By four o'clock, ten youngsters had been smuggled out, heading for prearranged overnight accommodation on the outskirts of the city, from where they would go to safehouses in Limburg and Friesland.

On the opposite side of the street, the SS guard outside the theater was watching intently as the entrance door to the day-care center regularly opened and closed, but he was surprised that few people actually walked in or out. He was not aware that Rachael was situated immediately behind the door and was pulling and pushing it with the specific intention of distracting him. In his peripheral vision, he noticed the college emptying at the usual time, but paid no heed.

Gezina de Wolf waited until the last child had gone before taking her leave from Johan.

"Good luck," she said. "With those extra contacts within the Resistance, let's aim to smuggle a dozen children every single day from now on. May God be with you."

"Thank you," he replied. "May God be with you, too."

He intended to go into the garden to tell Henriette about his discussions with the surprisingly helpful inspector, but first he thought he would walk over to the theater, offer the SS guard outside a cigarette, and engage him in a suitably diverting conversation. He did not want the man to be paying too much attention to the trams between four and five.

FORTY

Amsterdam – March 1943

Seyss-Inquart found himself in Rauter's Amsterdam office, and it had immediately become a source of aggravation to him. Firstly, as he was a guest, he was on the wrong side of the desk, perched on a plain and uncomfortable wooden chair that bore no comparison with that of his rival. Not only that, but the SS soldier's office was by a large margin superior to his own.

The Reichskommissar's office in The Hague was markedly utilitarian, situated as it was in a functional government building. Amsterdam was not the seat of government, but it did possess a larger number of grand, historical buildings, many of which had been commandeered by the Nazis soon after their invasion. Rauter's office was located in an eighteenth-century building in Museumplein, the view from his window an open vista of green lawns and columns of lime trees stretching to the magnificent Rijksmuseum in the far corner of the square.

In addition, Seyss-Inquart soon discovered that Rauter's plush leather chair was several inches higher than his, so he was continuously looking up at his rival. For that reason, he rose and made his way over to the window, wincing due to the stiffness in his leg. He watched the people in the square below.

"Over recent months, the Reich has been very satisfied with our progress," the commissioner said. "Despite their requests for ever-increasing numbers of deportees, we've still been able to satisfy demand. Eichmann himself has praised our efforts." He added begrudgingly, "He asked me to pass on his congratulations to you as well."

"It's highly satisfying that our work is being recognized," the soldier responded.

"However," the Reichskommissar continued, "they expect the high level of deportations to be maintained for the foreseeable future." He paused for a moment, deep in thought. "The civil service records have been of great assistance in rounding up Jews. The exemptions, the yellow stars, the ID cards, transferring their savings into our Lippmann Rosenthal bank, the regulations we've introduced—they've helped us gain almost complete control over all aspects of Jewish life. There's no doubt that we're victims of our own success since it's now proving problematic to find enough Jews to transport. As the number of deportations has increased and the credibility of the Jewish Council has decreased, many of the remaining Jews have gone into hiding. So we need alternative approaches to enable us to achieve our deportation targets."

The soldier rose to his feet, walked over to the window, and stood beside his colleague.

"I've been speaking with my officers and we've come up with a couple of compelling suggestions. With many of the Jews already deported or in hiding, they have very little presence in public during daylight hours, so we can transfer a sizable proportion of our SS resources from daytime to nighttime working. That way, we'll be able to raid more houses and restrict opportunities for them to move between safehouses. The less they move about, the more chance we have to catch them."

The two men stood side by side for a few moments, their backs turned slightly toward one another. Rather than engage in polite conversation, they silently watched the street scene below. The commissioner confessed to himself that the presence of bunkers and barbed wire in the square was a blight on this pleasant, natural landscape, notwithstanding its undoubted military importance. "You mentioned a couple of solutions?" he asked finally.

"Well, the other solution is perhaps more contentious," Rauter replied. "It's proposed that we appeal to mankind's capitalist tendencies."

"What on earth do you mean?"

"The idea's simple. We offer an incentive payment for every Jew that's found, arrested, and registered at the theater."

"Never! That would be wholly unacceptable for members of the SS. The SS should be able to vigorously pursue Jews with one hundred percent effort and diligence, without the need for monetary reward. Every SS soldier should recognize the absolute need to purge them from society."

"I fully agree with you. This sort of activity would be well below the high standards of the German SS. But it would be easier for a Dutchman. A Dutchman who knows or suspects where Jews are hiding and has so far been keeping quiet, might well divulge their whereabouts if there's a financial incentive on offer. Some guilders might encourage him to unearth some Jewish worms."

"What exactly do you have in mind?"

"We intend to select a small group of ardent Dutch Jew-haters who work in the civil service for the Central Bureau for Jewish Emigration. The incentive will be a straightforward payment of seven and a half guilders for every Jew registered at the theater. They'd be like modern-day bounty hunters.

"We've found the right man to lead this group, a truly fanatical antisemite who'll gather a team of like-minded colleagues. He'll be our sole point of contact. I'd like our association with this group to be kept at a distance. These fanatics might behave excessively and erratically, but they'll pursue Jews with great enthusiasm. There will need to be some cooperation between the group and us. The SS will continue with its own raids but will provide support where necessary to apprehend the Jews they dig up."

Still looking at the street below, Rauter smiled. "There's a final positive aspect to this plan. The incentive payments will be made out of the Lippmann Rosenthal bank, so the Jews will be paying for their own capture!"

For a moment, Seyss-Inquart forgot his animosity toward the other man and laughed. "The more Jews that are arrested, the more it costs them! And it always costs us nothing!" He laughed again. "And what's the name of the man who will lead this group?"

"His name's Wim Heinneicke. Needless to say, he's a member of the NSB. He's also connected with a substantial network of informants."

"Okay, let's see what happens with your so-called bounty hunters," the commissioner said. "I'll arrange for the necessary paperwork to be drawn up."

FORTY-ONE

Amsterdam – March 1943

Franck Kisch woke to the familiar sound of a raid taking place in the street. He clambered out of bed, went to the window, and peeked out from behind the curtain. He saw three groups of SS soldiers at work, accompanied by three trucks waiting to transport apprehended Jews to the Dutch Theater.

He watched and heard them knocking loudly at the door of Salomon Dukker, without success, since that family had gone into hiding a week earlier.

This section of the street had been transformed in recent months. Almost every house had been home to a family, and the street used to echo with the laughter and tears of children playing and adults talking as they strolled to and from the park, stopping to pass the time of day with friends and neighbors. Nazi restrictions had become ever more severe over the last two years but had worsened significantly during the latter part of 1942, when the number of deportations to Westerbork had risen steeply, and young and fit Jewish men were being forced into faraway labor camps. As a result, many families had gone into hiding.

The only people now residing on his street were associated, directly or indirectly, with the Jewish Council and still enjoyed the protection of an exemption. Even so, nobody went outdoors unless it was strictly necessary. In reality, many no longer had a reason to go out, having no money and no job. The risks were also too high, especially at night, after curfew.

The professor watched as the dark, featureless shapes of four men approached the front door of his next-door neighbor, Samuel Roozentaal. He smiled to himself, knowing that this, too, would be a fruitless exercise. Samuel and his family had quietly slipped out before dawn that very day. Although it was dark, he noticed these men were not members of the SS, as they bore no rifles and lacked the bulk and shape given by military uniforms. He was puzzled.

He heard another thudding on a door, only this time, it was louder. Much louder. He craned his neck and pressed his forehead against the cold glass of the window and peered down. A man was standing there, not at Samuel's door but at his own. He thought the man must have climbed over the low fence that separated the two properties. Wherever he had come from, this man who was now banging at his door with a pistol butt.

"Okay, okay!" he shouted from the top of the stairs. "I'm coming! There's no need to knock the door down." Despite his requests, the thudding continued to reverberate through the silent house until Franck unlocked and opened the door. The stranger in the doorway flashed his ID card and walked straight into the hallway. Dressed in civilian clothing and with a dark, wide-brimmed hat pulled tightly down over his forehead, this man only needed to incline his head slightly for his entire face to be screened from the sight of others, save for his stubbly, pointed chin.

Franck thought it strange that the man was on his own; raids usually involved groups of two or more, as they liked safety in numbers.

The man drew a piece of paper from his inside pocket and unfolded it.

"This is the residence of the Kisch family, am I right?" the man asked curtly.

"Yes, it is," Franck replied, recognizing his Dutch accent.

"And there are five members of the family living here, am I right?"

"There used to be five members of the family living here, but now there's only one. I'm quite alone."

"What?" the man bellowed. "Where the hell are the other four members of your family? And when are they coming back? They're breaking the curfew and could be arrested and transported for being away from the residence." There was a nervous agitation in the man's voice that unsettled Franck.

305

"They've been gone for days. And if they had broken curfew, what would be the difference between being deported for breaking curfew or being deported because of this raid?" Franck asked.

"Don't get smart with me, Jew!" the man scowled. "The difference is that this raid leads to the Dutch Theater, whereas breaking curfew is a crime, leading to transportation to Mauthausen. Believe me, there's an enormous difference."

"In this case, it makes no difference. The rest of my family has gone permanently. I'm on the Jewish Council and I've decided to stay. I have an exemption."

"Are you hiding them here, Jew?" the man spat out the words. "I was told that there are five of you here. I can have this house torn to pieces to uncover the rest of your family. If I find one person hiding, you'll all be sent to Mauthausen. That's a promise! Do you understand?" He lifted his head to reveal a pair of dark, beady eyes. He leaned forward, so close that the brim of his hat touched Franck's forehead.

"It doesn't matter how hard you look, there's nobody else here except me," he replied, staying calm in the face of this man's barrage.

The intruder retreated a step and lowered his head. Franck could hear him mumbling under his breath and noticed that the sheet of paper was shaking in his hands.

"I want five people," the man said almost inaudibly. "I need five people." He paused. "I need five people!" he repeated with emphasis.

"Why is it that you need five people?" Franck asked. "Sometimes, there are five people in a house, sometimes houses are empty, and sometimes there's only one person there. It's potluck. Tonight it's only me."

"What, what?" the man started and looked up as if he had only just become aware of Franck's presence.

"You said you needed five people? Why is it such a necessity?"

The man appeared to be speechless, and his face reddened. Franck was not certain if it was rage or humiliation. Or both. He had never seen a Nazi, Dutch or German, react in this manner. He sensed he might be able to take advantage of the man's loss of composure. "There's only you and me here. Nobody can hear us," he whispered. "Tell me why you need five people. Perhaps I can help you. I'm a member of the Jewish Council, which gives me a good deal of influence."

"A Jew can't help me!" the man scoffed without conviction, looking at him with an expression that was not so much aggressive as hapless.

The professor thought the man looked about thirty years of age, but his face was gaunt and troubled, which aged him considerably. He continued to probe, hoping to calm the man's anger. "There's nobody else in the building who can hear us. There's nothing to lose in your telling me why you need five people, is there?"

He edged forward and gently patted the man on his coat sleeve. The man opened up his mouth, as if to speak, but hesitated.

"There's nothing to lose," Franck said as sincerely as he was able.

"I need the money," the man blurted out. It was as if a dam in his mind had been breached and the words were flooding uncontrollably out of his mouth. "I need the money. I've got gambling debts. Owed to a gang of very nasty people. Who need paying. Quickly. Capturing five Jews will help me pay them off. Heinneicke agreed I could raid on my own tonight so I don't have to share my incentive payment."

"What payment?" Franck asked.

"From the Nazis." The man's words continued to gush out. "They're paying a group of us seven and a half guilders for every Jew we can round up and deliver to the theater. They'll do almost anything to keep their deportation numbers up. And they'll pay me cash." The man's eyes were wild and desperate. "They'll pay me cash! And quickly!"

"So you really need money, not Jews?" Franck inquired, sensing an opportunity.

"But without the five Jews, I can't get the money!" the man moaned. "Heinneicke told me there'd be five Jews here. It's on this piece of paper he gave me!"

"What if you could get the money without the Jews?"

"What do you mean? Are you trying to trick me? I know you Jews can't be trusted."

"I've got money," Franck said. "I can give you the money equivalent to five Jews at seven guilders fifty each." He paused, then continued. "It's in the house right now. As long as you promise to leave on your own, you can have it."

"Prove it and show me!" the stranger shouted. As he did, he withdrew his pistol from his pocket. "No mucking about, Jew!"

This man wasn't in control, Franck thought. He would need to tread cautiously. He slowly made his way up the stairs. There was an envelope of cash in his bedroom. Elizabeth, Hendrik, and Rachael had taken the other stashes when they left. This last one was partly earmarked for bribes to permit him to join Elizabeth and Hannes in the hidden village. There was more than sufficient to pay this man his bounty for five Jews.

He entered the bedroom, closely followed by the Dutchman. They did not speak; the house was quiet, save for the padding of their shoes on the carpeted floors.

He had hidden the money behind a loose panel in the oak-lined wall, next to the dressing table. Kneeling, he plucked the panel clear with his fingernails and withdrew a brown envelope, strapped tight by an elastic band. He plucked out fifty guilders and offered them to the man.

"Here you go," he said. "I've given you a little extra."

The man made as if to take the notes, then paused to ask, "How come you've got money, Jew? You should've handed all your money to the Lippmann bank."

"Okay, okay, I understand." Franck smiled through gritted teeth. "Let me offer you something extra. Another fifty perhaps?"

"I want it all!" the man demanded excitedly. "You shouldn't have any money, so you need to give me the lot!"

"Now, that's a little greedy, isn't it?" Franck said, immediately regretting his words.

"You, a Jew, calling me greedy?" The man sneered angrily. "Give me the envelope or I'll arrest you for breaking regulations by hoarding cash!"

"I simply can't give you everything. I need it. You need guilders, so do I."

"You simply can." The man nervously raised the pistol. "And why do you need money?"

"I just do! I can't explain."

"That sounds suspicious. Perhaps I should arrest you and take you in for questioning?" They stared at each other. "Give me the envelope, and I'll let you off. I won't arrest you. That's a deal?" He beckoned with his free hand, the pistol pointing at Franck.

Franck was conscious they were not making any progress. He glanced at the open bedroom door.

"Make one step that way, and I'll shoot you!" the man warned him, almost hysterical.

Franck placed the banknotes on the dressing table and added a further fifty guilders from the envelope. This man was only counting on five lots of seven guilders fifty. One hundred and fifty guilders would be a windfall for him. No strings attached.

Franck took a step toward the door. There was a loud roar that filled his eardrums, like when an errant Allied bomb had landed in the alley directly behind the house. He threw himself to the floor, his ears ringing.

He was confused, in shock. The scene seemed unreal as he watched the man slowly walk forward and reach out for the envelope. He tried to hold on to it but somehow couldn't, and it slipped from his grasp. The man lingered above him. There was a yellow glint as a stray ray of light ricocheted off the barrel of his gold fountain pen before the man slipped it into his inside coat pocket.

The man's lips were moving, but the professor heard nothing. Franck looked down at his hand lying across his chest and saw a dark stain spreading across his white nightshirt. He put his head back, slowly scanning the familiar room. The brass bedstead, the glistening ceiling light. It was a very pleasant room, he thought.

His gaze drifted drowsily to the dressing table and lingered on the antique silver-framed picture of his family. Then his eyes gently shut.

FORTY-TWO

Leeuwarden – May 1943

"Why do we have so many of our Resistance meetings in bakeries?" the man asked, laughing nervously. The faces of his companions who were sitting or standing around the room were like stone. Hendrik pitied the man whose attempt to lighten the mood had fallen on deaf ears.

"Because they operate at unusual times of the day, so our activities do not appear suspicious," Kramer replied, before adding, "This is the most difficult and dangerous mission we've ever undertaken." He ran his fingers through his thick, dark hair and knitted his bushy eyebrows in concentration.

"Let's go through the plan one more time, then we'll make our way to the Blokhuispoort," Kramer said.

The Blokhuispoort was a sixteenth-century fortified citadel with two imposing steepled towers bookmarking its entrance and a canal that had been dug to provide a moat around its perimeter. In the late-nineteenth century, it had become a detention center and prison, and in 1941, the Nazis had commandeered it. They built the citadel around a rectangular, cobbled courtyard, with sturdy wooden doors on two sides, one marking the entrance to the prison, which housed civil criminals, the other to the detention wing for political prisoners.

Since a significant majority of the inmates had been tried through the local courts, the Nazis had allowed the prison warders to remain in their posts to supervise both sections of the facility. SS officials only attended the site to interrogate political prisoners in the detention cells. This could happen at any time, night or day.

"Hendrik, Willem, and Arie, are you ready?" Kramer asked. "Willem, do you have the forged arrest warrant?" He looked at the three men, who were dressed in standard-issue Leeuwarden police force uniforms. They each nodded in return. "Then let's go! The longer we wait, the more our nerves will be frayed. There are nineteen of us. Every single man has a vital role to play. If one fails, we all fail."

He patted the breast pocket of his gray raincoat. "The list of detainees and their cell locations are here. There are two hundred and fifteen men being held, but we only have safehouses for thirty-nine, so whatever's said to you, no matter how much the prisoners beg, we can take not one more. Not one more. Is that understood?" He glanced around the room at the silent, studied faces, which in the half-light looked like rows of death masks.

"Our top priority is Jurjen Dreeuws. Our informant tells us he's being so severely tortured that the Nazis may well break him soon. He knows too much about Resistance activities for us to risk that. If, in the end, we've saved only Jurjen, then our mission will be a success. Saving thirty-nine would be a triumph.

"Finally, don't indulge in any non-essential conversations. Willem used to work in the police force and will do all the talking until we're in the prison. You will only speak in response to me or Willem."

He placed his cap on his head, buttoned up his coat, and walked to the door without uttering another word. The three men followed close behind.

Once outside, Willem led the group with Kramer following behind, flanked by the other two. Hendrik thought Willem looked the part, marching purposefully along in his dark-blue uniform and long, black leather boots. He and Arie, on the other hand, struggled to keep up and their strides were not synchronized with those of the former policeman.

Within a few minutes, the imposing stone facade of the citadel loomed in front of them, and soon after, they were approaching the bulky wooden door of the prison entrance.

Kramer noticed the two men at his sides straightening their backs and pushing back their shoulders.

"Remember, you must be convincing. I'm your prisoner, so you need to manhandle me with the disdain I deserve," he quietly urged as they came to a halt.

Willem rapped on the door three times. A wooden flap positioned at eye level opened, and a pair of eyes peered out.

"What do you want?" the guard inside asked brusquely.

"You know exactly what I want!" Willem retorted angrily. "We're delivering a prisoner to you. It was phoned in to the prison administration an hour ago. Here's the bloody warrant! Let us in and be quick about it!" Willem shoved the forged document through the slit, crumpling it as much as he could. The flap closed.

It seemed the world had stopped still as the four men waited outside. Birds that had been singing fell silent and the gentle rustling of leaves ceased.

Eventually, they heard the metallic clunk of a bolt being drawn and the door creaked open.

"Get in there!" Willem shouted, pushing Kramer over the threshold and past the guard.

For a fleeting moment, the guard thought that it was odd for the prisoner to be wearing a raincoat on such a warm and pleasant evening. And then he turned to see the man withdrawing a revolver from his pocket.

"Hands up!" Kramer demanded.

The guard complied and felt his own weapon being removed from its holster. He glanced around to see Willem looking impassively back at him. "You traitor!" the guard spat.

"I think you'll find that you're the traitor," Kramer responded calmly. He estimated the man was around sixty years old, his bulging belly obscuring his trouser belt. There was hatred in his face.

There was a firm rapping on the entrance door, and the remaining fifteen members of the group were let in. It was a quiet Sunday evening, and, as soon as the coast was clear, they had dashed across the bridge that spanned the citadel's moat.

The guard, hands still held high, watched with increasing bewilderment as each of the newcomers revealed their weapons.

"What's going on?" he asked, his voice still defiant.

"We're taking some of your detainees," Kramer replied. "If you cooperate, you'll have no problems with us. If you don't, we'll execute you, and if your colleagues oppose us, they'll suffer the same fate."

The guard looked down at the warrant he was still clutching.

"It's a convincing forgery, isn't it?" Kramer asked, snatching it from the man's hand. "I think that's better staying with me."

A phone was attached to the wall. The Resistance leader lifted the receiver and passed it to the guard.

"Call up the guards on duty in the detention wing and order them to bring Jurjen Dreeuws here. If they ask why, tell them the SS have made an impromptu visit and wish to take him away for further interrogation."

The guard made the call with the cold barrel of Kramer's revolver prodding his ribs. Meanwhile, the Resistance workers waited in silence, remaining well clear of any windows that might betray their presence. The detention wing was only across the courtyard, and when there was no sign of their colleague after a few minutes, they started to become nervous. In fact, the prisoner, having assumed he was being led to another torture session, had collapsed, and two guards were obliged to drag him out of his cell and haul him to the administration office.

The guards were preoccupied with escorting a semiconscious Dreeuws, and the office door slammed behind them before they realized they were surrounded by a group of men, including three police officers, pointing their guns at them. They surrendered immediately, and their arms were tied behind their backs. The sets of keys hanging from their belts were removed.

Dreeuws collapsed once again, but this time with joy and relief. A member of the group, Ronald van der Hoeden, was a doctor, and he dropped to his knees to tend to the tortured man. Aware of his comrade's condition in advance, Ronald was carrying a medical bag. But first, he helped him swig from a small bottle of brandy he had also brought.

"That leaves the three remaining guards in the detention block," Kramer said. "And one of those is our informant." He took the list of names out of his pocket, laid it on a nearby table and beckoned the entrance guard over.

"Kramer, is it wise to reveal our informant?" Hendrik whispered almost inaudibly.

"It's okay," Kramer whispered back. "We've actually got two informants among the prison staff. If we reveal one and take him away with us, the SS won't think for a moment there's one left behind!" He winked.

"This is the list of thirty-nine detainees. One's here, and you're going to help us free the other thirty-eight," Kramer continued, looking at the stout guard.

"You can go to hell!" the guard replied.

"I haven't time to debate with you." Kramer turned to the two men directly behind him. "Take this man's uniform off him and tie his hands. Lock him in one of the holding cells over there. The same applies to those two," he added, pointing to the other prison guards.

"Of course," replied Smits, a short, thin man, grabbing the guard roughly by the collar.

Five minutes later, a group of prison guards, policemen, and prisoners walked across the courtyard toward the detention block. Anyone looking carefully would have seen a short, thin guard with exceptionally baggy trousers held up by a belt that almost stretched around his waist twice.

They arrived at the door to the block and, after several unsuccessful attempts with different keys, managed to open it. Three guards and three prisoners waited outside while the rest rushed in. There was the brief sound of raised voices, then silence. They locked two of the remaining guards in an adjacent cell, leaving the last one with Kramer.

The Resistance leader surveyed this guard for several seconds. The rest of the men watched nervously. Suddenly, he extended his hand.

"Erik Tiemersma?" he asked.

The guard, a man in his mid-twenties, with fair skin, blond hair, and black-rimmed spectacles, nodded, smiled, and shook the outstretched hand.

"Pleased to meet you," Kramer said. "Without the support and information you've provided, this mission would have been impossible. Thank you!"

"I'm glad to have been able to serve the cause."

With the young guard's knowledge of the detention block, the Resistance workers were able to move methodically along its corridors, opening specific cells and releasing confused but euphoric prisoners. As the other prisoners became aware of the commotion outside their cells, the air was filled with the shouting of voices and the clattering of metal cups and dishes against cold steel cell doors.

They had given Hendrik and Arie the keys to cells 53, 59 and 68, which were situated on the first floor. The occupants of the first two cells bounded out as soon as the keys turned in their locks, hurrying unaided down to the detention block entrance.

There was no such reaction when Hendrik opened the door to cell 68. He poked his head inside to be met with the foul stench of human excrement. He could make out the shape of the prisoner cowering under a tattered old blanket. Together with Arie, he entered the cell but had to cover his mouth and nose to prevent himself from retching.

Hendrik gently tapped the prisoner on the shoulder, but the man recoiled, pulling his blanket tightly around his shoulders.

"It's okay," he said soothingly. "We're from the Resistance and we're here to liberate you. You're safe now."

A pair of frightened, blinking eyes peeked over the frayed edge of the blanket.

Hendrik smiled down at the man. "Shall we carry you?" he asked.

The man shook his head determinedly.

"That's fine, but we need to move quickly. Everybody's ready to go."

The man raised himself up to sit on the edge of the bed, allowing the blanket to fall from his shoulders. Hendrik took a sharp intake of breath. The man's shirt was ripped so badly, it looked more like thin strips of cloth, making it impossible not to notice his emaciated arms and chest beneath.

He had known that the SS habitually starved its victims and meted out severe beatings. However, both of this man's hands were covered in bloodied rags, which made Hendrik surmise that his fingers had been smashed or his nails removed. His eyes had sunk into hollowed sockets. They had been told this man was thirty years old, but Piet ten Hoven's features were those of an old man with thinning hair.

"Bastards!" Hendrik said.

Nonetheless, ten Hoven managed to stand up and make his way to the entrance to join the others. Whenever Hendrik or Arie sought to offer support, he shrugged them off. It was only when walking away from the citadel itself that Hendrik placed his hand under the former prisoner's elbow and found that instead of repelling the assistance, the man accepted it.

The extended group would have looked conspicuous on the streets of the town, so the men departed the prison at intervals of several minutes and headed off in different directions. Those who were in reasonable physical condition were taken straight to safehouses. The others, such as ten Hoven, were guided back to the bakery for additional medical attention.

Within an hour of knocking on the entrance door of the prison, all thirty-nine detainees on Kramer's list had been released without a shot being fired or an injury suffered on either side. By the time the next shift arrived and discovered the guards locked in their own cells, all the escapees were on their way to safehouses well beyond the town limits.

FORTY-THREE

Westerbork – June 1943

Schlesinger had never been invited to the commandant's house. It was situated about fifty yards beyond the barbed-wire fence next to a small coppice. Constructed of timber, its exterior was painted green except for its gable ends, which were brilliant white, a condition maintained by regular visits from a workgroup of camp inmates. A veranda stretched the length of its facade, permitting Gemmeker and his mistress, Elisabeth, to spend their evenings sitting and relaxing while sipping Scotch and surveying the camp which stretched out before them.

As the CSO approached, he was surprised and pleased to hear chattering voices and even the shrill laughter of a woman, along with the unmistakable clinking of glasses. Surely alcohol, he thought.

The front door was open, no doubt to ventilate the building on such a warm day, and he ventured cautiously into the hallway. From there, he could see into the sitting room where a group of people stood, casually conversing, each holding a glass of wine or liquor. Soldiers, civilians, men, and women were all mixing together.

Before he could venture farther, the commandant darted through the doorway, took hold of his arm, and swept him into a room on the opposite side of the hall. He did not even have opportunity to salute.

"Thank you for coming," the SS officer spoke politely but briskly.

"It's a pleasure, sir," he replied. "I'm honored to be—"

Gemmeker interrupted before he could finish his sentence, closing the door with a finality that extinguished his hopes of joining the party.

"Look, there are a couple of matters I wish to discuss with you, face-to-face. As you can see, I've got visitors. We're having a little celebration."

"I see that," he replied with a tone of disappointment.

"I'm going to have a documentary film made about Westerbork," the commandant announced.

"Excuse me, sir?" he replied, hardly able to conceal his disbelief. "A film?"

"Yes. The camp's exceptionally well run. It's an outstanding example of how to run an efficient operation. One of our inmates is a professional photographer. A man called Breslauer. I've bought the equipment, camera, tripods, and the like, and asked him to film the camp during its everyday activities."

"All its activities, sir?" he asked. "Even the transportations?"

"When I spoke to Eichmann recently, he once again complimented our transportation process. Rather than grainy, blurred photographs, we'll have moving images of the highest quality," Gemmeker said, leaning eagerly toward him.

"You wish to film the deportation of the Jews for posterity?" the CSO asked, wondering if this was an elaborate joke.

"Well, yes. Breslauer's going to film the entire camp, all its activities, including the transportations. Westerbork could become the benchmark by which other camps will be measured. I wanted to tell you so that you can inform the OD and the other inmates that this will be taking place, and that everybody should behave perfectly normally when they see the filmmaker moving around the camp with his equipment."

Schlesinger bit his lip. "There was a second matter you wished to discuss with me, sir?"

"The other matter's related in a fashion," Gemmeker said, an expression of satisfaction creeping onto his face. "Yesterday, we reached the milestone of seventy thousand inmates transported from Westerbork. It's an achievement we should all be proud of. That includes you, Schlesinger! We've regularly been exceeding our target of one thousand Jews per transport. On a few Tuesdays, we've even reached three thousand, and observing from the platform, I've noticed almost no disruption to the loading process. It's fine. Very fine indeed."

The OD leader could not respond. The smell of freshly cooked meat had drifted into his nostrils, taunting him.

Gemmeker smiled, and briefly, the Prussian's hopes of an invitation were rekindled like an unrequited lover chasing the merest glimmer of affection. Instead, his boss promptly walked over to the door, opened it, and gestured toward the exit. It seemed as if he had barely gone two paces before the commandant scurried back to his guests, closing the sitting room door behind him.

The CSO started to walk slowly back. With each step, the noise of the revelers subsided, and his anger grew. He believed those celebrations were entirely unjustified. The commandant was right: he had been a mere observer. At this moment, there were over 10,000 inmates in the camp, piled high inside cramped, dilapidated barracks in sanitary conditions that would not be deemed acceptable for animals. It was he, Kurt Schlesinger, who had coordinated and managed a process that deported between one and three thousand Jews every Tuesday. And now Gemmeker was going to have it filmed and take the credit for it all.

As he entered through the camp gates, he noticed a loose stone that had rolled away from the railway track, and he took an angry kick at it. That would undoubtedly leave a scuff mark on his shiny black boots. No matter.

A few steps on, he spotted another misplaced stone and kicked that too, with equal, if not greater, force.

*

The Hague – June 1943

Adrenaline was pumping through Rauter's veins as he marched into Seyss-Inquart's office. He had just returned from an SS assembly meeting, which took place in a mess hall and was packed to the gunwales with soldiers, officers, and dignitaries. Himmler had personally asked him to give a speech to motivate the men and to provide an update on the occupation.

The men had been drinking beforehand, which freed them from their inhibitions. Rauter stood on a raised platform, and the words he spoke had them cheering and banging on the tables in appreciation. He told them they had contributed to the efficient transportation of over 70,000 Jews from all corners of the country.

"You have purged the Jewish plague from the Netherlands!" he shouted. "You've helped solve the Jewish question, for which the Führer and the Reich will be eternally grateful."

Having then promised free beer, he left the platform with enormous cheers ringing in his ears and a sense of euphoria that came from addressing such a group of men.

The Reichskommissar noticed Rauter's undisguised good humor but decided to ignore it. "I've been looking at the very healthy deportation numbers over recent weeks," he said.

"So have I!" The soldier smirked.

"The Heinneicke Column and its informants have been able to locate and arrest four thousand Jews in only three months," he added. "Unfortunately, even their numbers are beginning to decline."

"That's true," Rauter said. "They're victims of their own success."

"However, we do have another large group of Jews which we can deport." He paused for effect, trying to establish if his rival had come to the same conclusion. Rauter sat still, a contented smile on his face. It appeared nothing could spoil the soldier's mood.

"We've still got the Jewish Council employees," the Reichskommissar added. "There are still around twelve thousand on the books, but there are very few Jews left for them to support. The council's served its purpose. Or should I say, it's served our purpose?" He smiled. "How many exemptions are still in existence?"

"Fourteen thousand," Rauter replied. "If you recall, the council originally asked for thirty-five thousand. That was far too many, so I granted them eighteen thousand. That was meant to cover everybody running the hospitals, the schools, working on the *Jewish Weekly*, arranging deportation lists, managing the issue and cancellation of exemption cards. The number has decreased as Jews have been transported or gone into hiding. We allowed eighteen thousand exemptions when their population was one hundred and forty thousand. What's the population now, fourteen or fifteen thousand? In the same proportions, we should only need about two thousand now.

"I remember arguing with Asscher and Cohen for hours about when those damned exemptions would expire. I'm convinced they agreed to *bis auf weiteres* in the hope that the war would end before the exemptions did. It appears that's proved not to be the case. *Bis auf weiteres* is here right now, today."

"Fourteen thousand exemptions," the Reichskommissar mused. "Based upon your calculations, we can cancel thousands of exemptions immediately. Given our excellent performance and record-keeping, I suspect a target of ten to twelve weeks to complete the transportation of them all isn't unreasonable. Of course, there will be Jews in hiding dotted around the country, but not enough to bother us."

"I'll summon the co-chairmen in the morning," Rauter said. "It should be straightforward to draw up the deportation lists."

"Then all the Jews will be gone, the Netherlands will be *Judenfrei*, and my job will be complete," Seyss-Inquart said, standing up and rubbing his hands together. He mused that only twelve short months ago, the transportation of 100,000 Jews would have seemed an enormous undertaking. Yet today it was so straightforward that it scarcely warranted any discussion at all.

*

Amsterdam – June 14, 1943

"Seven thousand's far too many!" Asscher complained. At his side, Cohen nodded, taking off his glasses and inspecting their lenses.

"I'm tired and frustrated with this," Rauter said, rapping his fingers on the desk. "The number of Jews has decreased considerably and so must the employees of your Jewish Council. So let me make it clear. Your council will send out a request for seven thousand deportees to be available for transfer to work camps by the end of the month. If you choose not to send this out and the requisite number of Jews fail to attend, then we'll conduct as many raids as are needed and send seven thousand to Mauthausen instead. I'm being generous. I'm within my rights to demand more. We'll take members of the council itself, with their families, to make up the numbers if necessary. The choice is yours. You tell your community what you wish. But remember this," he continued pointedly, "you've already provided us with the names and addresses of every employee of the council. Make no mistake, we can carry this off without you."

Cohen continued to inspect his glasses. "I'd like to be included in this series of deportations. I think it's only right that, as co-chairman of the council, I should be treated in the same way as my fellow Jews."

Asscher watched in silence.

"Yet another conversation is repeated!" the soldier said, his voice now threatening. "As I've mentioned before, and on numerous occasions, as co-chairmen of the Jewish Council, you're the leaders of your community and need to remain here."

Silence hung like an invisible wall between them, Cohen continuing his preoccupation with his spectacles, Asscher sitting upright, staring straight ahead, and the SS officer glancing around disdainfully.

"So, gentlemen, what will the council recommend, and what will be the message of the next *Jewish Weekly*?" Rauter asked.

Asscher slowly turned his head toward the German. "We'll recommend that our citizens comply with the request to attend for deportation to work camps on June thirtieth in order to avoid being arrested and sent to Mauthausen." There was no emotion in his voice.

"I'm sure that's the right decision," he replied. "I'm sure it's the right decision for the co-chairmen of the Jewish Council as well."

Neither chairman stirred, so Rauter stood and left them sitting. They might be there for hours, he thought.

FORTY-FOUR

Scheveningen, The Hague – July 1943

Hendrik Seyffardt was in his study, standing next to an ornately decorated wooden mantelpiece. He glanced down at a small glass case situated on a table to his left, in which three medals had been mounted on a red velvet backing. The Knight of the Order of the Netherlands, Grand Officer of the Order of Orange-Nassau, and the Officers' Long Service Cross. He had been proud of them, once.

Although he had retired in 1934, he remembered his times as a soldier with deep affection and pride. The leadership and discipline which he had demonstrated and enjoyed had been the foundation of a successful military career and led to him reaching the elevated rank of major in the Dutch Army.

The years immediately after his retirement had been challenging as he had sought to adjust to civilian life. He found the world to be a disorderly and disrespectful place. From being responsible for the stewardship of thousands of men, he had become the master of one solitary household.

The situation had improved somewhat when he joined the NSB, an organization that was small and lacking in organizational competence, and where he had hoped to put his skills to good use. The rise to power of Adolf Hitler had served to increase his optimism for the NSB's future, and the Nazi invasion of the country had reinforced this.

Although he held a low opinion of Anton Mussert, it was evident that the NSB was the sole political organization in the Netherlands that unequivocally supported Nazism. Then, in June 1941, Hitler had approved the formation of a Dutch unit of the SS, which would travel to the Eastern Front and fight the Russian communists. The retired major had been delighted to be appointed head of this legion.

He recruited a sizable number of patriots to join up, but he himself had not been permitted to travel east. Instead, he was obliged to follow events from his office hundreds of miles away in The Hague. He had reluctantly accepted that a man of sixty-nine years of age could not engage directly in military action, even though he felt that he was still physically and mentally able to do so.

Moreover, the younger German SS officers always seemed to ignore his advice. His carefully polished medals meant nothing, he thought, as he watched them glinting by the light of the chandelier that hung from the study ceiling.

The sound of knocking at the front door broke his reverie. He continued to gaze at his medals while listening for the sound of his wife, Alida. He waited a few moments longer and, with no indication that his wife was responding, strolled across the varnished oak floor toward the hallway.

He let out an obvious sigh of exasperation on seeing that his wife had indeed made her silent way to the door, wearing her carpet slippers. She raised her hand toward the latch, but thinking better of it, she paused and turned to look at her husband. He shook his head firmly, and she let her hand fall. He reached out and opened the door.

Seyffardt's house was a substantial eighteenth-century detached property with a black iron railing running around its perimeter. Its imposing facade was accentuated by a flight of steps leading up to its front entrance, several feet above street level.

Upon opening the door, he saw two people partway up the steps but was not able to see their faces from his elevated position, with only the flat caps on their heads visible.

It was ten o'clock now, and the light of that spring day had long since dissipated. The dark was punctured by the lights of the neighboring properties.

"Yes, what do you want?" he asked curtly. As he did not have any acquaintances who wore flat caps, this interruption was unlikely to be of any consequence to him.

"Hendrik Seyffardt?" the taller of the two strangers asked in return.

"*Major* Seyffardt," he replied.

The taller man appeared to be rummaging in his pockets. After several seconds, he lifted his head, allowing the lights from within to shine on his face. This revealed a man in his mid-thirties with a narrow, lean face and a smattering of unshaved whiskers that made him look unkempt. His expression was impassive, and his staring eyes cold.

"Hendrik Seyffardt!" the man announced, as if reading from an important legal document. "By the authority of the true Dutch government in London, and by reason of your collaboration with the illegal Nazi invasion of the Netherlands, you have been found guilty of the crime of treason against the state." He hesitated. "The sentence for which is death by execution."

The man withdrew his hand from his pocket to reveal a revolver. He extended his arm and leveled the gun at Seyffardt, the barrel pointing directly at his chest.

Until she screamed, the retired major had temporarily forgotten about his wife. It was a scream so shrill it sent a shiver through his body.

The assassin was also distracted by Seyffardt's wife but quickly turned his attention back to the retired major.

There was a moment's silence, followed by the single blast of a gun firing. Then a second shot rang out, and Seyffardt fell backward, thudding onto the oak floor. Two circles of red appeared on his immaculately ironed white shirt, spreading like ripples on a pond.

The gunman pointed his weapon at Alida Seyffardt.

"Not her," the other man spoke for the first time. "We came for him, not her."

"She's seen me," the gunman replied.

"He's a traitor and deserved to die. She's an innocent bystander!"

"She's seen my face and could provide a description to the SS. It *has* to be done. I'm sorry." It was not clear whether he was addressing his accomplice or Seyffardt's wife.

Another blast of gunfire sounded. And again. The woman slumped over the body of her husband.

The gunman turned and jumped down the steps into the street while the other man remained, head half bowed, staring at the scene before him.

"Come on!" the gunman exclaimed, tucking the gun back into his pocket. "We must go before we're caught!"

Hendrik harbored a deep hatred for the traitor and had enthusiastically volunteered to accompany Kastein on this mission, but there had been no discussion about killing anybody else, certainly not the man's wife.

"Now!" Kastein insisted.

Hendrik took one last glance at the couple lying in front of him before descending the steps. The two men ran down the side of the house, which formed the first part of their escape route, and in minutes, they stood panting in a gloomy alleyway about half a mile from Seyffardt's home.

While the decision to assassinate the retired major had been relatively straightforward, its location had been a cause for concern. He lived in Scheveningen, a middle-class district of The Hague, which lay on the North Sea coast. A few hundred yards to the west, the Atlantic Wall guarded the coastline. Designed to prevent the Allies from breaching the new borders of the Reich, the wall stretched over 1,600 miles from the tip of Norway to the southwest tip of France and was fortified with an array of gun turrets, bunkers, and thousands of German troops.

Amsterdam lay forty miles to the north, which at this moment seemed a world away to the assassins. They had been dropped off in daylight, masquerading as ordinary citizens, dining outside The Hague Kunstmuseum before making their way on foot to Scheveningen at dusk. Now they were fugitives, criminals in the eyes of the Nazis, with entire regiments of German soldiers only a short distance away.

"The Amsterdam Road's ahead," Kastein said, pointing.

A dark expanse lay before them. The road was flanked by farmers' fields. With the road likely to be swarming with vehicles, all searching for the fugitives, their plan was to avoid detection by crossing the fields, a safe distance away from people and lights.

Kastein poked his head out of the shadows, only to shrink back as a jeep sped by. "We'll run to the first field on my call," he said.

Hendrik knew the plan. He had memorized the signals, and they had rehearsed them many times, but his brain was disturbed and foggy. He could not shake off the image of the couple lying in the doorway, their bodies and limbs splayed like marionettes whose strings had suddenly been severed.

Kastein turned to his companion. "Okay?" he asked.

Out of the shadows, the young man spoke. "Did we have to kill her? She'd never have recognized you, and even if she had, they'd never have found you in Amsterdam, anyway."

"If you don't pull yourself together, neither of us will ever get back home," the other man warned. "Your only thought must be to cover the next three miles to Wassenaar, where we can take refuge in the safehouse. Then, and only then, can we discuss at length why an attack of conscience is the best way for a member of the Resistance to get himself and his comrade killed."

The alleyway fell silent.

"Now," Kastein whispered. "Listen hard, as hard as you have ever listened in your life. When I say *ready,* and you can't see or hear any vehicles, you reply to me *ready.* Then we both run as fast as we can."

It was so quiet Hendrik thought the world had stopped. Even his heart seemed to stop pounding like a drum.

"Ready?" Kastein asked.

Hendrik closed his eyes and listened. Hard. He heard no vehicles.

"Ready," he replied and was surprised at how quickly Kastein set off. He was immediately several yards behind. But one reason he had been chosen to participate in this mission was because he was strong and quick, and he soon drew level with his companion. His eyes focused upon the wooden five-bar gate that marked the entrance to the field, he was completely oblivious to his surroundings. He could only hope they would not be spotted or heard.

Although it seemed like an age, it took only seconds for him to reach the gate, vault over it, and crouch behind a hedge. He heard Kastein noisily clamber over after him.

Once more, the two men found themselves together in the dark, bound by a fearful breathlessness. To their right lay the silhouetted buildings of the outskirts of Scheveningen, to their left a black, featureless expanse.

"Come on!" Kastein said. "Let's keep moving."

The two men rose and started walking, treading warily. The field had recently been plowed, and finding a solid, flat foothold was difficult in the dark.

"If I say *down*, you drop into the nearest furrow and lie perfectly still. Even with a spotlight, we'll not be discovered."

As they stumbled on, Hendrik's mind could not help but drift back to Alida Seyffardt. Several times, he opened his mouth to speak but resisted the temptation. Although her facial features had already become blurred in his mind, he could not shake the image of her blood-soaked dress. Its floral pattern reminded him of one his mama used to wear in the summer.

Vehicles flashed along the road at regular intervals. The men could see their headlights well in advance and were lying low by the time they passed. One time, a jeep stopped, and a searchlight panned across the countryside. They lay motionless in their respective furrows until they heard the jeep driving away. They waited a few moments before climbing to their feet and carrying on.

Neither man spoke until they neared a small town with a number of houses silhouetted against the horizon.

"This will be Wassenaar," Kastein said. "We'll need to be vigilant. We're going to have to leave the fields and venture on the roads. The safehouse is on the far side of the town." He paused and drew a breath. "Follow me."

They edged forward, soon reaching the road, where, sure enough, they found a sign indicating *Wassenaar.*

The town was swathed in darkness, except for the odd glimmer of light escaping through the gaps in people's shutters.

The two men proceeded cautiously, moving from one doorway to the next. They paused on a street corner, tucked behind a wall, with the outline of a large, imposing building directly before them.

"There's the town hall," Kastein whispered. "The bakery's a short way beyond."

"We're almost there," his companion said. "We just need to—"

"Stop!" Kastein uttered a stifled scream as the young man took a step out from behind the wall. He had heard a barely audible rumbling, and in the near distance, a vehicle drove around a sharp bend, its bright headlamps beaming light along the road as far down as the town hall.

"Did they see you?" Kastein demanded, eyes wide.

"Possibly," Hendrik replied, lacking conviction.

"Then we must run for cover. In separate directions. We'll meet up at Sluij's bakery in an hour…if we stay out of harm's way. Good luck."

Before Hendrik had a chance to answer, Kastein took off, following the very first turn on the left, so Hendrik ran too. He had no option other than to go right. His only thought was to keep as far away from the town hall as possible. He would have to double back to the bakery later.

As he ran, the gloomy streets seemed to merge into one another, and he lost his bearings. The more he ran, the more confused he became. Now, the intermittent patches of light seemed to throw a spotlight on his every movement, and his hurried steps rang out like a tolling bell. The village had transformed into a cruel maze.

A crossroads lay ahead of him, and he turned left without slowing. He looked ahead and, to his relief, saw a black, featureless mass, the darkness and safety of the fields.

Somewhere behind him, he heard screeching brakes and muffled voices.

Almost there.

The noises grew louder. He imagined a five-barred gate coming into view, then vaulting over it and being swallowed by the dark.

Almost there.

He suddenly slowed down. And smiled. The blanket of night beyond the town filled his field of vision, until a vehicle turned into the street to face him, its headlamps blinding him and making his eyes smart.

He did not need to turn around as he sensed the insistent, throbbing motor of a second vehicle approaching from behind.

"Hands up!" somebody shouted.

Slowly, he raised his hands. It was over.

FORTY-FIVE

Amsterdam – July 22, 1943

The SS soldier stationed outside the Dutch Theater spotted the fast-approaching Walter Sueskind and was surprised to see that, instead of turning right toward the theater, he turned left toward the day-care center. Upon reaching the center, he proceeded to rap on its front door, creating a noise that was easily audible from the opposite side of the street.

Walter burst into Henriette's office without knocking.

"Walter, what's wrong?" she asked.

"Henriette, we need to be quick!" he said, panting and with beads of sweat running down his forehead. He placed his hands on the back of a chair to steady himself.

She had a glass of water on her desk, which she offered to him. He drank the water in one hasty gulp, which caused him to cough and splutter.

"We must act fast!" he said.

"Stay calm. Slow down and catch your breath."

"We can't slow down! We've only got a day left!"

"What on earth do you mean?"

With every passing moment, he was regaining control of his breath and ability to speak. "I've heard the Nazis are planning to close down the center." He gathered himself together and looked directly at her. "It's going to be tomorrow!"

"That's too soon!" she gasped, picking up a pen and starting to write. "We must help as many children as possible escape today and tonight. Even if that means taking more risks."

"We'll have to involve Johan," he said. "I'll go and see him at once and ask him how many additional children he can accommodate in the college. How will we obtain forged papers at such short notice? And what about the theater paperwork? Will you be able to remove the names from the registers?" she asked.

"I'll do what I can in the time available," he replied. "However, if we've reached the last hours of the center, then the theater will surely suffer the same fate soon. In these circumstances, you should remove as many children as you possibly can, and I will bear the consequences if my work is discovered by the SS."

"Of course, you know the risks," she warned.

"They're the same as you're facing," he countered. "I'm aware of the risks and am willing to accept them."

"So am I. So am I," she said. "Let's get down to business. It's nine o'clock now. If you go and see Johan straight away, shall we reconvene at ten?"

"Agreed," he responded, moving swiftly and purposefully toward the door.

*

"I don't know how many of the Resistance groups I'll be able to contact at such short notice," Johan explained. "But you know I'll do my very best."

"The Nazis will close the center in the morning and transfer the remaining children to the theater," Walter said. "Those children will then be transported to Westerbork. It's as simple as that."

Henriette was sitting behind her desk, with the two men opposite her. She was staring at a small pile of handwritten sheets. She coughed gently, "Gentlemen, these are the lists of the children currently staying with us, including those housed in the college."

The two men watched her intently.

She drew a deep breath. "The list contains the names and ages of one hundred and eight children." Her voice wavered, and she blinked back tears. "There's too many...we can't save them all."

"There are fifteen currently in the college," Johan said, "and we've already planned for them to be taken out today. They've been allocated places in safehouses. This morning, I've spoken to every supportive student and teacher and asked them to come in and help get the children off the premises by tomorrow. I've spoken to as many of my Resistance contacts as possible to ask them to take these extra children. We can smuggle out another twelve, although they may not all receive forged papers in time. That would be twenty-seven in total. Henriette, how many can you smuggle out of the center?"

She stared blankly at the lists. "I believe we can take sixteen kids today. Some will go on the tram run, the rest will go on a walk with a carer and not return."

"That makes forty-three!" Walter said. "That's more than I had hoped!"

"It will still leave sixty-five children behind," Johan murmured.

"We must focus only on saving the forty-three," Henriette said. "The sooner we start, the better. Walter, do you have a plan for the theater registers?"

The theater manager rubbed his chin. "Well, we have already dealt with the fifteen children currently in the college. We've received consent from their parents and falsified or destroyed their registration documents." He spoke clearly and methodically. "That leaves me with the other twenty-eight to sort out." He paused, gulping hard, before continuing with a quivering voice. "You two need to give me the names of the last twenty-eight. The sooner I know, the more time I'll have to do my work."

Henriette nudged the sheets toward Johan.

"N...no!" the principal stammered. "I can't possibly choose which children stay or go! Just give me the names."

She took the sheets back and picked up her pen. She closed her eyes for a few moments. When she opened them, she steadily worked her way up and down the lists several times, stopping periodically to place a tick mark by a name. Eventually, she put down the pen and pushed away the sheets as if they repulsed her.

"How? How did you choose?" Johan asked with trepidation.

"The youngest children have the longest lives ahead of them. And smaller children are easier to smuggle. They'll fit inside small bags. Perhaps one adult could take two babies at the same time. So I've chosen the twelve youngest remaining here. It's as simple as that."

Johan picked up the sheets, scanning them briefly before passing them to Walter, who wrote the twenty-eight names in a small notepad he had concealed in the lining of his jacket.

"Henriette, do you wish me to manage the center tomorrow?" Walter asked.

"It's fine," she replied. "Thank you for asking. You're a good man. But no, I'll be here in the morning."

The two men rose to their feet and made their way to the building entrance. Walter leaned over and grabbed the door handle, turning to his companion as he did so.

"You go first," he said. "I'll wait a few minutes so we're not seen leaving together."

"Thank you. By the way, why did you offer to manage the center tomorrow?"

"If the Nazis take the remaining children tomorrow, they'll probably close the center as well. Henriette's going to tell her staff not to come to work. She may well be the only member of staff in attendance."

"But surely, they'll arrest her?"

"Almost certainly. We're both Jewish, but she's Dutch and I'm a German who's on the Jewish Council. I'd be much less likely to be arrested."

"Why not flee while she can, like the rest of her staff?"

"She's spent most of her working life in the service of young children. She wants to make sure we've smuggled out every child possible, and she'll need to attend to those left behind."

"She's an angel," Johan said.

"She certainly is," Walter agreed, pulling the door open.

"Good luck." Johan gently placed his hand on Walter's.

"Good luck to you, too."

The principal darted through the doorway and was gone. Walter let go of the door and allowed it to shut slowly. Then he stood and waited.

FORTY-SIX

Amsterdam – July 23, 1943

It had been a long and terrible week.

After his meeting with Henriette and Johan, Walter went straight to the theater, where his first task was to seek the consent of twenty-eight sets of parents whose children they had earmarked for escape. He then made his way to the registration room where the records were kept.

Having made sure he was alone, he started skimming through the individual records in the first filing cabinet, notebook in hand. These were stored alphabetically, so it took him a matter of minutes to locate the twenty-eight relevant documents.

There was a second cabinet nearby, a remnant from when the building had been a flourishing venue for drama and art. It was crammed with theater programs, invoices, correspondence, posters, and scripts. It was in the bottom drawer of this cabinet that he carefully concealed the twenty-eight documents, on top of the others that he had been stashing there since the smuggling began. This task always made him nervous, but destroying the documents or smuggling them out of the building would have presented an even greater risk. Concealing them in the recesses of a cabinet that was no longer used would at least delay their discovery. For how long, nobody knew.

Modifying the register was always a much trickier proposition. Each registration sheet contained fifty names and was pre-numbered. Discarding one sheet would remove a child but also forty-nine other people. Moreover, the SS officers insisted on signing every single one and were sticklers for tidiness, asking for a sheet to be rewritten rather than permitting the manual correction of an error. Simply crossing out the names had never been a solution.

He made himself a cup of coffee and sat at one of the tables with the forty or so register sheets in front of him. Placing his elbows on the table, he rested his chin on his clenched fists and stared down.

"What are you doing here, Sueskind?"

He was so surprised by the voice of the SS guard that he lurched backward and almost fell off his chair. He needed several moments to recover his composure.

"Good morning, sir," he replied, recognizing the face of Fischer, the soldier with a taste for Glenlivet single malt. Before uttering another word, he kneeled and retrieved a bottle of Scotch from one of the filing cabinets. For a fleeting moment, he was terrified by the image of the SS man scouring the cabinets in a desperate search for Scotch.

He unscrewed the lid and tilted the bottle from side to side, hoping its fumes would tease the nostrils of the soldier.

"Would you like a Scotch, sir?" he asked, picking up a clean glass he had placed on the counter earlier.

The soldier's attention was diverted, at least temporarily. "Yes, thank you, a small one. It's still early."

He poured a generous measure into the glass and gave it to the soldier.

"So what are you doing here?" Fischer asked again, gesturing with his glass at the papers on the table.

"The Jewish Council informed me that the day-care center might be closed down tomorrow," he replied, trying his hardest to recall the explanation he had rehearsed in his mind. "We've got over thirteen hundred inmates in the theater. It's really overcrowded. With the transfer of the children, it'll make matters worse. I want to make sure that everything is set up in advance so we can re-register the children in the theater as quickly and smoothly as possible. I'm led to understand up to sixty children are expected to return."

"Sueskind, you're a good man," the soldier replied, apparently satisfied with the explanation. "And you're very efficient. I'm sure you'll easily deal with sixty children. It's not so many." He yawned. "I'm going to take my Scotch and rest in the box." The SS had commandeered one of the private boxes in the theater, and this was where he was now heading.

Each child would be registered with its parents at the theater before being transferred to the center. Once the smuggling had begun, Walter had always endeavored to keep the children's registrations as close together as possible. As a result, the twenty-eight names given him by Henriette were spread across only nine pages of the register. He also made sure the same pen was used whenever the SS officer applied his signature.

Walter was a reasonably proficient typist and could soon recreate each of the nine pages, excluding the twenty-eight. Then he carefully placed one of the original sheets on top of a new one, and with a blunt pencil, he traced the date and signature, being sure to exert enough pressure to leave an impression underneath. As he lifted the original away, rays of morning sunshine highlighted the indentations left behind. He took the pen and carefully followed the grooves to replicate the words and numbers. He rolled the page up a couple of times, folded it in two, and worked its corners between his fingers. This sequence he repeated until the new sheet took on the appearance of the well-thumbed original.

He then applied the same process to the remaining sheets.

*

Amsterdam – July 23, 1943

The following morning was an emotional experience for the theater inhabitants, beginning with unbridled joy when parents were reunited with their children. However, this was soon tinged with feelings of fear and foreboding when they realized the day-care center was being closed and there would be no more children transferred in either direction.

"Are there no more Jewish children left?" a man asked Walter.

He did not know how to reply.

He handed the re-registration sheets to Fischer for signing. Once this was done, his job would be finished.

"I'm not signing these," the soldier remarked, waving his hand in a gesture of disapproval.

Walter was suddenly paralyzed with fear, unable to draw breath into his lungs. Had he made a mistake?

It was the SS man who broke the silence. "We've not finished yet," he said. "We've still got adults to register. The day-care center staff. I'll sign all the sheets in one go."

Relief flooded Walter's his body. "I'll go and fetch some new registration sheets."

Fischer looked at him. "We have tipped the staff off about today's activity. Most of them didn't turn up for work. There were only four there." He shrugged. "I'm guessing that you and your colleagues in the Jewish Council might have had some involvement in that. Am I right? No matter, it's a small number. You might as well add these names to the sheets you've got there rather than fetch more." He rummaged in his pockets and withdrew four ID cards, which he handed to the theater manager.

Walter took a seat and laid the cards on the table. He read the names on each—Henriette Pimentel, Sara Hazes, Elizabeth Sluijs, Rachael Kisch. He gulped and opened his mouth to speak, but no words came.

Seeing Henriette's name there and having to type her details into the register upset him so much he could barely hold the pen. He felt as if he were personally deporting her.

And Rachael Kisch, he knew her father well. Why had she not saved herself by staying away from work? And why had Franck not intervened? Then again, nobody had seen him for weeks.

With council employees now being sent to the theater, it was inevitable that all of them would end up in Westerbork unless the war ended in the next few weeks. Even he would find himself there sooner or later. With his wife and daughter. Poor, sweet Yvonne, only three years old, an innocent whose heart was too pure for these horrors. A deep despair fell upon him, like an enveloping shroud, suffocating all hope.

*

Walter was reflecting upon these events as he exited the theater that evening. He glanced forlornly over at the center, its front door padlocked. A tram passed along the street before him, and he recalled the thrill, the fear, and the satisfaction he had felt each time he had learned of a child running with the tram.

His eye was drawn to the college. It was past seven o'clock, and the lights in the lobby were still blazing. That was unexpected. Johan had intimated that the last two children would be escaping at six.

Although his legs were so tired that he could hardly move, he crossed the street. Finding the entrance door unlocked, he entered and made for the principal's office, which was situated on the ground floor.

The college lay in silence, save for the gentle padding of his soft-soled shoes on the tiled floor. There was an atmosphere of eerie desolation.

He saw Johan's silhouette through the frosted glass of his office door. He knocked. "Can I come in? It's Walter," he asked softly. There was no reply, so he repeated the question. Still no reply.

He turned the handle and pushed the door open.

Johan was sitting at his desk, shoulders drooping like an old man, his head resting in his hands. He appeared to have physically shrunk. This was not the image of the college principal Walter recognized. A man of action, always making things happen, always positive. A man with youthful energy, managing the college while protecting and saving countless Jews from the heinous Nazis.

He was shocked when Johan lifted his head to reveal his face. His usual animated expression had disappeared. The bright, blue eyes that had once shone from behind his spectacles had been replaced by dull, blotchy slits. His complexion was so pale, the blood appeared to have drained from his cheeks, and Walter could have sworn he saw wrinkles on the man's forehead that had not been present the day before.

"Are you all right?" he asked gently. "Have you had problems with today's escapes?"

"All have proceeded as planned," Johan replied.

"Well done! Over the last few months, you must have saved hundreds of children's lives. You should be enormously proud of yourself."

He edged forward and noticed the red, raw skin around his friend's eyes, which betrayed the tears he had shed.

Johan slowly shook his head.

"I've not had a moment's peace since yesterday morning. And not slept for a second."

"That's understandable, given the great stress of planning and carrying out those extra twelve escapes."

"It's not the twelve that are the problem," Johan sighed. "It's the thirteenth."

"Thirteenth? What do you mean by thirteenth? We agreed twelve, and you completed twelve. That's an unequivocal success," Walter reassured him.

"But why couldn't I have taken thirteen? It's only one more. The little child or baby who would've been the thirteenth. What will their fate be now?"

"You're being much too harsh on yourself," the theater manager insisted. "You don't even know who the thirteenth might—"

"Kitty van Lochem," Johan interrupted. "Kitty van Lochem would have been the thirteenth. I saw she was next on Henriette's list. She's four years old. There's only one reason that she's not in a safehouse right now. And that reason...is me." The principal shook his head as he spoke. "Just one more! Why not just one more?"

Walter watched the tears rolling freely down his friend's face. He stepped forward, close enough to place a gentle hand on his shoulder. "You must think of the hundreds saved, not the one lost!" he reasoned. "You can't spend the rest of your days thinking about the thirteenth child, it will kill you! One day in the future, you'll feel differently. I'm convinced of it."

Johan rose to his feet. "Thank you." He smiled weakly. "Perhaps, sometime in the future, I may feel differently." He paused. "But not today. Not today."

FORTY-SEVEN

Mauthausen – August 1943

"For goodness' sake!" the man exclaimed. "Don't put the stone directly on your shoulder. It might seem easier to carry that way, but by the end of a twelve-hour shift, you'll have no skin left. It'll be red-raw flesh. Don't find out the hard way."

The man wore tattered shorts and a faded gray shirt. Bald, save for a few wisps of white hair flanking the sides of his head, his crinkled skin was red-brown and dotted with lurid-pink patches from exposure to the searing summer sun. From his skeletal features, Hendrik could not tell whether he was fifty or seventy years old.

The man threw him a backpack, which consisted of a square timber base, the size of a small tea tray, with two lengths of rope, which had been looped through holes drilled in each corner.

"Thank you," he replied, carefully maneuvering the roughly hewn block of granite off his shoulder and placing it on the wooden base. Then, from a crouching position, he placed his arms through the loops and stood up.

The uneven edges of the base instantly dug into his back, and the ropes rubbed uncomfortably on his shoulders. The stone was irregular in shape, so its weight was not evenly dispersed, and with every other step, he had to adjust the loops to make the burden more bearable. Nonetheless, it still seemed preferable to balancing the granite on his shoulder.

Hendrik had arrived in Mauthausen less than a week ago and was dreading his first journey up these steps. He had been told that dropping a stone during the ascent could have fatal consequences for both him and those in his immediate vicinity.

The laborers were scattered across the quarry floor, loading up their stones. Having completed this task, they made their way toward the base of the stairs, forming into rows of five as they neared.

"It's best to work yourself into the first few rows," the balding man advised. "At least you'll be one of the first up. Then there are fewer men who could topple back on you, and the men near the back may have to wait an hour in this damned heat before they even reach the first step. When they finally do reach the top of the stairs, they'll be dog tired, and the SS soldiers will be very bored. The death rate for the later rows is by far the highest."

Taking the man's advice, Hendrik advanced steadily, maneuvering himself into the fourth row, on the farthest right of five inmates. From here, he had his first sight of the full extent of the Stairs of Death. As he peered up, the stairs, dusty and bleached white by the sun, seemed to tower almost vertically above him before curving to the right and disappearing from view. Weighed down by his stone, he could not lift his head high enough to see farther.

The men waited quietly, contemplating the pain and anguish ahead. Some fiddled with their backpacks to maneuver them into the least uncomfortable position, while others jammed their feet hard into their wooden clogs to make sure they did not slip during the ascent. Some stood head down, lips trembling. Perhaps in prayer, Hendrik thought. Others stared blankly forward. No one looked scared. He wondered if anybody was as terrified as he was and, like him, trying to bury the fear deep inside.

After a few minutes, he heard the shouting of SS soldiers.

"Right, you bastards!" a voice yelled behind him. "Start climbing at once! Keep up with the man in front. Anybody who falls behind will be shot. Anybody who falls must get up at once or will be shot."

The voice of the soldier grew louder until Hendrik sensed a presence close at hand. He turned his head a few degrees to the right. The soldier was right beside him, his face barely a yard away, staring directly at him. A snarling, belligerent face.

The sparse stubble on his chin made him look like a teenager, a spotty, stubbly youth. The SS must be desperate, he thought.

"What are you smiling at, Jew boy?" the soldier demanded.

He dropped his gaze, hoping the soldier would depart. He looked at his own dirty feet in rough clogs and compared them with the adjacent pair of shiny black boots.

"I could shoot you now, Jew boy!" the soldier snapped, his face now so close Hendrik could smell the taint of stale cigarettes.

In the baking heat of a summer's day, the Resistance fighter was trembling as if it were midwinter.

"Come on, Bremmer!" a shout came from the left side of the stairs. "I've no problem with shooting Jews, but doing it before the first step's a bit much by any standards!"

The other SS soldiers laughed loudly.

Hendrik kept his head bowed and heard a whisper in his ear.

"I'm watching you, Jew boy! I think I might kill you today."

It seemed like an eternity had elapsed until the black boots stepped away.

The laborers started to climb the stairs, led by an SS soldier on either side. While the soldier on the left remained quiet, volleys of insults and threats spilled from the mouth of the young soldier on the right. Not one stair was overcome without the expression of some sort of invective.

"Go faster, go faster!" Bremmer exhorted. "You're all going far too slowly! The rest of the Jews are waiting. They're lining up in the quarry while you lot are dithering up here!"

It seemed to Hendrik that the closer they came to the summit of the stairs, the louder and more contemptuous the berating from the young soldier became.

By the time he reached the last few steps, Hendrik was sweating profusely and yearning for water. Yet he was young and athletic. He empathized with others who were not so healthy and wondered how they might cope.

Glancing around, he saw that those men nearest to him looked exhausted at best. Several seemed on the point of collapse. Two rows in front, he spotted the balding man who had helped him load his stone.

There were another two soldiers positioned at the summit of the stairs, both gripping rifles across their chests. When the first row of carriers finally reached the top step, these soldiers made no effort to move out of the way, meaning there was not enough space for all five and their stones to pass. Desperate not to disturb these soldiers, the carriers endeavored to shuffle around them but only succeeded in colliding with one another. For the balding Jew, his exhaustion was so great that a single bump from his neighbor knocked him off balance. Falling to his knees, it seemed as if his stone might force him right down.

The pounding of a thousand pairs of clogs ceased. For a moment, there was silence.

"Get up, Jew! Get up!" the young soldier screamed, a high-pitched shriek, almost hysterical.

The balding Jew was on his haunches, his shoulders heaving as his lungs strove for air. As the last of his energy deserted him, his head fell forward, and the stone rolled slowly and inexorably off its base, across his back, then toppled over his shoulder, making a thud as granite met granite.

"Pick up your stone! At once!" the soldier demanded. "Every single person's waiting for you to move!"

Apart from his silent gulping, the Jew did not move an inch.

"Come on, Bremmer!" another soldier shouted dismissively. "Just do him. He's holding everybody up."

Without raising his head, Hendrik glanced through the corner of his eye to observe the young SS soldier, who had removed his pistol from its holster. With arm outstretched, he was pointing it at the man prostrated before him like a supplicant in prayer, seeking mercy from God.

The young soldier's lips were tightly clenched, his cheek was twitching spasmodically, and his hand wavered noticeably.

"Come on!" another voice rang out. "The first one's always the hardest. But from then on, Jew killing's easy. If you don't do it soon, they'll have you on kitchen duty for a week!"

There was a peal of laughter.

Hendrik watched in horror as the young soldier squeezed the trigger. The echo of the shot bounced around the quarry and seemed to burst inside his head. He jammed his eyes tightly shut. Suddenly, his stone seemed twice as heavy, and his leg muscles turned to putty.

"You, pick up that stone!" he heard Bremmer shout. "And you two, pick this man up and throw him out of the way!"

There was movement nearby, a scraping and scratching against the dusty stone.

"Get moving!" the soldier ordered.

A thousand pairs of clogs shuffled and prepared to continue their ascent.

Head down, Hendrik opened his eyes and fixed his gaze on the heels of the man directly in front, moving cautiously up as the next step became vacant. After four more steps, he reached the summit. He lifted his gaze and saw the path stretching out ahead of him before it turned to the right and disappeared. A couple of paces to his right was the vertical face of the quarry. The prospect caused him an attack of dizziness.

He staggered a couple of yards farther, and the dead body of the bald man came into his line of sight, situated on the edge of the rock face and only inches from his own feet. The man's ragged gray shirt was drenched in fresh blood.

Suddenly, a sharp gust of wind blew, lifting a cloud of granite dust off the ground and lashing the men. He felt as if nails were being driven into his bare, raw skin.

"Stop!" Bremmer screamed. "Hey, Jew boy! I've got a job for you."

Hendrik remained as still as he could, his head bowed. He saw the shiny black boots next to the man's body.

"Hey, Jew boy!" the soldier repeated. "Are you deaf as well as subhuman?" He snorted, unable to conceal his mirth. "Perhaps this will improve your hearing?"

Hendrik shivered as the cold steel of the pistol barrel touched his ear.

"Look at me, Jew boy! Or I'll shoot you right now!"

He shuffled around and lifted his head upward, feeling the rough granite rubbing against the small of his back.

His eyes met the smirking face of the young soldier, who moved the muzzle of the gun away and pointed it at the body.

"This Jew's in the way. He's an obstacle for the men climbing up. We certainly don't want anybody tripping over him, do we? You need to push him over the edge and out of the way," the soldier taunted, looking straight at him.

The body wasn't in the way. It was lying on the very brink of the quarry edge. The balding man was small and skinny; gentle prod of the soldier's foot would have completed the task.

"Hurry up, Jew boy! Do it now, or we'll have another body to shift!" The soldier leaned forward and whispered in his ear, "It's true, killing a Jew's easy!"

Hendrik took a step forward toward the body and the edge. He spotted the soldier smiling triumphantly. One more step and he was so close to the body that his clog was standing in a creeping pool of blood.

Nobody survived Mauthausen, he thought. There were many things people weren't sure of in this war, but one thing certain was that nobody survived Mauthausen. Its survival rate was zero.

He bent down to roll the body over the edge. The SS soldier was positioned between him and the quarry edge. Suddenly, the Resistance fighter grabbed the wrist of the young soldier, gripping it with all the strength he could muster. In panic, the soldier clenched his arm muscles to wrestle his hand free, but Hendrik found he could keep the pistol pointing away with relative ease.

He heard the clicks of pistols and rifles being made ready behind him.

"Don't shoot! Don't shoot!" Bremmer shrieked. "Shoot him, and he takes me down with him!"

Hendrik took hold of the soldier's other wrist with equal force. It was like restraining a child. He smiled when he saw the desperate look on the young soldier's face. He took a step forward, and now his chest touched the soldier's. Their faces would have touched had the soldier not been writhing frantically like a wild animal caught in a trap.

Glancing down, Hendrik saw the crumbling edge of the quarry face and the soldier's shiny black boots, teetering on the brink. He looked up and over the soldier's shoulder. His gaze rose from the gray granite quarry and beyond to the cloudless azure sky, which radiated brightness in every direction. He closed his eyes and experienced a sense of release as the beautiful sunlight warmed his face. He recalled Jacoba's smiling face and his brother's playful laughter.

He re-tightened his grip on the soldier's wrists, leaned forward, and took one final step.

The other soldiers let off a volley of gunshots, but by then, nobody was there.

FORTY-EIGHT

Westerbork – October 16, 1943

In the gloom before dawn, the silhouetted shapes of the laundry hanging from the rafters remind Rachael of the Christmas bunting in Waterlooplein and put her in mind of her family, lighting the menorah candles together for Hanukkah. But as the morning light creeps into the barracks, she sees it for what it is, the ragged and stained clothing of the inmates, still damp and barely cleaned by water without soap. It hardly seems worthwhile, but at least washing is an activity which provides people with a tenuous memory of what their everyday lives used to be like. When things were normal.

She shuffles in her bunk, the corner of the suitcase she has been protecting digging into her side. She has been told that even on these fateful Tuesdays, baggage left unattended on the floor is apt to disappear during the night.

Rachael has not slept and is wide awake when the OD supervisor arrives. The others have warned her not to trust the OD since they are invariably German and protect the interests of the Nazis and German Jews first, with the Dutch Jews a distant third.

This OD man looks very much like the others. His green coveralls and cap are considerably cleaner than anything achievable in these barracks. He looks as if he is in his mid-twenties, and this youthfulness is accentuated by his clean-shaven face.

Her bunk is at the front of barracks 56, overlooking the spot where the supervisor is examining the deportation list. When she glances behind her, she sees the inmates gathering in the shadows like figures emerging from the fog. She hears the soft rustling of clothes and occasional quiet words of comfort.

Without any words of introduction or explanation, the supervisor starts to read out the names. "Assou, Lily. Auerbach, Ulrike. Auerhaan, Rachel…" As each person steps forward, he points toward the exit, and they dutifully make their way outside.

Her watch is broken, but she estimates it takes around ten minutes for her name to be called, at which point she rolls out of her bunk and jumps to the floor, the skeleton of her rickety steel bed squeaking plaintively as she does so.

She waits outside, lining up with the others for a further fifteen minutes while the rest of the list is called. Even the rising sun cannot warm her freezing bones. The shelter of the barracks is insufficient to stop the bitter wind lashing them.

There is another OD guard watching over them outside, slouched against the barracks wall, a continuous stream of cigarettes being lit, smoked, and stubbed out under his nonchalant boot. She wonders how many other deportees are yearning for a long drag on one of those cigarettes.

Number 56 is located between two other barracks. She watches the inmates gathering outside 57 to her left. The hospital, to the right, is still cast in darkness.

Finally, the supervisor comes out, slamming the door behind him, which flaps shut like a flimsy piece of cardboard.

"Right! Everybody follow me!" he shouts. "No funny business. There are seven watchtowers, seven machine guns, and the same number of guards watching your every move." He advances to the front of the group and strides ahead, with the deportees following. The smoking guard, not bothering to extinguish his cigarette, lazily brings up the rear.

In the freezing air, Rachael's senses are heightened. Walking beside them now, the size of the barracks surprises her. They must be a hundred yards long. As the phalanx of deportees trudges through the mud past the Jewish Council offices, she observes its employees peering nervously through the windows. They must have been called in to work in case there were any problems with the transportation paperwork. Once beyond the council building, they are almost immediately on the railway platform. There, inmates from across the camp are converging upon the train like ants thronging relentlessly to their queen.

"You're embarking on wagons thirteen, fourteen, and fifteen," the supervisor says, pointing to the cattle trucks about fifty yards further down the platform. "You must enter the wagons in a civilized and quiet fashion and in the same alphabetical order your names were called. But under no circumstances embark until I have tapped you on the shoulder to confirm I have ticked you off the list."

Lists, lists, lists, she thinks. The whole of the Nazi regime seems to have been founded upon lists—the civil service records, the Aryan attestations, the exemptions, the Dutch Theater registers, and now the deportations. It feels as if the Nazis have managed to subjugate the whole of Dutch Jewry by means of a series of lists. No doubt there will be more lists when they arrive at the labor camp.

She watches as cattle truck 13 is being filled. The sliding door is half the length of the truck, yet even when it is open, much of its interior is swathed in a cloak of darkness. She can see or hear nothing. It's as if a black hole has swallowed the deportees up.

"Get in! Get in!" the supervisor demands. "There's no room for anyone to sit or lie down. Everyone must stand." He peers into the gloom for a few moments. "Even the elderly must stand. Lean against the wall if you must!" Obediently, the inmates place their suitcases on the wagon floor and stand upright like human skittles.

As each person climbs into the wagon, Rachael watches the supervisor making a pencil mark on the list. In due course, he steps forward to block the next person from embarking.

"Stop! This truck's full!" he shouts, then walks on a few paces, leans his shoulder against the rusty metal handrail of the door and pushes. Then pushes again. Nothing happens.

"Werner, don't just stand there! Come here and give me a hand! The fucking door's jammed. It won't budge."

Rachael peers over her shoulder and spots the other guard, still smoking and now leaning against the wall of the maintenance shed beside a station sign showing *Westerbork to Auschwitz*. He casually makes his way past the waiting deportees. Without speaking, he puts his cigarette in his mouth and places his hands on the door handle next to those of his colleague. They push together and the door begrudgingly slides shut, screeching like a tortured cat. The supervisor rummages in his pocket, withdraws a piece of white chalk and, directly beneath the small, barred window, writes the number *58* on the black and rusted exterior of the truck. "Truck fourteen is next," he shouts, moving swiftly along the platform.

As Rachael draws closer to the front of the line, she gains a clearer view of the interior of the truck. She watches rivulets of water dripping from its floor from when it was recently washed out. However, a splash of water has not been enough to extinguish the stench of human ordure. The kindly man who had registered her arrival in the camp had warned her of this and explained that, should she be deported, she should stand as close as possible to the single barred window of the truck to give herself the relief of sporadic gusts of fresh air.

There is an old lady standing directly in front of her, quite alone. She is mumbling to herself and, as she approaches the truck, the sound becomes louder and she begins to fidget.

"It's all right, I'm right behind you," Rachael says, leaning over the old lady and gently squeezing her shoulder. In the woman's faltering words, she recognizes a rural Utrecht accent.

"Come on, speed up!" the supervisor demands, looking straight at the old lady, who does not respond.

"I don't think she understands the language," Rachael replies in her best German accent. "I'm Dutch and teach German. Would you like me to help you? Unless you can speak Dutch?"

The supervisor shuffles uncomfortably.

"Your spoken German's very good," the OD supervisor replies. "A few weeks ago, the Jewish Council would have given you an exemption and a job as a translator."

"A few weeks ago?" she asks.

"Now we've started to deport Jewish Council employees as well, they've stopped recruiting. Anyway, do speak to her. I need her on this train." And then, as an afterthought, "And quickly."

She bends over to converse with the old lady, then informs him, "She says her husband was in barracks 57, and she wants to be in the same truck as him. They've never been apart in fifty-two years."

"That's impossible," he replies tersely and officiously. "We can't have OD guards wasting their time reuniting two old lovebirds. That would cause a delay I can't afford."

"What if I were to do it?" she asks. "I'll move her away so you can keep loading people. There would be no delay and no commotion, especially as the filmmaker's here today." She points at Rudolf Breslauer, whose camera is slowly panning across the platform.

"Okay, get rid of her," he says. "But remember, you're being watched like a hawk!" He gestures toward the smoking guard, who has returned to his previous leaning position and is himself watching the filming.

She puts her arm around the shoulders of the old lady and escorts her away from the line. The two of them walk along the platform, Rachael asking each OD guard whether he's loading barracks 57. Shortly, they come across a tall, thin guard whose coveralls do not fit him properly, leaving his legs and arms sticking out well beyond their hems and cuffs. She addresses him in her most professional and assertive German accent.

"There's been a mix-up with the deportation lists for barracks 56 and 57. Are you loading either of those?"

"Fifty-seven," he replies without taking his eyes off his list.

By the time he does look up to address the speaker, Rachael's gone, weaving in and out of the lines of deportees who are waiting to board the truck. He shrugs and returns to the loading.

Every few steps, she asks the same question, "Does anybody know Josef Krieker? Josef Krieker?" She is met with blank faces but presses on until she finally receives a positive response.

"I know Josef Krieker. I helped him board that wagon a few minutes ago." She catches sight of a pointing finger, hurries to the open side of the wagon, and leans inward.

"Josef Krieker! Are you there? Can you hear me, Josef Krieker?" she cries.

*

At the back of the wagon, it's like dusk. As each additional deportee is loaded, another patch of light is extinguished, and the surrounding gloaming deepens. He hears a voice and moves slowly forward, breathing in, twisting and turning his body to squeeze past the others. The truck's filling up and they're packing ever more tightly together. Some of them can't move, so he has to retreat and take a different route. He focuses on the sliver of slate-gray sky at the truck opening.

"Stop pushing!" somebody mutters.

He pushes on.

"Josef Krieker! Josef Krieker!" she repeats.

He puts his hands together, as if in prayer, and pushes them out in front of him to forge a path through the last few people. After standing in the gloom, even the weakest morning light makes his eyes sting. He perceives nothing more than blurred outlines. He shields his face with his hand and looks down.

There's a figure that grabs his attention. It's not a shape that's been captured by his straining eyes, but a color. Against the hues of gray, in this dull morning light, he recognizes what his papa calls "red hair." It matches perfectly with the voice he has been hearing.

"Josef Krieker! Josef Krieker!" she calls.

"Rachael!"

Now she's scrambling into the truck, her frantic limbs barely under control. She's inside but not yet on her feet when Hannes collapses into her arms. They hug tightly, with a love intensified by absence.

Wrapped in each other's arms, the stench of the wagon is dissipated. He is sure he can smell her lavender perfume. Her face nestles in his sweet, innocent hair.

"My beautiful baby brother!" she gasps joyfully.

After a few moments, she murmurs in his ear. "Where's Mama?"

"I don't know! She fell. She said she'd come and find me. But she never came." He begins to sob. "I left her in the woods…"

"And Papa?" she asks.

He shakes his head. "Is Papa not with you?"

An uncontrollable feeling of dread rises within her. "The Jewish Council staff told me he'd disappeared. I assumed he'd gone to be with you and Mama…" Her voice tails off.

There's a long pause.

"And Hendrik?" he asks.

"The Nazis took him away," she says, fighting back her tears, her face still buried within the locks of her brother's hair.

He recognizes the way his sister is tousling his hair, and this makes him feel more bereft. A profound sense of longing and loss consumes him.

They are still embracing when the cattle truck door screeches shut, the shriek of a whistle pierces the air, and the train lurches forward.

POSTSCRIPT

Although the Nazis occupied the Netherlands for five years, from May 1940 until May 1945, most of the damage inflicted on Dutch Jewry occurred during a relatively brief period. The first transportation by train from Amsterdam to Westerbork took place on July 14, 1942, and the last one barely more than a year later, on September 29, 1943.

In that period, 107,000 Jews were transported. Except for the 800 inmates still alive in Westerbork when the camp was liberated on April 12, 1945, all the transportees were sent onward to camps in the east, 58,000 to Auschwitz and 30,000 to Sobibor, forming the biggest proportions. There were 800 survivors among those dispatched to Auschwitz (a survival rate of one percent) and, almost unbelievably, only 18 survivors from Sobibor (effectively a survival rate of zero). Survival rates in the other camps, such as Theresienstadt, were approximately 50 percent.

Of the total number transported, approximately 5,000 people survived and 95 percent perished.

Of the estimated 140,000 Jews living in the Netherlands during the Nazi occupation, around 38,000 survived by going into hiding, escaping the country, or enduring the various labor and extermination camps. In a period of less than two years, the Nazis murdered around three-quarters of all the Jews living in the Netherlands (including German Jews who had sought refuge there). Unfortunately, Eichmann was correct when he stated that the Dutch deportation trains ran like a dream.

Very few people survived Auschwitz and Sobibor, but most of those who did attested to the fact that they did not know they were extermination camps until they arrived there. The Nazis in the Netherlands managed to put in place a web of regulations and communications that lent plausibility to the story of labor camps in the east. By the time people really appreciated what was happening, it was too late.

As I have mentioned previously, all five members of the Kisch family are purely fictitious.

It is important to add that, although this work concerns the fate of Dutch Jews under the Nazi regime, the Nazis killed a vast number of people from different nations, religions, and backgrounds in places such as Auschwitz, Sobibor, and Mauthausen, including Sinti, Romani, Poles, Russians, and anybody whose views did not accord with their own.

Obergruppenführer Arthur Seyss-Inquart was the Reichskommissar for the Netherlands during this period. With his "velvet glove and iron fist" approach, his actions were fundamental to the extermination of the Jews. By manipulating the Jewish Council, he was able to introduce increasingly prohibitive regulations to alienate and isolate the Jewish population. After the war, he was prosecuted at the Nuremberg trials and found guilty of war crimes and crimes against humanity. He was hanged on October 16, 1946, still proclaiming, "I believe in Germany."

After the war, Höherer SS- und Polizeiführer Hanns Rauter continued to demonstrate his animosity toward Seyss-Inquart by attempting to pass the responsibility for his own actions on to his superior officer, claiming he had been merely following orders. Rauter, by virtue of his reporting line to Heinrich Himmler, in fact wielded almost as much power and influence as Seyss-Inquart. This was proven at his trial in The Hague, where he was found guilty of war crimes and sentenced to death by firing squad, which duly took place on March 24, 1949.

The leader of the Dutch Nazi Party, Anton Mussert, was a weak and much disliked official who carried little meaningful influence. As a Dutch citizen, he was tried and found guilty of high treason. He appealed to Queen Wilhelmina for clemency, which, given his demand for her to be assassinated in 1940, was predictably denied. On May 7, 1946, he was executed by firing squad in Waalsdorpervlakte, an area of dunes close to The Hague where hundreds of Dutch citizens and Resistance fighters had been killed by the German and Dutch SS during the war.

Wim Heinneicke's group of about twenty bounty hunters succeeded in capturing around 8,000 Jews in the seven-month period from March to September 1943. This was of significant benefit to the Nazi regime, which was striving to increase deportation numbers when the majority of the remaining Jews had gone into hiding.

Heinneicke himself, a mundane car mechanic prior to the Nazi invasion, became a notorious and despised Jew-hater, willing to hand in Jews of all ages for the sake of a few guilders. He and his colleagues would often return to the homes of those they had recently arrested and steal their property. He was assassinated by the Dutch Resistance in 1944 and two of his group were executed in 1947. Most of the remaining members of the Heinneicke Column were sentenced to death but subsequently pardoned.

The actions of Abraham Asscher and David Cohen, as co-chairmen of the Jewish Council of the Netherlands, have attracted a significant amount of debate since the end of the war. Many discussions and arguments have not led to a consensus as to whether they were self-interested collaborators with the Nazis or earnestly acting in the best interests of Dutch Jewry while being subject to immense pressure and threats from the invaders. When the Nazis no longer had a need for the Jewish Council, both men were sent to Westerbork. However, they were not transported to Auschwitz or Sobibor, but to Theresienstadt, which probably enabled them to survive the war.

After the war, neither Asscher nor Cohen was ever put on trial by a legal authority, but some Jewish organizations reprimanded them for their management of the Jewish Council. Given the low survival rates resulting from deportations compared to the relatively high survival rates among those who went into hiding, the argument has persisted that if the council had actively advocated going into hiding or displaying vigorous resistance to the Nazis rather than offering compliance, the overall survival rates of the Dutch Jews would have been higher. This point of view appears compelling but has the advantage of over eighty years of hindsight.

After a period of exclusion, Cohen eventually returned to his professorship at the University of Amsterdam and died in 1967. Asscher was less able to cope with the postwar recriminations and did not re-assimilate into Dutch and Jewish societies in the way his colleague did. He died in 1950.

The reputations of Asscher and Cohen continue to fluctuate from their being feted as heroes to being shamed as traitors.

The releasing of the prisoners from the Blokhuispoort detention center was one of the most daring and successful operations conducted by the Dutch Resistance during the Nazi occupation and took place with absolutely no bloodshed. Despite their concerted efforts, the Nazis and local police could not capture a single one of the escapees or the Resistance members in the aftermath of the raid. Unusually, the Nazis did not seek any reprisals. The raid on the Blokhuispoort actually took place on December 8, 1944 (for the purposes of narrative flow, the novel takes some license with this date).

The hidden village of Vierhouten was founded by a Resistance worker, Edouard von Baumhauer, in early 1943 with the assistance of a local farmer, whose farm was located on the edge of the forest of Soerelse. In time, there would be around one hundred people in hiding there, and the number of huts grew to twelve. At that point, many of the inhabitants of the town itself were engaged in supporting and concealing the hidden villagers.

Two SS soldiers did indeed discover the village while out hunting in October 1944 (again, my story has taken some license with the start and end dates of the hidden village). By the time reinforcements arrived, all bar eight of those in hiding had managed to escape. The SS subsequently destroyed all the huts with explosives and murdered all eight captives within two days, including a six-year-old child.

SS-Obersturmführer Albert Gemmeker was a complex and ambiguous character. His boyish smiling face, gentlemanly demeanor, and support for many of the cultural and educational activities taking place within Camp Westerbork need to be reconciled with the image of him standing on the railway platform, cigarette in hand, placidly watching tens of thousands of Jews being loaded onto cattle trucks and shipped to the east. Gemmeker also attended and supervised the evacuation of the Apeldoornsche Bosch psychiatric hospital, from where the patients and staff were not sent to Westerbork, but straight to Auschwitz.

Gemmeker was arrested after the war and at his trial claimed he had been ignorant of the fate awaiting the Jews in the east, and that he had treated the inmates of Westerbork well, in comparison to other camps. Because of these claims, he was found guilty of the much lesser crime of deportation for the purposes of forced labor. He received a sentence of ten years in prison, which was ultimately reduced to six for good behavior. There are many who believe it was inconceivable that Camp Commandant Gemmeker was not aware of the gruesome fate that awaited the Jews, and that he lied his way to an inequitable judgment.

Gemmeker commissioned one of the camp inmates, Rudolf Breslauer, to make the film of Westerbork. Breslauer, a photographer by profession, was provided with new equipment and materials by Gemmeker in order to capture all aspects of camp life. He himself was ultimately deported to Auschwitz, where he died in 1945. However, the film was saved by a camp acquaintance, who was exempted from deportation because he had a Gentile wife.

The camp film is available to view on YouTube:

(https://www.youtube.com/watch?v=ZiLNDziwEtc).

Breslauer recorded the broad spectrum of activities taking place in Westerbork; the dentists and doctors at work; the building of the water filtration plant; the construction of barracks and greenhouses; the operation of the hospital; the playing of sports; the tilling of the land and the tending of farm animals; the factories making shoes and clothes; and the aircraft recycling facility. Then there was Gemmeker's favorite: the revue shows with the orchestra in suits and ties; the comedians, the actors, the singers, and the dancers; all taking place on the specially erected wooden stage (manufactured from the timber of a destroyed synagogue) often on Tuesday evenings after a transportation that very morning.

With the benefit of hindsight, the ordinariness of these filmed scenes of camp life is chilling. Yet it is nowhere near as disturbing as the footage of the deportations, where the Jews are milling around the platform, chatting with each other, calmly boarding the cattle trucks, then waving their fond farewells in complete ignorance of their impending fate. All the while, Gemmeker stands by, hands behind his back, in relaxed conversation with his entourage.

Kurt Schlesinger, the unscrupulous self-server and Gemmeker's Jewish right-hand man, avoided prosecution and escaped to New York, but not before he had given evidence in support of Gemmeker at his trial. He died in the United States in 1964, aged sixty-two, never having been subjected to trial.

As a founding refugee in Westerbork at the age of only seventeen, Leo Blumensohn was an important member of the Jewish German population in the camp, being instrumental in the creation and provision of ongoing education for the younger inmates. In September 1944, he was deported to Auschwitz, then transferred to the labor sub-camp in Gleiwitz.

The Nazis subsequently sent him on a forced death march of some eighteen miles to Blechhammer, another sub-camp. All this he survived and went on to live in Israel, where he died in 1993, aged 72.

On April 12, 1945, Westerbork was liberated by the Canadian Army, having been abandoned by Gemmeker and his staff the previous day. With certain parts of the country still at war and the survivors needing to undergo security checks, it was not until July of that year that the last inmate was released. By then, everybody had learned what had truly happened to their family and friends who had been transported to supposed work camps in the east.

SS-Standartenführer Franck Ziereis and SS-Gruppenführer Oswald Pohl built an extensive network of work camps, from those able to produce advanced manufactured equipment to those created solely to detain people and work them to death. Ziereis died in 1945 from gunshot wounds received while trying to escape from the American soldiers who had liberated Mauthausen. Pohl was put on trial and executed for war crimes in 1951.

Henriette Pimentel, working together with Walter Sueskind and Johan van Hulst, was responsible for saving the lives of hundreds of children through the teacher training college and the day-care center, both "over the hedge" and "running with the tram." On July 23, 1943, the Nazis arrived at the center to arrest her, any staff present, and the remaining children.

Pimentel was transported to Westerbork and perished in Auschwitz two months later.

Until the rise of the Nazis, Walter Sueskind had led a respectable life as the manager of a margarine factory in Germany. He fled to the Netherlands in 1938 with the intention of emigrating to the United States. Unfortunately, he missed his visa application by a week, so he, his wife, and daughter were stranded in the Netherlands when the Nazis invaded.

After the invasion, Sueskind obtained work with the Jewish Council, which included managing the Dutch Theater. At great personal risk, he manipulated the records in the theater, which allowed hundreds of children to escape undetected via the day-care center or the teacher-training college. His good relations with the SS leadership and Jewish Council meant that he avoided transportation. However, when his wife and daughter were sent to Westerbork, he chose to join them. All three were subsequently transported to Eastern Europe, where they were murdered in 1945, his daughter aged just five.

Johan van Hulst survived the war and served his country as a politician in the Dutch Senate and European Parliament. Despite his achievements in saving the children from the Dutch Theater and protecting a considerable number of Jewish teachers and students from the Nazis in Amsterdam, van Hulst always regretted not having done more. When he died in 2018 at the age of 107, he was still plagued by the thought that he could have saved "just one more."

Although Kitty van Lochem is an historical figure, she was not van Hulst's "thirteenth child." Kitty was deported to Westerbork in 1943 and then sent onward to Sobibor extermination camp where she was immediately murdered, aged seven. Nobody, perhaps not even van Hulst himself, knew the name of the thirteenth child.

ACKNOWLEDGEMENTS

My thanks go to Gary Dalkin, my first professional editor, who looked at the manuscript, saw potential and helped me mould it into the completed work. Your sage advice and supportive words kept me going when my inkwell seemed to be running dry. I am also indebted to Tanya and Richard, who were brave enough to read the draft manuscripts, give constructive feedback and still remain friends. Thank you to Linda for guiding me through the PR and marketing maze. I would also like to thank Estelle and Michelle at TAUK Publishing and Phil at Novel Websites, who took a manuscript and transformed it into a superbly presented printed book supported by an equally brilliant website. I never thought this would happen, but it did because of you all. As I raise my pen to begin the sequel to The Thirteenth Child, I hope you will all be with me on the next stage of this journey.

Lastly, I want to thank Karen and Alex with all my heart for tolerating my moods and the haphazard mounds of papers, books, and computers strewn across the kitchen table, far larger than even someone with ADHD should be able to justify. And Pippa, our cat, who has sat silently nearby, sphinx-like.

AUTHOR BIO

Born in Manchester but now living in Cheshire with his wife and daughter, Mark wrote his first draft novel when he was 17 years old. It still lies—untouched—in a box in a dusty loft space. Like many other aspiring authors, he fell in step with a 'steady' career and income, but the yearning to write gurgled away in the pit of his stomach.

When a shaft of light presented itself in his busy life, he started writing short stories and was lucky enough to have many published or praised in competitions. (Some of these stories are available via his website.)

In May 2022, a convenient break in his steady career appeared, and, at the same time, he discovered the dreadful truth about his Jewish ancestors' plight under the Nazis in the Netherlands. He then embarked on his first full-length novel, *The Thirteenth Child*, a piece of historical fiction, but with the experiences of his ancestors permeating every word.

Silently supported by his black and white cat and often distracted by his ADHD, he completed *The Thirteenth Child*, published in January 2024 by Bebetter Publishing. Suitably invigorated, he has started its sequel, which will be released later in the year.

MY STORY

If you are interested in my writing, research, ADHD, then please register for my newsletter via www.markdemeza.co.uk.

You can stay in touch with me via:

TikTok – mdm82442
X – @markdemeza
Facebook – www.facebook.com/MarkdeMezaauthor
Website – https://markdemeza.co.uk/

TAUK Publishing

TAUK Publishing is an established assisted publisher for independent authors in the UK.

With hundreds of titles including novels, non-fiction and children's books, TAUK Publishing is a collaborative-based team providing step-by-step guidance for authors of all genres and formats.

To sign-up to our newsletter or submit an enquiry, visit:
https://taukpublishing.co.uk/contact/

For a one-to-one advice, consider scheduling a Book Clinic:
https://taukpublishing.co.uk/book-clinic/

Connect with us!

Facebook: @TAUKPublishing
Twitter:@TAUKPublishing
Instagram:@TAUKPublishing
Pinterest:@TAUKPublishing

We love to hear from new or established authors wanting support in navigating the world of self-publishing. Visit our website for more details on ways we can help you.

https://taukpublishing.co.uk/

SCAN ME

Made in United States
Troutdale, OR
05/08/2024

19732215R00243